A Bleeding Heart Arrives with the Bride Train

STAND-ALONE BOOK

A Christian Historical Romance Book

by

Olivia Haywood

Table of Contents

Prologue

Maysville, Virginia, May 4, 1865

The coins bit into Lydia's hands through her thin gloves as she clutched them against her chest. She was walking by rote, her mind firmly locked on the scene at the Dressmakers she'd just left, her ears ringing with her employer's last words. Well, former employer now. Mary had explained that she wasn't making enough money to support her family and that her husband had taken a job at a mine in Pennsylvania after the war.

They were leaving Maysville and going to be with him. She was closing the shop this morning to pack. "I'm sorry this is so sudden," she repeated as she'd pushed a month's wages into Lydia's hand and guided her out the door.

When her parents moved here, it was a great place to start a business. With the railroad growth came more families, and with the families came more business. Then the war destroyed all of that. Families were broken, and fathers and brothers perished, leaving women like Lydia to fend for themselves. She shouldn't have been surprised that Mary was choosing to relocate rather than stick it out in Maysville, hoping it would recover soon.

Harsh reality pulled her out of her thoughts and she stopped walking to look down at the coins in her palm. Seven dollars and fifty cents, a month's wages, lay against the threadbare cotton of her glove. She took a deep breath, feeling desperate, and curled her fingers around them, again, closing her eyes and whispering a prayer for guidance.

Seven dollars and fifty cents was barely enough to pay for her room at Netty's Boarding House for another few weeks. As it was, it didn't leave much for food. She had a little of the money from selling their house left, but it wouldn't sustain her for much longer.

"What am I going to do now?" She asked no one in particular. Saying the words allowed some shock to seep out, which felt great, though she winced at the high-pitched whine that snuck out with them.

When she opened her eyes, the reality of Maysville greeted her. The memories from her childhood in this town faded into the nearly abandoned streets and the half-covered windows of empty storefronts lining them. The crisp morning air did nothing for the picture in her eyes. Even the trees looked like they'd abandoned hope of growing here. Their spring buds were still a few weeks away, and until then, they looked like gnarled hands, bursting through the ground, bony fingers stretched toward the heavens.

Forcing herself to look away from the bare trees, her eyes took in the cracked windows, the peeling paint, and the dusty appearance of the buildings around her.

Her eyes caught her reflection in the window next to her, and she stepped closer. People in town had always commented that she looked like her mother, but Lydia had never understood why until recently. Her eyes scanned the tall woman reflected in the window, taking in her willowy frame, her shabby day dress doing nothing to hide the narrowness of her shoulders and hips.

Her eyes continued up, meeting the curls of caramel ringlets lying on her left shoulder, the petite bow of her lips, the slight uptilt of her nose, finally landing on the gray-green eyes that looked tired and worn from days bent over a sewing job or other. At twenty years of age, Lydia was considered an old maid. She leaned closer to the mirror, lifting her hand to the dark circles under her eyes. The woman looking back at her looked every inch an old maid indeed.

She would know, too. Her father had said that her mother had keen eyesight, which made her very good at needlework, and that Lydia seemed to have picked up the skill. It's what led her to Mary's Dressmaker's shop when her father and brother's letters and money stopped coming a year ago. She had never met her mother.

General Lee's letters came a few months ago, written in his own hand and informing her of their deaths. She hadn't seen them since they'd left and now wouldn't be able to say goodbye or pay her respects with their graves too far away for a hired carriage to make the trip. Not that she could have afforded it, of course.

The grief she'd been holding back since reading of their deaths gave way to disbelief, chased by anger, and finally despair as those realizations slashed through her mind. She lost track of time. Days blurred together. She threw herself into work, partly for the distraction but also because she'd had to accept that she had to earn her keep now.

In those times, she didn't have time to think of the future, and her dreams of meeting and having a family of her own got swept aside as she simply tried to stay alive.

You've got nothing but time now, her reflection seemed to say, and Lydia blinked, returning to the present. Her eyes focused on a flier on the window next to her face in the reflection, and Lydia's gaze narrowed.

OBJECT: MATRIMONY

FRANKLIN, UTAH TERRITORY

FEMALE COMPANIONS NEEDED FOR NEW TOWN IN THE UTAH TERRITORY. TRANSPORTATION AND ROOM AND BOARD WILL BE PAID FOR THOSE WILLING TO TRAVEL TO OUR TERRITORY TO FILL THIS NEED. CATALOG OF BACHELORS AVAILABLE AFTER SIGN UP LOCATED INSIDE.

REQUESTED AND VERIFIED BY: BISHOP SILAS DAY

Lydia read the sign twice, tilted her head, then looked at the sky overhead. "Are you trying to tell me something here?" She asked with a shaky laugh. She'd prayed every morning and night since she could speak, prayed over every meal, and even added a few prayers throughout the day while her father and brother were away fighting in the war. Never had she felt this scoffing sarcasm dripping from her lips.

Was the lost job the last straw to break her resolve? Still shocked at herself, she whispered, "Go West?" She considered it for half a breath and then on her way back to Netty's, her head shaking at the idea. She couldn't shake the coincidence, though. Was the fact that she'd noticed the sign seconds after her exasperated question a coincidence?

"As if the Lord would ask a young woman to travel into a place very few people knew about and try to make a place for herself among the people there!" She scoffed, then tilted her head in thought. "Or would that be exactly what He would want me to do?"

Lydia was still contemplating that hours later when she poured her afternoon tea on the small balcony her rooms afforded her. It looked away from the town, over a garden Netty lovingly tended every day, and allowed her a sense of privacy. Netty would be by in a few minutes, as they'd taken to sharing afternoon tea each day after Lydia finished work.

As if on cue, Netty knocked on the door to Lydia's room and let herself in, as usual. Her square jaw lacked the feminine structure that would've made her beautiful, but otherwise, her face was as perfect as an angel's. Her eyebrows were both arched perfectly, one shade darker than her hair. Her deep brown eyes reminded Lydia of the cake her father would bake for her birthday each year.

Lydia told Netty about losing her job as Netty arranged the tray of finger foods she'd brought along for their visit. "On the way back here," she paused, taking a sip of tea, "I saw a sign in the Stage Office window advertising for women to leave their homes, go west, and marry a man they've never talked to!" She laughed as if the coincidence between the loss of her job and the sign in the window weren't still bothering her, but it held a nervous edge that gave away how much it did.

Netty was quiet for a long moment as she mulled over the situation. "The way I see it, you need to examine the good things against the bad about accepting the offer and moving west." She pulled a folded butcher paper sheet from her pocket and spread it on the table.

"On one hand, you have no job, no family, and very little money left from selling the house. The salary Mary gave you before she pushed you out of the shop this morning won't hold for long. And with job prospects in Maysville growing slim, it makes sense to find a family that also comes with financial support." Though her words were frank, her voice stayed conversational, telling Lydia she wasn't trying to upset her. She was just starting the facts as she saw them.

It would also give her a purpose since she currently had none, but Netty didn't say that. "On the other hand," she continued, her pencil scraping on the other side of the large 'T' she'd drawn on the page. "Moving so far away from your memories and your friends to marry a man you've never met... The very idea makes me shudder."

She paused, looking up from the table and pinning Lydia with a hard stare that made her squirm. "You realize that your dream of marrying for love would be gone, don't you? And not just for now, but forever? You'll never get that chance again." She frowned and dropped her eyes to her list for a second before widening and shooting back up to meet Lydia's gaze. Lydia flinched at the look of panic in her eyes and the slightly squeaky tone of her voice when she spoke. "What if you don't like the man who meets you on the other end of the trip?"

Lydia had considered that. "What if he isn't a Christian?" She whispered into the silence, following Netty's question. She'd heard the stories of lawless, Godless men. They were enough to burn her ears. Then, again, the advertisement was sent by a Bishop, so there had to be some of God's influence out there – at least in that town. "Even if he is a Christian, is that enough to make a marriage work?"

Netty nodded, tearing off the edge of the paper she'd been writing on and leaving it on the table as she collected the tea tray and moved to the door. "You have a lot to think about," she turned as she reached the door, balancing the tray in one hand while opening the door with the other. Netty's eyes gleamed at the prospect of sharing gossip. "I'll save you some extra food in case the noise from the couple in the corner suite keeps you up!"

Laughing, Lydia shook her head at the closed door behind her, her face flaming at the innuendo. Netty always tossed inappropriate comments in when she couldn't retaliate.

Intent on working on her mending pile, Lydia rose from her chair. Her mind immediately snapped back to the matter of traveling West. Pa used to say that when he had questions with no easy answers, he turned to prayer to figure them out. "Give it to the Lord," he'd said. "There's no better problem solver."

Worrying about it hadn't worked. Talking it out with someone else hadn't, either. Of course, she'd intended to add it to her evening prayers, but perhaps this couldn't wait. Lydia sank to her knees on the small balcony, her hands clasped in front of her as she faced the sun moving behind the trees lining the garden. "If this is what you want of me, Lord," she murmured, her eyes sliding closed and speaking from her heart. "I need you to give me a sign and leave no room for misunderstanding.

The flier in the window could be a coincidence. This is a complete change in my life. There are many risks involved, and I'm not discounting the rewards. But I need a sign." She imagined the words lifting to His ears and remained where she was with her eyes closed until her knees ached.

When no answer came, she stood and returned to her room, leaving the door to the balcony open so she could enjoy the light breeze.

She used the distraction of mending the torn hem of a dress that had been caught on a nail in the step the day before to pull her thoughts away from the idea of moving West. The repetitious movement of the needle moving in and out of the fabric became their own song, with the smooth portico of the needle through the fabric and the rap of the cotton thread she was using sliding through it as she pulled it through to begin the process again. Prick. Rasp. Prick. Rasp. It was a song her senses knew like a hymn she'd learned as a child.

She stopped mid-stitch and pinched the bridge of her nose, only then realizing that the sun was setting and the light was leaving. She lit an oil lamp that hung on a wall sconce next to her chair, then settled back into her work. Prick. Rasp. Prick. Rasp. The regular pattern started singing to her, and she was yawning by the time she finished closing the hole with hidden stitches.

After tucking the dress neatly among her other clothes, she swept her Bible from the dressing table on her way back to her chair. Intent on doing a little reading before bed, she opened the Bible to the spot where she'd tucked in a scrap of ribbon to hold her place. Focusing her eyes on the words was more difficult than she'd bargained for, and she leaned her head back and closed her tired eyes.

"Get thee out of thy country," whispered a voice that seemed to come from nowhere and everywhere at once, piercing the darkness of her dreaming mind. "And I will bless thee." Before her, a train of people was traveling across a dusty land – their animals herded along after them. Again, she heard the voice, "And I will bless them that bless thee, and curse him that curseth thee, and in thee and thou shalt be a blessing." Her hand reached for them, and she gasped as a woman who looked very much like her mother turned her way.

A loud thud nearby shocked her awake, and Lydia sat up straight in the chair, eyes searching the room for the source of the noise without recognizing her room. Her eyes fell on the Bible that had fallen from her lap. It lay open on the floor next to her foot, creating the noise that had startled her. A flush of chills froze her body as her eyes focused on the words just beyond her fingertips.

8: By faith Abraham, when he was called to go out into a place which he shoulder after receiving for an inheritance, obeyed; and he went out, not knowing whither he went.

9: By faith he sojourned in the land of promise, as in a strange country, dwelling in Tabernacles with Isaac and Jacob...

Lydia knew then that the sign had been delivered. Hebrews, Chapter 11; Abraham getting instructed by God to leave Hanan and strike out to found more cities. There was no way to deny this sign.

Lydia sat back in the chair, a small bloom of excitement starting to unfurl inside her. She knew what she had to do tomorrow morning. She had only a few hours before the Stage Office would open and she could follow through on her promise.

"Thy will be done."

Chapter One

One week later

Lydia beat the morning coach to the stage office, eager to begin her adventure. Netty had helped her pack up the night before and hugged her with tears in her eyes before leaving Lydia to rest for the evening. She'd demanded letters, too.

The reminder made Lydia smile slightly as she stood in front of the Stage office, her trunk by her feet, her travel bag atop, and her reticule clutched in her gloved hands. Her bonnet was tied on the loop of the plaits she'd twisted into her hair before leaving her room. Her new traveling dress made her look slightly older than her twenty years.

"Might early, ain't ya, Miss May?" Mister Perkins, the stage office clerk, asked as he saw her on the sidewalk in front of the office. He was just coming into work, so he held the keys to the door in his hand as he stepped out of the road and onto the sidewalk. He was an older man with wrinkles lining his face.

His white hair ringed his head, leaving the top shiny in the early morning sun. He smiled as he paused in front of her, a few inches shorter than Lydia in her boots. His smile was wide, making his blue eyes twinkle behind his spectacles, and she found herself smiling back at him, knowing where most of the wrinkles had originated.

"I'm afraid I just couldn't sleep. I held out as long as I could this morning," Lydia added.

His laugh made her smile widen, and he shook his head. He held his hand towards the stage office. The nearly pressed cotton shirt nearly gleamed – it was so white. "The stage should be here any time, Miss. Would you like to come inside and get comfortable in the waiting room until it does?"

She politely declined, and he nodded his understanding. She didn't think she'd be able to sit still inside, so the waiting room may become a bit of a cage. Here, the morning air kissed her cheeks, giving them a slightly rosy hue. Her nose tingled, and her lips were chapping, but she'd still rather stand outside with the feeling of freedom. Freedom to take risks and make decisions that would change her life forever. He went in to begin his work, and she remained on the sidewalk, the butterflies swarming in her stomach.

She both wanted the coach to arrive and didn't. Mister Perkins hadn't known any details about what awaited her on the other end of the train ride, so she was still going in blind. Was that where the eagerness that curled around her gut came from? It was just enough to tantalize her and keep her from bolting back to the Boarding House.

A few minutes before the scheduled departure time, the coach rolled to a stop in front of her. Mister Perkins came out of the office and met the coach driver, handing over the post that needed to be taken into the post office at their next stop and introducing Lydia, their only passenger.

She passed them her tickets, and they loaded her trunk onto the top of the coach as she settled inside. The coach was appointed for a long journey, with plush seats covered in crushed velvet worn in a few places by travelers. She studied the pattern in the wallpaper as Mister Perkins conversed with the driver and his assistant.

There was no one to see her off, no goodbyes at the door of the stagecoach. The driver thought it strange, at first, but when all she'd said was, "I lost them in the War." Both he and his assistant understood easily enough. She clutched her travel bag and reticule in her hands as they both climbed back into their seats on top of the coach and gave the horses the orders to start rolling.

Lydia watched the city she'd grown up in disappear in the distance, knowing she'd never see it again. Her heart clenched. She felt the prick of tears in her eyes for what could've been if the war had not come and taken away so much of their lives. She knew that all her memories were either gone or packed into her things and traveling with her, but it was cold comfort, knowing that she wouldn't see the trees bud or the dogwood trees bloom. She wasn't losing anything, but there was a great chance to gain much more. And if the Lord had told her to go and leave all that she knew behind, then that was the right thing to do.

***

Hours later, her trunk was returned to her at the stage office in Gordonsville, where she barely made it to catch her train. She was directed to a particular car on the train and carried her baggage with her as she climbed aboard. The steward told her that everyone in that car was part of the journey to Franklin, so she had her choice of compartments. She turned to move down the corridor as he handed her tickets back to her. She had never been on a train before, so she had no idea what to expect.

This car had a long walkway down the side with tall windows dominating the outer wall. What little wall they had above and below the windows was covered in blue wallpaper with a scroll-like pattern in black on top. The other side of the car was divided into compartments, with the same blue wallpaper with black scrollwork framing the door with its large window, allowing one to see inside. Oil lamps hung between each door with posters advertising other locations this line made.

As she passed each door, she noted the benches that faced each other were a soft cream color in what looked like leather, and each bench was occupied with girls much younger than she, talking to each other, their faces and hands animated in excitement. She kept moving past them, favoring something a little less... loud. She found a compartment near the other end of the car that had only one woman in it and opened the door.

"Do you mind if I sit with you?" Lydia asked quietly. She'd ducked her head and taken half a step inside but didn't go any further than that.

The woman, who'd been watching the foot traffic outside the window of the compartment, turned her way and smiled. Her blue eyes danced with humor, and her deep brown curls bobbed as she nodded. "I don't mind at all. I'd appreciate the company. I just couldn't handle all the chatter from the girls back there, so finding a quiet place worked just fine for me. I'm Birdie, Birdie Quinn. Are you heading West to find a husband too?"

Lydia laughed softly at the stream of words flowing from the woman who professed to want a quiet place, but she entered the compartment and stowed her trunk.

She took a seat on the bench opposite Birdie and returned her smile. The woman was petite but had curves that would draw a man's eye with the correct cut of her bodice. She wouldn't have to lower the neckline to get attention like some others Lydia had altered clothes for, and the thought made her own eyes dance with humor. She stretched a hand towards Birdie. "I'm Lydia May, and yes, I'm heading West to find..." she swallowed the word 'husband.' It seemed to be a strange way to find one, after all. "A new life, at the very least." Was she ready to admit that she was hoping for marriage to a man she loved and not just one she met just before the vows were spoken? No, best to keep that to herself. "I had no idea there would be so many women willing to take part in something this..." she searched for a word to match what she was thinking and simply couldn't.

"Something as reckless as traveling across the country for the prospect of marrying a man they've never met?" Birdie supplied a musical laugh. "There aren't a lot of choices for an unwed girl since so many men didn't return home. Some of us are a bit long in the tooth to find a husband these days, but it's even worse when the choices are so slim! This Bride Train idea started a few months ago. The first girls who went out West were married within the week after they arrived. Do you think we'll be so lucky?"

Lydia blinked back the sting of tears that bit her eyes at being one of those women whose men didn't come home from the war. She had to admit she was right about the lack of men. Even Maysville had a steep shortage of unmarried men to set a cap for, not that it had ever had a plethora of them. She refrained from thinking about the men on the other end of the journey. "Where are you from?" She asked conversationally. Maybe, since it seemed that Birdie was going to Franklin, too, they could be friends? It would be nice to know someone and not be alone in a new place.

"I'm from Fairfax – the city, not the county," she answered. It didn't sound like it was the first time she'd said it that way. She answered without looking at Lydia, fidgeting with the rifle on her dress. "It's only two stops back, but with how long it takes them to get people on a train, I swear, it's been hours since I left Mama at the Depot." And with that, she launched into a string of tales about her family that made them both laugh.

Lydia almost didn't notice when they passed Appomattox. The courthouse steeples caught her eye as they did, though, and she looked out over the fields and forests. She silently said goodbye to her father and brother buried out among the graves left by the battle before Lee's surrender in sixty-four. She'd most likely never see them now. That would have to do. Even Birdie grew quiet as they passed by.

With a prayer to the heavens, she hoped their souls were resting and that they knew she loved them, but mostly, she prayed they were with her mother in heaven, watching her do this reckless thing with people she didn't know. As she did, she thought she heard her father's voice reading from Deuteronomy. "Be strong and courageous. Do not fear or be in dread of them, for it is the Lord, your God, who goes with you. He will not leave you or forsake you."

She sniffed, her hands still clasped before her in prayer as Appomattox disappeared beyond the view of their window. As she finished her prayer, she added another: that what they found on the other end of the train ride didn't change the way Birdie smiled or laughed and that maybe, just maybe, she'd find love there, too.

Chapter Two

Franklin, Utah Territory, May 9, 1865

Isaac let out a scream, sorrow, and frustration filling his lungs with a painful stab, and he sat right up in bed. His thigh cramp felt as sharp as when the bullet passed into him two years ago. Sweat covered his chest as it heaved, trying to force air back into his lungs.

He cast his eyes to the window that he'd opened last night before. He'd been uncomfortably hot and had taken his shirt off, too, hoping the chilly night air would grant him some solace. It had been enough to allow him to fall asleep, at least. The morning sun hadn't warmed it yet, as it was barely peeking out on the horizon.

He scrubbed his hands over his face and turned to the side, placing his feet on the floor. He contemplated the window for a minute before hunting for his shirt. He'd kicked it off the end of the bed in his fitful sleep and found it on the other side of the bed, half hidden under the mattress.

He bent and swept it off the floor, pulling it over his shoulders to hang open as he shuffled, still barefoot, to the kitchen. He stretched as he walked, trying to work the stiffness out of his leg, leaning into the steps and stretching the muscles along the back of his knee as his weight shifted to the other foot.

He drew a deep breath and stood for a few moments, enjoying the peaceful early morning stillness inside the house. The first day's sunlight soared through the window, casting shadows from the vases and trinkets his mother kept on the windowsill. The shadows stretched across the plank floor to the table on the opposite side of the kitchen.

The large iron stove stood to the right of the cabinet under the window, giving off random hisses and pops from the coals of the fire he'd banked before turning in for the night. He added a few small logs from the wall rack next to the stove and stoked the fire back up.

He opened the pantry and cabinets on the other side of the sink basin, collecting what he needed to get breakfast started. A few minutes later, eggs were frying in one pan, a few links of sausage already cooling on a plate nearby. He sliced a few pieces of bread and used the egg pan to brown the bread. He loaded two plates and left a smaller one in the oven covered with a cotton napkin to stay warm until Ma woke.

He tucked into his breakfast, his mind on the list of things he knew had to be done that day, both around the homestead and the Sheriff's Office and Jail. He needed to mend the fence on the southern end of the eastern grazing lot before moving the cows there next week and get his deputy, Jack Sharpe, to check the hinges on the cell doors. "May as well send him out to check the Northern side of the border between town and the next town over," he said aloud into the silence of the kitchen.

He'd heard some rumbling about the Natives harassing the farmers on that side of town. The reports carried enough similarities to warrant checking out, and Jack was as good as any to spot trouble, be it between two people who were about to fight or figuring out what the Natives were doing around those farmhouses. He'd also need to check the arrival of that train this morning since he'd promised Bishop Day that he'd–

"The Bride Train," he snorted. That was the name Jack had given the train bringing the new townsfolk this morning. It was such a big deal that the mine in the next town had given men the day off to find a wife and marry her if they were back at work the following morning! They'd filled the hotel, and a few were camped outside town just to be here when the train arrived.

He left the plate on the table, returning to his room to dress. He didn't have much time. He still had to take Ma her breakfast, so he just buttoned up his shirt and pulled on his trousers. He buttoned on a vest, put his boots over his wool socks, and then went back into the kitchen for his mother's breakfast.

He paused in the doorway, seeing his mother sitting in her usual chair, the plate of food sitting on the table in front of her and a steaming cup of tea resting by that. "Good morning, Ma." he stopped next to her chair to drop a kiss on her upturned cheek, then took the seat where his food still rested. "I was bringing you your breakfast just now."

Cora Branson was almost forty years old and had been a widow for nearly a year. When Isaac left for the war, she still had a youthful air, a spring in her step. Her blue eyes, so much like his own, danced when she laughed. Her deep brown hair didn't have a single strand of gray, and she always wore it in a loose bun on the nape of her neck. The woman he'd met when he came home was very different. Her eyes still danced when she laughed, but she didn't laugh nearly as often, and they seemed to have sunk back into her face a little more than he remembered. Her hair was still in a loose bun on the nape of her neck, but there were streaks of gray starting at her hairline and moving into that bun. Where once she was lean like a woman used to doing housework without help, now her form was frail and thin. It had only gotten worse when his father got sick. His passing ensured those frailties were a permanent reminder of the loss she'd experienced.

She laughed, the high-pitched musical sound pulling him from his thoughts. Since he'd been home, he'd learned that when her laugh was that high, it was a bad sign. "Oh, Isaac. You know I don't need you to spoil me. I am a grown woman. I can handle walking to the table for breakfast."

"Yes, ma'am," he said, his voice softening and his smile spreading across his lips. They'd had this conversation before, and he'd learned not to argue with her about the necessity of restricting the distance she had to walk. Especially when all the signs of a seizure were starting to show. Her hands shook slightly as she held the fork to her lips.

She kept swiping her nose with her free hand as if it were itchy. He knew the next sign was rubbing the rest of her face. That's when it was too late. He'd carry her back to her bed if she needed him to, just like he'd done dozens of times in the last year. He just wished he knew how to keep these things from happening.

She returned his smile and returned to eating the breakfast in front of her. She delicately scooped up her eggs. He pretended to go back to his, though his eyes tracked her free hand every time it came above the table line and monitored how much she ate. Sometimes, if she got enough bread or meat before the face rubbing started, she could avoid the seizures that came afterward. He relaxed a little as more and more of the eggs and toast disappeared.

The Bride Train could wait a little while longer, he decided. He needed to ensure she wouldn't need his help back to her room first. Her appetite was nowhere near what it had been when he was younger. His father had said it was her worry for him that had started it. The way she'd fussed when he got home, pieces of the Minnie ball still lodged in his thigh, he could believe it. She scooped up the last of her eggs, set the fork aside, then folded her hands in her lap, just staring ahead.

He sighed inwardly, taking in her vacant expression. Definitely a bad day for her episodes, but maybe she was just picking up on the energy the whole town was experiencing in anticipation of the train's arrival this morning. He'd noticed that, sometimes, when the town was buzzing about something, the excitement affected her, too. Even without going into town, people came by during the day to see her and their excitement would wear off on her. On days like these, she had all the same indicators as a bad day, but it rarely turned out the same way. He set his fork aside and scooted his chair back.

He helped her up, holding her hands and helping her navigate the furniture as they moved her back to her room. Once she was in bed and resting, he closed the door softly and returned to the table. He scraped the breakfast scraps into a bucket on the counter for the chickens, then took it, his hat, and his jacket out to the stable. His horse snickered at him as he opened his stall's gate and nuzzled his shoulder, looking for apples or sugar cubes as he tightened the saddle girth around the stallion's belly. Then he hooked the bucket over the pommel, pulled his jacket and hat on, and swung into the saddle.

"She'll be okay, Boots. She's resting. Essie will be over to check on her in a little while, and we'll be back for lunch. She'll be asleep until then." While his voice sounded confident, he felt anything but – and the horse knew it. "C'mon. Let's get to town and see what the 'Bride Train' business is all about."

He clicked his tongue, and Boots walked to the stable doors. His head swiveled to the house a few times on his way to the tree line and the road that cut them in half, praying Ma would be alright until he returned.

***

Bishop Day walked through the door to the Sheriff's office just before noon, his head bobbing in response to Jack's greeting. "Good afternoon, gentlemen. Is everything in order for the train's arrival?"

"Unless they spring something new on us or the train's hijacked, we've got it covered, Bishop!" Jack interjected, rising to cross the room as Bishop Day turned toward Isaac's desk. Jack Sharpe had a sharp wit and an easy smile, and when you paired those with a jokester who enjoyed ruffling people's feathers, it wasn't always well received, especially not in Franklin.

At nineteen, he had been too young to join the war – a point that had frustrated him greatly. He was from the next town over and had reminded Isaac so much of himself at eighteen when he'd shown up in town that it just seemed natural for the Sheriff to try guiding him away from the trouble that would find him if he kept letting his pride get between him and the right thing to do.

It didn't stop Isaac from wanting to lock him in one of those cells and bury the key most days, though. He knew he was far from the only person with that opinion either. Isaac had taken him on as a deputy not long after he had been elected Sheriff and told himself that he did it because he didn't want to spend his days arresting him.

Isaac shot Jack a look that would've been daunting to anyone else, but it did nothing to dampen the grin that nearly always split Jack's face. Shaking his head, he met the Bishop's eyes and gestured to the chair across from his desk. "Everything is running on time, Bishop," his voice was level, and he watched the man settle into the chair.

Bishop Silas Day was thirteen years older than his twenty-two years, but he still looked at the world through hopeful eyes. Perhaps it was the nature of the work, but Isaac had that innocent outlook stripped from him early in the War. Whenever he felt it creeping up again, it would get crushed by whatever unholy mess awaiting an army unit around the next bend in the road.

Isaac blinked, and Bishop Day's clear blue eyes and stiff-backed appearance returned into focus. "What else brings you by, Bishop?" The way the man's hands curled around the edges of the wide-brimmed hat in his hand revealed something was on his mind.

"Yes, well," Bishop Silas Day wasn't a quiet man within the bowery, but he seemed a bit uncomfortable in spaces where instruments of violence, at least the ones specifically made for it, are kept and worn openly. The Sheriff's office and cells that could house more violent people made him more visibly anxious than anywhere else in town. Maybe it was the gun rack behind Isaac's desk or that neither he nor Jack were ever without a pistol on their hip, but he'd never seen Bishop Day relax in his presence – not since he'd come home, anyway.

"He wants to know if you are ready for a wife, Sheriff," Jack supplied helpfully from where he leaned on the corner of Isaac's desk. He was still wearing that smile, and Bishop Day squirmed uncomfortably, his eyes sliding from Isaac's face to flick angrily at Jack before dropping to the floor.

"I received word that there were more women on the train that I had prepared for," he shrugged, still focused on the grain of the wood plank floor. "I promised them a place in our community when they arrived. I fear for the unmarried women who find themselves without a chaperone in town."

"Surely you have matrons willing to take a girl in, Bishop," Isaac suggested. "Most would relish the idea of a fresh young lady to mold in their image." Isaac wasn't sure why this had become his problem since he'd not been privy to Bishop Day sending the infamous telegram about the Bride Train. The likelihood of an orderly arrival and departure with chaperones to keep the time the women spent with men they didn't know from going beyond the acceptable level of propriety was very slim. There was so much potential for trouble that it made his jaw ache.

"Yes, well," Bishop Day repeated, glancing sideways at him. "I would feel better if they got what they lacked at home."

"A man?" Jack, ever the helpful one, supplied, pinning the Bishop with a look that bordered on incredulity. His smile never faltered. "I'm not sure, Bishop. Is it the women you're giving away or the townsfolk?"

Bishop Day spluttered, lurching to his feet. "I am not giving anyone away, Deputy Sharpe! I am merely trying to help both communities out of a tight place. We have men; they need men. They have women; we need more women for our young men. It's as simple as fitting the pieces together."

Save me from people who feel they know what's good for me! Isaac lowered his eyes to keep his exasperated frustration at yet another well-meaning community trying to find him a wife to himself. Jack kept Bishop Day busy, firing back, "So, God called you to be a matchmaker, Bishop? I didn't think He was in the business of finding wives for men, these days with the prayers that must be keeping him busy noon and night after the war!"

"Jack," Isaac said one word, jerking Jack's eyes to him. He raised an eyebrow, and Jack shrugged, launching himself off the desk, his teeth flashing in the smile that never seemed to leave his face.

"Why don't I go check on that train for you?" he offered, heading straight for the door. There was anger in the lines of his shoulders, something Isaac only caught because he knew the kid. Why was he so worked up about the Bride Train? He didn't wait for Isaac to say anything. He stepped out and closed the door behind him.

Isaac watched him go, making a note to talk to him later to figure out what was bothering the kid so much about the Bride Train. He turned his attention back to the Bishop. "Did you say you were going calling today, Bishop?" He changed the subject smoothly without answering the question Bishop Day had been trying to get an answer to earlier. His lack of response should do well to convey his position on the idea of marriage.

"Indeed. I need to call on a few farms along the western side of town. It will most likely take me all day, but after the–" he paused, looking for the right word, "Incident last week, there are some bearing injuries that I need to tend to. Doctor Bradford is going along to check on the injuries to their bodies. I fear the injuries to their souls may be worse."

"Would you mind stopping in to check on Ma? I know we're not one of your flock, but" There weren't many in town who didn't love his mother. The ones that didn't. still held her in high regard. Her health over the last five years had been in the prayers of the farmers who had found their way to Franklin and settled among them.

They had clung to the idea of "wherever three gather to worship me, there shall I be," and held regular prayer circles and Bible studies. His mother looked forward to Bishop Day's visits, and that was reason enough for Isaac to ask The Bishop to make a stop and check on her.

"I would be delighted to call upon your Mother, Sheriff Branson. We owe your parents a good deal for giving up their lives to come to protect the folks of Franklin. I always believed that while you may not be part of my flock, you are part of my family." His smile matched the warmth in his voice, and Isaac found his own lips stretching.

They'd walked toward the door of the Sheriff's office, and Isaac reached his hand out to the Bishop. "I'm much obliged," he said as Bishop Day's hand slid easily into his. The Bishop did not hesitate to shake the hand of a man who'd given up on God and all his teachings in the aftermath of the war.

"You know, if you need anyone to talk to, Sheriff," Bishop Day started before their hands parted. He was interrupted by the door flying open, nearly smashing into his shoulder, and Jack bursting through it.

"The train is early, Sheriff! There's already a gathering at the train platform." He jerked his thumb out the door where it was still open behind him.

A sharp whistle sounded in the distance as if punctuating Jack's announcement, and Isaac bit off a curse before it got past his lips. Bishop Day nodded, acknowledging the deference to his presence, and moved to leave.

If he was a praying man, this was the time to offer up a dozen that whoever was meeting that train had a plan. Since he wasn't one, he moved a little faster instead. Something about the size of the crowd he could see swarming around the tracks made him very uneasy. Memories of similar crowds of men with guns in their hands started to stir in his thoughts. The noise from that crowd pulled them from the depths where he'd shoved them down before he'd left the house that morning.

"Ya know, I'd half consider sweet-talking a woman off that train. I'm not sure I'd wade through that to get one, though." Jack huffed as they drew closer to the growing excitement of the crowd, and the train pulled into its place on the platform.

"That's not even funny, Jack," Isaac spat at him, not even looking as he launched onto the platform from the side and started pushing his way into the crowd. "Not funny at all."

Chapter Three

"Chaos," Lydia whispered in shock as she stepped onto the platform. "Absolute chaos."

Behind her, Birdie gasped. "Looks a bit like a feeding frenzy, doesn't it?" she mused. She stepped down, and they both took a step to the side to let others behind them exit the train. "Who do you think is in charge here?"

"Bishop Day is the person who sent the request," Lydia mused, looking around for anyone who looked like clergy. It had all the makings of a feeding frenzy as girls were scooped up within steps of the train and pulled away. Lydia could see only those in front of her, pale-colored skirts mixing with black or brown trousers.

But the crush of bodies from behind was still going as they lurched forward. Shouts and curses filled the air, teaming with the sound of excited voices. The smell of sweat and dirt hung heavy in the air, while the floral scents worn by the women getting off the train clashed and threatened nausea. "I'm not sure how this is supposed to go..."

"...But this isn't right." Birdie finished the sentence, her eyes as wide as Lydia's as they scanned the seething mob before them. One woman shrieked to their right, and the sound of a slap echoed across the sudden quiet of the crowd. As she watched, an older woman stepped in, looped her arm through the young woman's, and gently pulled her away. The presence of chaperones did very little to make Lydia feel better. "This is not what I expected at all."

Not a minute later, they heard another scream as a woman fell off the platform, landing on the packed dirt road with a sickening crunch. Lydia pressed back, her hand to her chest. She hoped to find the doorway to the train and get back on board before the crowd of men noticed the two of them standing outside its bubble and surged to wrap them inside too. She clasped Birdie's arm and pulled her back with her. Maybe they could make a run for it before they were embroiled in it. They could get back on the train and hide in another car. Perhaps they could hitch a ride back to Maysville, and she and Birdie could open a shop of their own.

Instead of the steel wall of the train, she ran into something completely different. Arms wrapped around her, pulling her roughly to the side. She screamed, kicking her heel back and scoring a strike on the shin of the beast that held her. She thrashed in her attempts to get free, but nothing loosened the arms that banded her middle like steel.

She heard Birdie scream behind her, but she couldn't release herself from the man holding her to see what had happened. Then she was passed from one beast to another. This one, at least, looked her in the eye. Well, for a second, anyway. His leering eyes moved down her front, and Lydia shuddered at the predatory gleam she saw in them. Then Birdie was beside her again, and Lydia reached for her, her lips parting to ask if she was alright.

Birdie had a small tear on the arm of her jacket and her hair had been pulled out of her bun. The man leering at them was faster, though, grabbing each of their arms and pulling them closer to him. He smelled as bad as he looked, with pudgy jowls filling the space between his chin and the collar of his shirt. Even with the top button undone, the second strained to stay closed. His hair was a greasy pile of black so dark it could only be fake on top of his head.

"You will do nicely, I believe," he sneered at them, shifting his eyes between them with wicked light in his eyes. "Very nicely, indeed."

His breath was enough to make her gag. Lydia lifted a handkerchief to her nose and pulled on her arm. But her iron-fisted captor just tightened his grip, lifting her upper arm a little higher and no doubt leaving bruises on her arm under the sleeve of her coat. Her lips parted to tell him off, but she drew up short as they caught the eye of a man standing in the center of the slowly emptying platform, watching them.

Under the brim of his hat, the man's cinnamon-color hair hung in soft waves to his shoulders and around his ear to brush a strong clenched jaw as his gaze shifted to the man clutching her arm. His strides ate up the distance between them quickly as he shot into motion, even with the slight limp she caught as his weight shifted from his right thigh to the left. She bit her lip as he approached, momentarily forgetting the man bruising her harm.

"Burns," he gritted out as he stopped before them, obviously talking to the man between Lydia and Birdie. "It ain't right to manhandle a lady. I would think you'd know that. But then again, you probably don't get many ladies in the saloon." Burns, as the man had called him, loosened his grip on her arm but didn't release her completely. The lines around the man's eyes deepened as he narrowed his gaze on Fred. His voice was even more menacing when he continued talking. "Why is it that every man here was content with one woman, but here I find you with two?"

"I was sent out to fetch wives for a pair of men inside the saloon." Lydia repressed a shudder at the oily sound of his voice and pulled on her arm again. He still made no move to release her.

"That's not how this works, Burns," the newcomer said flatly. His voice was gravely, and it rumbled with something akin to malice. His hand hovered over the pistol on his hip while his eyes pinned the man next to her in place. Her heart beat a little faster, and she had to look away from his face and the way his jaw squared when he clenched it. It was her nerves, naturally. Anyone in her situation would have an anxious heart thudding, right?

Her eyes moved away from his face and landed on a silver star just over his heart. She breathed a small sigh of relief. A lawman had come to their rescue! The Lord was looking out for them after all! "Bishop Day arranged this so each man chose his bride from among the ladies on the train. There aren't any options for substitutes this time. You'll have to let the ladies go find other husbands."

Burns' fingertips bit into her arm, and she released a small cry, turning to stare at the man holding her arm. "I do what I can for my customers, Sheriff, you know that. Business isn't what it could be, so I merely sought to keep the few customers I have comfortable while they enjoy my establishment. Besides, there aren't any other men here looking for women. It seems this train was overbooked."

The Sheriff barked a laugh and shook his head. He shot a look between her and Birdie, swept his gaze over his shoulder, and then pinned Burns with a glare. With resignation, he muttered, "One woman, Burns. For yourself.

No passing her off to customers or whatever else you had planned." That was too much for Lydia to take.

"Excuse me, but are we cattle?!" She snapped. "Don't we have a say in the matter?"

Burns didn't give anyone a chance to reply. He simply released her so quickly that she stumbled to the side. She caught herself before anyone had to help her and turned on the man, intent to give him a piece of her mind. Before she got a sound out, though, he was addressing the Sheriff. "This one, then. She is easier on the eyes and has a feisty temperament." He looked back over Lydia, his lips quivering. "Since I know you've no interest in a wife, Sheriff, and I don't see anyone else needing a husband, perhaps I can offer her a job?"

He leaned toward Lydia but didn't take a single step away from Birdie, who looked horrified. "With a little training, you'd do well in my saloon. What do you say? Two cents a week to work for me?"

Irritation spat from Lydia as she searched for the right words to cut this man to the quick. She'd not lower herself to work for him for any amount of money, no matter what business he owned in town! Her hands curled into fists at her side, and she stepped toward him, intent on slapping the leer from his lips.

"I need a wife too," the Sheriff announced then, drawing Lydia's attention and stopping her before she could assault Burns. The world seemed to pause and look at him, dumbfounded. She blinked a moment, looking around her. There weren't many people around, but those gathered had slack jaws and were frozen by the announcement. What was going on here?

Then a fissure of electricity jolted through her. Was the sheriff suggesting that he would take her as his wife? Was he not only rescuing her from this slimy Burns fellow but also offering to give her what she'd come all this way for? A family? A home? A husband? Her palms were suddenly damp, and she curled her hands back into fists. She'd never considered what the man she'd marry out here might look like, but she knew this rugged lanky sheriff with the most beautiful eyes Lydia had ever seen wasn't what she'd expected!

"You?" Burns laughed. "C'mon, Sheriff. We both know you have no intention of ever–"

"That's where you're wrong, Burns. Not that it's any of your concern, but I find myself in need of a woman." He paused, blinking, then corrected himself, "A wife. That's why I agreed to help Bishop Day with this Bride Train business to begin with."

Burns' face lost all humor, and he nearly growled at the Sheriff. "Come, boys. We have customers." He spat on the ground next to the sheriff's booted foot and stalked away. He dragged Birdie along, trailed by the two large men that had pulled her and Birdie away from the train. Lydia longed to reach out and help her friend. Wouldn't the sheriff save her too?

She turned to look up at the sheriff and blinked in wonder as his gaze met hers in the shade caused by the brim of his hat. The eyes that had caught hers were the softest shade of blue she'd ever seen. His jaw relaxed, and he broke eye contact to watch Burns disappear into the saloon.

It gave her a moment to take in his height and his clothes. They were made for him, sure, but they were far from professionally tailored. That jacket needed to be taken in at the shoulders to fit better, for one. She noted it was also very bulky on his torso as her gaze slid down his chest. The hilt of a pistol peeked out from under the jacket, and she wondered if that was the reason the jacket was so much larger than it should be. The vest under that jacket looked worn but was of good quality.

Would this man become her husband now? Did he really want a wife, or had he said it just to protect her from... whatever Burns had been offering? She cast a look down the street to the saloon where her friend had disappeared and chewed the corner of her lip.

What was she supposed to do now?

Chapter Four

Isaac watched Fred Burns until he'd disappeared into the shadows of his saloon, his unease growing. He'd been unable to get both women, and he should be glad he'd managed to save one. His concern for the other grew, though, and a stone of guilt lodged in his stomach. His mind whirred, trying to think of a way to get the other girl free, too, without breaking any laws.

He clenched his jaw again and scanned the empty platform. There should've been more organization to this mess. If people were going to get married without knowing each other, the least they could do was be offered a choice of the woman or man they ended up with. "It's just going to end in disaster," he muttered, checking his pocket watch.

"I'm sorry?" the woman standing next to him asked, drawing his gaze back to her. He cleared his throat, forcing his thoughts back to where he was.

The lady beside him had a build not far from what was considered average for a woman back East. But around here? She wasn't exactly delicate. Still, there wasn't a single thing about her, from her clothes to the tight bun she'd pulled her hair into under that pert little hat that hinted at anything short of a pampered East coast lady. What had he gotten himself into?

"My apologies, Miss..." He let the question draw out, tilting his head a bit and leaning closer as if presenting his ear to better hear her answer.

"May," she answered, a smile stretching her lips. "My name is Lydia May. And you are?"

He nodded, standing straight up again and checking that his badge was still visible. "I'm Sheriff Branson. We're not much on the formality here, so I guess you can call me Isaac."

"Then you must call me Lydia." Her voice held a soft southern accent, the softly rounded syllables curving into a warm tone that sounded like she was smiling. It soothed a bit of his irritation at the situation.

"Of course, Lydia," his voice sounded as if he were testing the name in his mouth to see if it fit the woman standing in front of him. He cleared his throat and nodded toward the train still standing at the station behind them. It would leave within the hour, and he intended to remain here until it did. "How was your trip? Did the train lull you to sleep?"

Her lips twitched slightly, and she nodded, her eyes over his shoulder. He followed her gaze to a trunk, and he guessed it was hers. He held his hand out toward it, palm up, inviting her to walk with him, and she started walking toward it. "Once we passed Virginia, I had a difficult time staying awake. Birdie, the woman..." she paused, her eyes returning to the saloon down the street. "Birdie decided to leave one side of our cabin in the sleeping position, and more than once, I found myself curling up for a nap while the sun was up. It was just too difficult to stay awake!"

"I can't sleep on a train," he admitted, his eyes scanning the street, though every other sense seemed focused on the woman next to him. "Not for longer than an hour or so, anyway. There's too much to see. The mountains that flatten over the plains, the rivers raging under the train bridges." He cast a look sideways to see her looking up at him as they walked. "It's just too distracting."

She smiled, making him wonder what he'd said that was amusing. He was saved from asking by Jack, who hopped onto the platform and approached them. Jack's smile was wider than ever as he caught up with them.

"Well, that's the last of them, Sheriff. I got the men camping outside of town to take their women to lunch at the hotel, so we can keep a bead on them until they leave. We can make sure they don't take off with the women that way." Jack's gaze slid to the woman at Isaac's side. "I heard a rumor that you were taking a bride from the train, after all. Is this her?"

The way he looked at Lydia made Isaac uneasy, and he barked a sharp," Yes," before clearing his throat. "This is Lydia May. Lydia, this is my Deputy, Jack Sharpe."

"A pleasure," Lydia responded, accepting Jack's outreached hand in welcome without hesitation.

Jack's gaze slid back to Isaac, a silent question in them. He parted his lips, and Isaac leaped into the space left vacant by his silence. "Now I need to introduce Miss May to Ma," he said quickly, swiping her trunk off the platform as he walked toward the end closest to his office and horse. "Can you check the hinges on the cell doors and then ride out and check the lines along the border? There have been complaints." He didn't supply anything else. He didn't want to influence Jack's investigation.

He also didn't want to wait on the answer, and he passed Lydia's trunk to Jack as he hurried to his horse. He heard the rustle of skirts behind him, letting him know she followed closely. "And bring this by the house on your way out there? I don't have room for it," Isaac fought to keep his voice from sounding nervous as he pulled himself into the saddle. "I need to check on Ma, anyway, so I can take Lydia..." he paused, looking down at her from the saddle.

Her eyes seemed like deep pools as he looked into them, and his voice trailed off mid-sentence. She was pretty, he realized. Her wide eyes, softly curved lips, and the hairs that had broken free of the tight pull of the bun and curled gently around her face. He found himself wondering if her lips were as soft as they looked and if she would taste like... He snapped himself out of that thought before he could finish it. No, he was not marrying this woman.

He would give her a place to stay tonight and get her back on the train in the morning. Thinking about marrying her and kissing her were the thoughts of a mad man – and he had no time or room for madness in his life. Or another woman, for that matter. He had enough on his hands with the town and his mother.

"I apologize, Miss May, but I wasn't expecting..." To be the least bit interested in any woman who'd come out here without guarantee about her future? No, he wasn't interested. He just appreciated a beautiful woman.

He shook the thought from his mind and stretched his hand out toward her. "I wasn't expecting to be taking anyone home with me," he finished as she slid her gloved hand into his. He took his foot out of the stirrup, and she slid her boot into it, knowing how to swing herself into the saddle behind him without him saying anything. She knows her way around horses then.

The rest of his argument dissolved in a whoosh when her arms wrapped around his middle. For the second time that day, he nearly wished he were the kind of man who prayed for help from the Almighty. He needed as much of it as he could get with her pressed against his back. Already, her warmth against his back made his skin heat up. His pulse danced a bit, and his thoughts strayed to places they really shouldn't have gone about a woman he had no intention to marry.

He tipped his hat at Jack, still standing there with that grin. "I'll be back to close up. Folks know where they can find me if I'm not around. Just lock the door before you head North."

"Will do, Sheriff," Jack drawled. "It was nice to meet you, Miss May. I hope we will see you in town once you're settled and all."

Isaac shot him an icy look that only made Jack's grin grow. Without another word, he nudged his horse and headed home. Isaac didn't live far out of town and he was thankful for that. He wasn't sure how long he could handle feeling her behind him before he forgot every reason why he didn't need a wife. He ran through the list of reasons why he wasn't a married man a few times. He silently reminded himself why Miss May would get back on that train and return to Virginia as soon as possible.

The nightmares that woke him, his job that meant she may well be a widow younger than most other women, his temper, his long hours at work, the crazy times people came banging on the door needing help. It was a long list that he'd been building since he'd come home. Many local matrons did their best to match him with this cousin or that sister who would be more than happy to move to Franklin to be with him.

He had no intention of marrying any time soon. He had his hands full with his mother and his job. He didn't have time for a wife, either. Not another person that he was responsible for. Not another person he could lose.

***

He held open the door to let Lydia inside, and she stepped through the doorway, her curious eyes scanning the living space. He tried to imagine how it would appear to her, suddenly self-conscious of their meager living habits. He and Ma had done their best to keep the place clean, though it was far from spotless. The furniture was well made. Most of it was purchased in nearby counties as they'd settled in when his father had taken the sheriff position here and moved them across three states.

They'd left most of the furniture in the house he'd grown up in, taking only the sentimental pieces with them as they'd packed their belongings into the train car they'd rented space in. The high-backed chairs gathered around the fireplace were sturdy, the tables flanking them a golden pine that matched the coffee table.

A quilt lying over the back of the chair, memories stitched into each inch. Curtains hung at the windows, and a rug lay across the floor under the low center table. Aside from portraits of his family on the walls, there was little else of note about it.

"The kitchen is through there," he was still holding her trunk and gestured toward the doorway on the other side of the living area. He didn't say anything about the sitting room just to the right of the doorway. She wouldn't be staying long enough to need to know about that, anyway.

Then he turned and pointed to an open doorway to the right. He moved toward it and didn't turn to see if Lydia followed. He laid her travel bag on the end of the bed and turned, looking around this room, too. There wasn't much to it: a bed, a dressing table, and a highboy in the corner, but the window looked over the side garden. "I'll let you get settled. I'll be in the kitchen if you need anything."

As he moved the cornbread into the oven, he heard someone come into the kitchen behind him. Based on the click of her boots, he knew it was Lydia. He swiped the towel off the counter and wiped his hands, turning to meet her eyes. She'd shed her traveling coat, though she still wore the skirt of her suit. Her crisp white shirt seemed out of place, but he didn't mention it. He tried his best to mimic one of Jack's smiles instead. "All settled?"

"Yes, thank you. I feel better after a quick wash in the basin." She smiled. "Would you like any help?"

She reached toward the basket of peas and the potatoes he'd set on the table to get started after the cornbread was in the oven. He nodded, gesturing to the table. "I would appreciate it," he said, sitting across from where she settled at the table and reaching for a potato and a knife, the towel tossed over his shoulder. "I didn't know if you cooked or not, being a southern–"

"I do," she snapped. Isaac flinched. He had assumed she was the daughter of a plantation owner. If she wasn't, then how had she been able to afford clothes like these? She continued before he could say anything, her tone slightly annoyed. "Pa never brought enough money home for us to afford a cook. He made sure Theo, my brother, and I could handle ourselves in the kitchen. When the war came, I had to do it all myself." For the brief minute she allowed herself to meet his gaze, her eyes held anger.

Was it due to his assumption, or was there something more? The tightness around her eyes didn't match the simple slip he'd made. There was something she wasn't telling him. Under other circumstances, he'd have pressed to find out what it was. Reminding himself that she would be on a train by the end of the day tomorrow, he let the curiosity go.

"My apologies, Miss... Lydia. I was wrong to assume anything about your past." He corrected his slip on her name and tilted his head to the side, trying to show her his sincere attempt at being friendly. "Well, since you know your way around a kitchen, what is your favorite way to cook..." he grinned wider and held up the potato he'd just peeled, "...the humble potato?"

Her smile hit him in the chest, and he fought to keep his expression the same for a second. Then, her smile fell back into the near scowl she'd been wearing since he'd commented about her ability to cook. He studied her as she told him about the many ways her father had taught her to fry a potato. She paused, bit her lip, sniffed slightly, and continued her chatter, and he nicked his finger with the knife in his hand.

Was that... was she crying? Her voice gave no hint as she continued speaking. "My favorite, though, is when he'd sauté them in butter and garlic. He'd cut them into wedges that were the size of my thumb. You must cook them until the centers are starting to brown, but the edges can't cook too long, or they'll burn. It's not the easiest way, but the work is worth it when they're ready."

He looked at the pile of peeled potatoes. "I have garlic and butter," he offered. "Would you like to help me cook them that way? We have some salted pork in the smokehouse behind too."

"That sounds lovely." She cut in with an easy smile, dropping the last peas she'd shelled back into the basket. "I'll handle these and keep an eye on that cornbread while you go out for it." She stood, collected her basket, and headed for the stove. He followed her to the other side of the kitchen with the potatoes.

"The butter is in the pantry on the top shelf," he said, backing away from the stove where she began hunting for the right pan. The scowl was back, and he didn't trust her not to accidentally hit him with one when she found it. "Garlic is in the corner cabinet." He pointed to the pie safe, the cabinet his father had built that stood in the corner of the kitchen, his eyes leaving her for the smallest of seconds.

"Thank you," Lydia said, her voice suddenly tight, like she was having trouble getting the words past her lips. It drew his eyes back to hers as she turned toward him, dropping her hands away from the stove and lifting her gaze to his. Was it the light, or were her eyes a little watery?

"It's just garlic and butter, Miss May," he said, bumping into the chair he'd left pulled out at the table to stand up a few minutes ago. He'd backed across the kitchen to get away from those tears. He'd never handled his mother's tears very well. The few women he'd had time for when he was younger hadn't changed his ability to not feel like the worst kind of man when he saw their eyes turning red. "No need for thanks for those."

"It's more than that, and you know it. Thank you for agreeing to take me in. Thank you for saving me from whatever Mister Burns had planned. And..." she paused, her gaze dropping. "Thank you for agreeing to marry me."

"Um, Miss May, there's something I should–" Why did this woman have him fumbling like a fool? His voice wasn't steady, his balance was off, and his nerves were dancing like the first time he'd helped his father catch a criminal. Were her shoulders suddenly stiff?

"Lydia," she interrupted him, her voice a bit sharp. "I asked you to call me Lydia."

"Yes, well, Lydia." He cleared his throat. How do you tell a woman that even though you announced that you needed a wife and brought her home, you had no intention of marrying her? How do you look her in the eye and tell her that you're not marrying her? That you're sending her back East as fast as you possibly could?

"Isaac?" she asked, concern filling her voice as she stepped toward him, her hands reaching as if to catch him before he fell. "Are you alright?"

His eyes avoided hers, but he knew he had to be honest. She deserved that much. He took a deep breath and closed his eyes, blurting the words just to get it over with. "Lydia... I can't marry you."

Chapter Five

"Excuse me?" she asked, leaning forward as if she hadn't heard him.

"I can't marry you," he repeated, this time a little louder. "I only said that to keep you out of Burns' hands and..."

"What do you mean you 'can't' marry me? Are you already married?" She stepped toward him, now, definite lines of anger beginning to seep into her expression. "I'm afraid I don't understand, Sheriff Branson."

"Fred is bad news," he fought to keep his voice from becoming angry. He needed to sound as logical as his intentions had been. "I do not doubt that he has less than savory plans for your friend, and I couldn't stomach the gleam in his eye when he had his hands on two women. I tried to rescue you both but, without someone else for your friend to be claimed, but my hands were tied..."

"Claimed?" she hissed. "You think you claimed me? Or that he claimed Birdie? Without either of us being given a choice? I was given to understand that arrangements had been made to see to the women who arrived on this train to leave them some room for propriety to preserve their reputations. Is this not so?"

The anger danced in her eyes, and it took his breath away. He'd heard of women being even more beautiful when angry, and he'd never understood it before now. The rosy color rising to her cheeks made the pale gray of her eyes even more impossible to look away from. The quiet woman who'd followed him back to his horse was gone and in her place was... he wasn't sure what! But he found it difficult to keep his thoughts in line because of it. He scrambled to focus on what she'd said and form an answer. "No, I mean... Yes, but–"

"I am not baggage, Sheriff. You can't claim me like you'd pull a trunk from a coach. I came out here to find a family, a place where I was needed. Now you're saying that even though you offered it to me with an entire town full of witnesses and brought me to your home, you have no intention of honoring your offer? Not even after I had accepted it?" Her voice rose as she progressed through her speech. By the end, she was shouting at him, her chest rising and falling as if she was having trouble breathing. He had no idea what was happening behind those eyes as they shifted frantically around as she kept pacing a small circle on the floor and wringing her hands together. Her movements confused him as he tried to place what was going on to approach the situation. The angry lines of her shoulders and the fire that lit her eyes made his heart thump wildly in his chest. The worried twist of her fingers as her hands knotted together in front of her chest brought out every protective instinct he'd ever professed in protecting his town and his regiment during the war.

He was afraid to interrupt her, though he'd lifted his hand to get her attention to do just that. She paid him no heed, and just as his patience wore off. He opened his mouth to halt her pacing, and she stopped still, her face melting into a look of shock as if she put pieces of a puzzle together. Her eyes flicked to his with a stare that froze him on the spot and any impression of passion he thought he'd seen vanished like smoke from a snuffed candle. "Is THIS what you meant when you said you hadn't intended to bring anyone home with you today? I assumed..."

"I made no offer!" He yelled his interruption back at her, finally finding his voice under the cold fire of her stare. "Everyone just assumed that I meant you on that platform. I never asked you to marry me, Lydia. I was just trying to save you..."

"From what?" she demanded, still no hint of the fiery passion he'd seen in her eyes just moments ago. He stared at her, dumbfounded for a moment before he answered. "Fred Burns tries to skirt the law every chance he gets. He hired a substitute rather than join the war back East. He came West, thinking to get rich, and somehow landed here in Franklin.

He tried the gold mines, and when he didn't make money fast enough that way, he opened a saloon here. The only reason the community didn't run him out of town is that he's the only place in town that serves food they don't have to cook long after the kitchens in the hotel are cold. Some folks who live in town..."

"I don't care about some folks in town, Isaac! I care about why I'm standing here making potatoes and snapping peas for a man who brought me home with no intention of carrying through on the unspoken contract that that action entailed! You could've done any number of things with me, from putting me back on the train to finding a place for me to stay. Instead, you brought me home like a lost pup!" She was shouting again and had taken a step toward him.

"I arranged a place for you! Even at the last minute, I arranged a place for you!" He shouted back at her, leaning forward in answer to the fiery heat in her eyes. Her anger had brought her closer to him, and his had refused to give an inch to her. He refused to concede even a fraction of fault for misleading her. His fists were clenched at his sides as he fought for control of his temper by whatever shred he could muster while the temptation to grab her and shake some sense into her was held in check by the thinnest of lines. "It just happens to be that the place is my place—"

"Isaac?" came a thin voice from the doorway. His head whipped to the door and the sight of his mother standing there in her night dress. "Oh..."

The heat of his anger washed out of him as if he'd been doused in cold water. His voice was little more than a whisper. "Ma?"

The woman in the doorway groaned, pressing a hand to her head and another to her stomach. He felt Lydia move at the same time he did, and they both launched at her as her eyes rolled back and she slumped.

Chapter Six

Isaac scooped his mother off the floor, hurriedly pushing in a bedroom on the other side of the living room. Lydia followed close behind him, her mind whirling around what had just happened. Fear sent her pulse into a frantic rhythm. Isaac's mother looked as thin and worn as her father had when his seizures had deteriorated.

That had been almost ten years ago, but the fear would feel while watching him collapse had buried itself deep into her memories. She'd seen the discoloration under this woman's eyes when she'd turned. Her rage and the feeling of betrayal had dissolved as soon as she'd heard the thin voice call his name. She felt the sharp pang in her chest as her heart lurched from the near panic of anger to the shock of surprise.

With a firm shake of her head, she focused on what she was doing. At that moment, it was chasing Isaac across the living room and into one of the doors that had been closed earlier. Why had his mother passed out? Had they caused this with their anger and yelling? Did she suffer from seizures because of a broken heart like her father? The questions tumbled like dice in her mind as she paused to let Isaac have the room he needed to lay the woman down on the bed that took up most of the room.

He stayed bent, his hands moving to her throat and then her forehead, checking her pulse and temperature. Content that he didn't need the space anymore, Lydia reached past him, her hands reaching for the bow tied in the strings at his mother's neck as if by habit. Her hands were shaking as she remembered her father's episodes. If Isaac's mother had anywhere near the trouble her father had...

Isaac slapped her hands away, and Lydia bristled visibly. "I know what I'm doing," she growled, reaching for his mother again. Again, he slapped her hands away, and she curled her hands into fists. "After my mother died, my brother said my father's health turned bad. He was afraid we'd be orphans, but then Pa got better. Years later, though, he still had episodes much like your mother's. The first thing we always did was loosen whatever tie was around his throat to help open his breathing passages. Then we'd prop him up and try to cool his skin."

He pinned her with a look. "Please, just... let me help you?" She felt the weight of guilt in her chest and heard the tone in her voice, begging him to let her help. He gave in reluctantly and stepped back to allow her to get closer to the woman, his mother, on the bed. Lydia did as she said she would, untying the laces at his mother's throat first, then adjusting her pillow at a higher angle. She pointed to the pillow in the rocking chair a few feet away, and Isaac passed it to her, wordlessly accepting that she knew what she was doing. Before long, his mother's eyes fluttered open again, and her lips tried to tilt into a smile as her eyes met Lydia's.

Lydia smiled back at her and felt confidence return to her. She'd helped Isaac's mother just as she'd helped Pa.

"Alright, doctor, what next?" Isaac asked. It was his turn to be grumpy, and his voice came out in a growl.

"Next, she needs some sugar water and a cool cloth. You stay here. I'll see what I can gather myself." She turned to go, but Isaac stopped her with a hand out.

"I'll get it. You won't know where to find things. I can get them and get back faster. Just..." he paused and ran his hand through his hair. "Just stay with her."

Lydia bit her lip at his retreating back and wrung her hands. Five minutes ago, she'd been yelling at him in anger and fear. And now?

She sighed, turning back to his mother and noting the woman had drifted asleep. Now, she was fighting off the urge to hug him and tell him everything was going to be ok. She'd make sure of it.

When Isaac returned, he had his hands full. He set the bowl of water down and pulled the cloth off his shoulder. "I'll go back for–"

"It's okay. I'll go get it. Stay with your mother. You'll see she's already so much better," Lydia smiled softly and left the room. She didn't close the door behind her as she crossed the living room and slipped into the kitchen.

The potatoes were still where they'd left them, though her chair was on the floor beside the table. When did that happen? She righted the chair, then turned to spot the glass Isaac had left on the counter. She dipped her finger into the water and tasted it. "Perfect," she murmured, pleased that he'd remembered the sugar water. She left the kitchen and headed back for the bedroom where Isaac and his mother were softly talking. His mother had woken up while she'd been out of the room.

Outside the door, Lydia paused, hearing Isaac narrate the day's events and how he and Lydia came to be arguing in the kitchen. She leaned against the wall, still holding the bowl and glass in her hands, eavesdropping on their conversation. She'd feel guilty about it later. For now, she needed to understand what he was thinking.

"'Don't forget to do good and to share what you have. Because God is pleased with these kinds of sacrifices,'" she heard his mother's soft voice reciting scripture and smiled. Hearing it eased her mind about walking into a Godless marriage. Not that this was going to be a marriage, she reminded herself. He was planning on sending her back East tomorrow. "You brought her here, Isaac.

Of all the things you could've done, you brought her here. Something in you knew that you were missing something and saw what you were missing in that girl. You must do what is right in the eyes of God. Your father would say the same, and well, you know it." She paused, and Lydia heard the humor in the woman's voice when she spoke again. "He might add a bit about upholding the honor of the family name too."

Lydia could almost hear the smile in the woman's voice, the fondness she felt for her husband. She spoke about him in the past tense, Lydia mused. Does that mean he'd passed on? She wrinkled her brow, adjusting her opinion of Isaac a bit. Had he taken on the responsibility of his mother's health as well as becoming Sheriff at such a young age?

"I couldn't care less about what God feels is right," Isaac grumbled. Lydia bit her lip to keep her gasp from giving her away. How had a woman who could quote Bible verses raised a son who was so opposed to the idea of Him?

She decided not to wait to find out and launched herself away from the wall, entering the room with the bowl and glass of sugar water. "Ah, you're awake." She smiled. "I brought you some sugar water to help you feel better. It always worked for my father, so I hope it will help you, too." She passed the glass to the woman on the bed. "If you'll allow it, I'll pass the damp cloth over your face and neck for you. You can continue talking that way."

Isaac's mother smiled warmly at her, accepting the glass. "Thank you, child. You're sweet to help someone you've never met."

"I was raised that you do what's right, ma'am," she smiled. "Helping others brings honor to God, for it was His son's work. I merely do what I can to help those who need it."

The woman's eyes twinkled, catching the reference to the scripture she'd quoted earlier and knowing Lydia had heard her. Lydia soaked the cloth in the water, which had begun to cool, and wrung it out. As she pressed it over the woman's forehead, Isaac startled them both by standing up and walking to the door.

She watched him go, unsure about whether she should let him tend to his mother or if there was something else he was going to get. Did she forget something? Was there something else that would help this woman relax from the exertion of the seizure?

He paused at the door frame, and she watched the fear leave his shoulders. She was still watching him when he looked back at them both. His eyes shifted to Lydia, where she stood next to his mother, the cloth still in her hand a few inches away from his mother's forehead. There was a heaviness to his posture that hadn't been there a few moments ago.

She drew her breath in, silently begging him not to say anything to his mother about sending her home tomorrow. When he spoke, his voice was quiet, but there was a tone of finality to it that made her shiver. "I will marry you, Lydia. I will honor the agreement I made by claiming you as my bride. We will speak with Bishop Day first thing in the morning."

With that, he turned and strode from the room. In the silence he left behind him, Lydia heard his boots cross the living room and the thud of the front door close behind him. Lydia frowned, staring at the open bedroom door as if someone was going to come along and make what happened make sense.

No one did.

Chapter Seven

Isaac turned his thoughts everywhere but where he was going. He'd hitched up the wagon to bring Lydia and his mother to the Bowery but fussed over his mother the entire trip to ensure she was comfortable. She and Lydia were sitting in the back, where his fiancée had piled blankets to make that trip comfortable for Cora. Cora swatted at them for making such a fuss, especially since this was their day.

He'd been silent for the last few minutes, listening to the soft murmur of voices behind him. Lydia had her head bowed close to Cora, and they were deep in conversation. Their hushed tones meant it wasn't a conversation for him, but his curiosity was getting the best of him. He pulled on the neck of his shirt, needing a little less restriction on his airway. Feeling the button and the tie reminded him of their morning thus far.

Not thirty minutes ago, Cora had swatted his hands away from his terrible attempts at a necktie and tied it for him. She pressed the necktie flat along the front seam of his shirt to make sure it was hanging straight. "There. That sweet girl won't know what hit her."

It hadn't taken long for him to realize his mother had it all wrong. His mother settled into a chair to wait for them, and Isaac excused himself to hitch the wagon and bring it around to the door from the barn. He took his time, giving her plenty of time to get dressed. She was a woman, and it was her wedding day. It was understandable that she'd need time.

When he brought the wagon around the front, Lydia was helping his mother down the few steps to the dirt drive. He slowed the horse to ensure he didn't kick up a lot of dust and ruin their lovely dresses, so he focused mostly on the horse and the dirt as it shifted under the wagon. That was his excuse as he turned to step off the wagon seat and help his mother into the wagon. As he landed on the ground and looked up, he met Lydia's eyes, and his knees nearly buckled under him.

Her hair gleaming in the morning sunlight made the curving strands leading the knot she'd tied her hair into seeming almost like a glowing halo. Where he'd assumed her eyes were gray the previous day, they seemed to be almost green this morning. It was difficult to see them clearly from this distance, but he felt the pressure of her eyes on him like a physical weight. It seemed odd, considering they looked more like fresh moss on the edge of a pond, light and soft. She and Cora had nearly reached the wagon by the time he snapped out of it and helped.

***

They reached town too soon, and he was drawing up the wagon in front of the covered pavilion that made up the town's meeting space and Bowery before he was ready.

Bishop Day erupted from under the thatched roof of the Bowery as Isaac came around the wagon. A wide smile on his lips and his hands rubbing together in glee. "Sheriff Branson! I was hoping to see you today," the Bishop said jovially as his hand clasped Isaac's in greeting. Isaac breathed a little easier as the Bishop turned his attention to Cora, who was hanging on to Isaac's arm for support. "And Mrs. Cora, so wonderful to see you out and about."

Cora fluttered a hand at his flowery speech and laughed. "If you'd move the town closer to our place, you wouldn't have to wait so long to see me in town."

Lydia laughed at the exchange, which drew Bishop Day's eyes to where she was standing a few steps behind them. His smile deepened, and Isaac saw the man's eyes darken in sincere happiness as he stretched a hand toward her. "You must be the bride-to-be," he said softly, his fingers curling around hers.

"Lydia," she responded. He didn't have to turn around to see the smile, it was evident in her voice. "Lydia May. It's a pleasure to meet you, Bishop Day."

"The pleasure is all mine, Miss Day." He patted her hand still clasped in his, his voice quiet. He turned back to Isaac and Cora, his arms sweeping wide as he released Lydia's hand. "You are the first couple here this morning, so you will be the first ones married today! Have a seat near the front, and we will begin shortly."

As promised, Bishop Day took his place behind the narrow podium within minutes and called the group together. Isaac looked around, having not noticed how many people had come in while they waited for the service to begin. Bishop Day spoke for a few moments on the sanctity of marriage, sounding just like every preacher Isaac had ever heard. Isaac looked around at the people filling the first few rows of the benches in a circle around the podium. He was snapped from his observation and growing dread about everyone watching when the Bishop turned to them.

"Isaac Branson and Lydia May?"

Isaac looked up to meet the man's kind eyes and nodded as Bishop Day waved them forward. Isaac stood, kissed his mother's cheek, then held his hand out for Lydia. She eased her hand into his like it was the most natural thing in the world. He couldn't help noticing how cold her fingers were, how small they felt in his. Her fingers slid easily between his, drawing their palms together as they moved toward the podium.

Bishop Day moved from his place and gestured them into the proper positions. Isaac felt even more out of place as he knelt on the bench across from Lydia. She hadn't released his hand as she'd knelt. He'd been too worried about looking like a fool before this many townsfolk to notice until that moment. He lifted his eyes to meet hers, and she smiled at him, the smile reaching her eyes and dancing in their crystalized depths. It closed the space between them, and he had to admit, he preferred this to standing awkwardly in front of people who stared holes in his back.

After that, the service became a haze in his mind, punctuated by the pinches on his hands when he missed a cue. Lydia was smiling, obviously paying more attention than he was and enjoying pulling him back into it. His free hand was curled into a tight fist on the tabletop next to their clasped hands as he fought off wave after wave of discomfort.

He hadn't stepped foot in anything close to a religious service since he'd left the field hospital on his way home. His wandering eyes fell on Lydia's concerned frown and followed her gaze to his free hand on the bench. Great, he thought. She saw his white knuckles. Irritated, dropped it to his side. Sweat beaded his forehead as scripture was recited by Bishop Day.

"But the salvation of the righteous is of the LORD: he is their strength in the time of trouble," the Bishop's voice drew his attention up to the man. His heart stopped, and he felt the rush of adrenaline that told him to run coursing through him. Isaac knew that scripture. It was Psalm 37:39. He'd used it to pray often while kneeling in the mud and half-starved. He'd spoken it to his unit to give them comfort when those times of trouble had come upon them in camp.

Those days when the rations were full of insects and the rain, like their marching beats, never seemed to stop. His eyes met Lydia's, and the words of salvation seemed to ring like a bell in his head. The calm smile on her lips and the way her hand was curled into his pulled him back from the brink of the nightmare that woke him from sleep at night. Was that what she was? Salvation? The quiet strength of the way she held his hand as if she didn't want to hurt him or draw his attention away from what was happening but with no intention of letting go.

"I, Lydia Evelyn May," her voice reached through his discomfort, and he found solace in its soft tone. There was no tremor in her voice, no hint of insecurity or fear. He lifted his eyes to see hers watching him. "Take you, Isaac Branson, as my husband." She promised to love, honor, and keep him, to be there with him until death separated them.

"I, Isaac David Branson, take you, Lydia May, as my wife." He repeated the words Bishop Day fed him while looking into her eyes. He couldn't promise to love her, but he could promise to honor and protect her. He amended the vow as he spoke it, earning a surprised gasp from the matrons watching. Bishop Day took it in stride and continued the service without comment. Somewhere in the haze, he produced his grandmother's wedding band from his vest pocket and slid it onto Lydia's finger.

"I hereby pronounce you husband and wife!" Bishop Day was nearly shouting in his joy. Clearly, this was one of his favorite parts of his job. "You may kiss your bride."

Isaac flinched, then leaned forward to press his lips to Lydia's cheek.

"It is my pleasure to introduce you to Mister and Mrs. Isaac Branson!"

***

Isaac ignored the looks the townsfolk threw at him as he passed them on his way to the Sheriff's office a few hours later. He knew what they were thinking. It was his wedding day. He had a new bride at home. Why was he riding into town like he did after lunch every day? What was he thinking?

In truth, he was thinking about how easily Lydia had slipped into the role of housewife. While he'd gotten his mother settled in her room, she'd made him a bowl of stew that she'd cooked early this morning and left on the stove. When he'd come into the kitchen to find her, the bowl of steaming stew and fresh slices of bread were waiting for him at the table, and she was at the sink working through the morning dishes.

She'd asked which chores his mother enjoyed taking care of so she might know which ones were left, nodding with understanding as he described the most mundane of tasks. Her easy acceptance of what she would be doing all day. "What is your schedule like each day? Is there a time you like to have breakfast and supper? Do you come home for lunch?" He could still hear her voice, and he'd been dumbfounded at her efficiency at taking up housekeeping. Her lack of surprise or anger that he meant to ride back into town and work on their wedding day – at her not bringing up that he'd never promised to love her in his vows. She didn't mention sleeping arrangements, either.

"Afternoon, Sheriff," his Deputy, Jack Sharpe said, his voice rising at the end like it was a question.

"I want to check out Burn's Saloon," Isaac answered the unspoken question. "I don't trust Fred Burns as far as I can throw him, and I mean to make sure the girl he took home is being taken care of."

"Today?" Jack asked incredulously, his feet sliding off his desk as he leaned forward.

"Do you have other plans?" Isaac shot back at him, his eyebrow rising. He didn't wait for an answer, just grabbed a pistol belt from the case next to his

Jack shook his head and rose to his feet. "Maybe so," he conceded. "Do you want to go now? I was reading reports of trouble along the western town border and..."

Isaac nodded. "Good idea. I'll look when we get back. We'll compare notes on both the reports and what we learn from Fred Burns. Let's head over to the Saloon."

Franklin was not a large town, though the streets were wide, and the four blocks inside the fort were lined with a mix of homes and businesses, most of them owned by the pioneers that founded the town. The Bowery stood at the crossroads at the center of the town, protected on all sides by the other buildings. Isaac avoided looking that way due to the reminder of his discomfort that morning. His eyes moved upward, and he wondered if God was offended by his lack of faith while pledging his life to a woman who obviously revered Him.

He shook that off, and they turned toward the Saloon. It was midday, so a few patrons were inside for a quick bite to eat and a drink before returning to work. Isaac nodded to them, plastering a smile on his lips to set them at ease. He wasn't there for them.

Birdie came around the end of the bar and stopped dead in her tracks, seeing Jack and Isaac standing there. She adjusted her direction and ducked behind the bar as if trying to avoid them. Isaac's unease grew.

He and Jack strode to the bar and took seats. The woman avoided them, so the usual bartender, Smiley, slung a stained towel over his shoulder. "What can I get you, Sheriff? Deputy?"

"Whiskey," Isaac answered easily.

Jack nodded and lifted his hand. "Same."

Birdie was trying to talk to walk past them without a conversation starting, but Jack turned on his charm, trying to get her attention. "I'm so glad you're settling in," he said jovially. She shot him a glare by way of an answer. She ducked around the other end of the bar, her hands full of mugs of sloshing beer. Jack turned raised eyebrows on Isaac, who glowered back. He downed the whiskey and dropped coins enough to cover both drinks and a nice tip for Smiley before he rose and followed the woman.

"A word, if you please?" he asked her, his tone sounding like the exact opposite of a question.

"I don't want to talk to you," she said stiffly, not looking at him as she cleared a table nearby. "Fred said you'd be asking questions. He just didn't say it would be this soon."

"I wanted to check on you. Lydia is worried and…" he let the sentence drift off.

"There's nothing to worry about," she snapped. "As you can see, I'm fine."

She looked at him, that time, and bit off a curse. There was a bruise running down her cheek, a haunting dimness in her eyes, and a pleading tilt of her lips. At least as much as they could move, given how swollen the top lip was on one side. She'd done her best to cover the deep purple lines, slathering on layers of rouge in a vain attempt at disguising what she didn't want anyone, especially not him, to see. He stepped closer to ask about it when Fred Burns' voice boomed out from the stairs to the rooms he let on the second floor. When he glanced back at Birdie, her head was down again, her hair falling to hide the damage to her face. "Why are you harassing my wife, Sheriff? Is she wanted for something?"

Jack slid out of his seat at the bar to stand at Isaac's shoulder in silent defense. "Your wife, eh?" Jack turned to get confirmation from the woman, his smile faltering as she nodded at him stiffly.

"Go upstairs, Birdie," Fred ordered the woman as he approached them. "Clean the first room on the left."

They all watched her nod, her head still lowered, and head up the stairs without a word to anyone. The whole interaction made Isaac's stomach churn and he turned his gaze to Fred, his jaw clenched. Fred turned back to them; his lips stretched into an oily snarl, talking before Isaac could get a word out. "If you've got a question, Sheriff, you can ask me. Leave her out of it."

Isaac felt his jaw tighten even more. "Are you afraid she'll tell me something you don't want me to know?"

"I don't want you making her upset," Burns shot back.

"Did you hit her??" Isaac fired at him, his hands clenching at his sides.

"She fell," Burns answered with a careless shrug.

He didn't elaborate and Isaac growled out, "Did you marry her?" Jack laid a hand on his shoulder, a silent reminder that he couldn't just attack Fred Burns in his own establishment. Even if he had hit his wife, there was no law against it. There was nothing Isaac or Jack could do if she didn't ask them for help.

"Did I not say she was my wife?" Burns responded, annoyed. "Now, if there's nothing else, I trust you know where the door is?"

Isaac nearly growled, but he nodded and left, Jack following closely behind. He had every intention of checking with Bishop Day about the wedding. Far from setting his mind at ease, he was now even more determined to find out why Burns wanted a woman badly enough to get one off the Bride Train.

He needed to know why Birdie looked so afraid of Burns when he'd appeared and why Burns felt so comfortable barking orders at her. Something was not right, and he had to get to the bottom of it before Birdie was seriously hurt.

He and Jack stalked back to the Sheriff's office, neither noticing the way the sidewalks cleared for them to pass. They entered the office, Isaac heading to his chair and Jack heading to his, both intent on finding something to calm them down, and both failing miserably. After an hour of shuffling paper around on his desk and pacing between his desk and Jack's on the opposite wall, one hand on his hip and the other at his lower lip, as if tapping it would help him figure out what Burns was up to.

He muttered and turned toward the door. "I'm heading back to the house."

Jack nodded quietly in answer, his brows furrowed as he read through the reports he'd been working on when Isaac arrived earlier. Isaac was nearly out the door when he heard Jack call his name. He turned and fixed his Deputy with a look that relayed his frustration and annoyance. Jack didn't even flinch. His lips stretched into a wide grin and his voice sounded a bit melodic as he said, "Forgot to say it earlier but... Congratulations on your nuptials!"

Isaac's scowl darkened and he slammed the door on his way out.

Chapter Eight

Lydia was singing to herself as she bustled around the kitchen. She pulled out vegetables and lined them up on the counter, then put another log on the fire she'd started to warm up the stew she'd started at breakfast time. She ran through her list of things to do, having already anticipated most of them, and started a few of them last night while Isaac was still spending time with his mother after dinner.

She'd stuck to cooking and washing dishes, then had gathered her clothes and the towels in the kitchen that needed washing. She hadn't done more than put them in a stack, though.

She knew a few girls in Maysville who had married and moved in with their husband's families before the war started. Once the men of the house weren't around to buffer the tension between the women, there was trouble. Mothers who didn't appreciate being reminded that they had been replaced as the lady of the house warred with new brides who were eager to establish the home they'd been taught to run from childhood.

During the war, they'd come into the dressmaker's and chatter while Lydia was working on their fittings, complaining about their mothers-in-law and the things that seemed to set them off on a rant. For some, it was moving furniture or changing out paintings. For others, it was far more simple things like their choices for what to put on the table at dinner time. No, Lydia wasn't going to move a grain of spice from the rack without talking to her mother-in-law first.

That thought drew her up short and she raised her left hand to look down at the ring on her finger. She was too focused on the odd weight of the ring on her finger that Cora startled her when she entered the kitchen. "It's lovely, isn't it? I loved looking at it when I was a girl." She walked into the kitchen and talked while filling up the tea kettle and putting it on the stove.

"My mother was so careful with it, never washing dishes with it on her finger. I would have been surprised if she took it off every time she washed her hands, truthfully. She said my father had spent his entire life's savings on it when they got married."

She laughed and shook her head, picking out two cups and sitting them on the table Without a single shake in her hands. "Do you take sugar or honey?" she asked Lydia, her eyebrows lifting in question.

"Honey, please," Lydia smiled and approached, helping gather whatever Cora forgot. The kettle whistled while Cora put her collection of cups, spoons, plates, a jar of honey, and a small bowl of sugar cubes on the table. Lydia removed the steaming kettle, swiped the canister labeled "TEA" from the counter next to the stove, and approached the table with them.

"I prefer sugar, but honey is easier to get out here," Cora laughed. She'd already set up the table for their tea.

Lydia settled the hot kettle on an iron trivet and opened the tea canister. A floral smell lifted from it, and Lydia's brow wrinkled as she tried to place the scent. "Chamomile?"

"And orange blossoms," Cora added, her smile widening. "You like herbal tea?"

"I do, indeed." Lydia laughed. "It reminds me of home." She meant the home she'd had with her father and her brother, of course. Netty had continued having tea with her when she'd moved to the boarding house, at times bringing new dishes she was trying for the dining room with her, to keep her from feeling so alone. Lydia had packed the remainder of her tea in her bag but hadn't brought it to the kitchen yet.

"I hope it will help you make this place your home, too," Cora said quietly. She dipped a teaspoon into the canister, scooped out a measure of leaves, lifted the lid from the teapot, and dumped them inside before putting it back on. "This is an oolong base, which is very hard to get out here. My brother mails canisters to me from St. Louis for my birthday and for Christmas because he knows how much I love it."

Lydia was silent as grief and loneliness shot through her at the mention of Cora's brother. It's the kind of thing her own brother would've done, too. She shook that out of her mind and changed the subject. "Isaac was glad I would be able to help you with housekeeping. I've handled the dishes, and I was going to work on the laundry next. Is that alright?"

Cora's brows were knitted together in concern, but she allowed Lydia to change the conversation. "Is there anyone in the world that would say no to someone else doing laundry?"

Lydia's lips twitched. "Yes. Well, I don't want to step on your toes. This being your house, I want to make sure I'm not being a bother. Is there anything you'd prefer I not do?"

"You're a sweet girl," Cora said by way of answering. "I haven't been able to keep up with everything, so I'm glad for your help, too. The help and the companionship. I have visitors every now and then, but I am generally here by myself for most of the day. It will be nice to have someone to talk to. Even if I was determined to do things myself, I would be so glad to have someone to talk to that I'd never say a word. I am not all that fussy, dear. As we get better acquainted, we can work out who is responsible for what. Does that suit you?"

Lydia knew she was really going to like Cora. "Very much," she responded, lifting the lid of the teapot and inhaling the scent. "It will be lovely to have someone to talk to. I haven't had many women to talk to in my life. Netty, the woman who ran the boarding house, and the woman at the dressmaker's shop who hired me, Mary, are the only ones who were more than a passing conversation."

Cora reached across the table and closed her hand over Lydia's. "Losing people is hard. We can grieve for them together. I lost my husband last year. I thought I'd lost my son a few years before that. For a brief moment, I had them both back under one roof." She shook her head and lifted the teapot, filling each of their cups with a practiced motion. "Then my husband got sick, and everything changed."

They were silent for a few minutes, each lost in their own thoughts, as they sipped their tea with one hand, and clasped hands with the other. The large clock in the next room dinged the hour and pulled them out of their memories. Cora patted the back of Lydia's hand. "So, if you're going to handle the wash, then I will start working on dusting. Have you already started dinner preparations? Is there something I can do to help with that?"

Lydia smiled, her voice a bit thick with emotion, "I would love to cook with you, Mrs. Branson. I haven't started it. I was going to take stock of the smokehouse to decide what to put on the table for dinner."

Cora winked. "Just wait until I'm burning the water I'm boiling, and then see if you feel the same!" Lydia laughed at the unexpectedness of her statement, and Cora continued. "The smokehouse is full of venison and beef. There is at least one chicken out there. I bet he forgot to tell you about the animals?"

Lydia blinked. "He mentioned something about the barn but didn't go into detail. He said that would most likely fall to him to do." She narrowed her eyes. "Does he think I can't handle the workload?"

"I'm sure he does, but he doesn't see what I see yet," Cora answered, gathering their tea cups and spoons and taking them to the sink. Lydia collected the tea box and kettle and followed behind her.

"And what is that?" she asked.

"Stubborn refusal to give in when the odds are stacked against you," Cora answered, turning toward her with a smile. "Most girls I know wouldn't have done what you did. Even when their prospects were not good, getting on a train and reaching the end of the line to marry a man you've never even corresponded with was a big chance.

Only someone with nothing left to lose would even consider it. That Bride Train of Bishop Day's was specifically targeted at women who were orphaned by the War. It sounds like you've known loss much longer than that."

Lydia nodded and laughed. She didn't answer the unspoken question, though. "I am, indeed, rather headstrong. It has rarely been a compliment when I'm reminded of it, though."

"It is a prized condition out here in the wild country," Cora sighed heavily and pulled a rag from a stack near the pantry. "Sometimes, it's all that gets you through the winter. I think you will do quite well here, Lydia, dear. Let's get to work before Isaac comes home. His supper still isn't ready!"

Still smiling about the encounter, Lydia gathered lye soap and the lavender she'd brought and headed out to the back porch. The wash bin waited for her to scrub her knuckles raw on the washboard. She'd been missing the mind-numbing effects of such work, and as she rolled up her sleeves to get started, she was looking forward to trying to figure her new husband out.

***

Over the next few days, they fell into a pattern. Having always been an early riser, Lydia was up before Isaac. When he entered the kitchen for breakfast, it was sitting on the table waiting for him. She would eat a little with him, and they'd talk about whatever came up, though nothing serious ever did. Then he'd leave for work, and she cleaned their dishes. Lydia had about an hour before Cora woke. She spent it walking out to the barn, getting to know the animals and learning their habits. There was one other horse, two cows, and an assortment of goats and chickens housed in the barn. Cora had said there were more out in the pasture, but Isaac usually handled that part.

When she returned to the kitchen, Cora was usually at the table with a plate full of whatever Lydia had cooked for breakfast and a warm smile on her lips. After breakfast, they would do a round of whatever cleaning task needed doing, and then eat a light meal around noon.

Cora would lie down for a nap afterward and Lydia had taken to sitting in her mother-in-law's room and handling the mending and sewing that always came with a household. It left her mind with free time to wander and try to align what she knew of marriage to whatever her relationship with Isaac was.

He hadn't mentioned sharing a bedroom, so she hadn't brought it up. He'd acted strangely at the bowery during the wedding ceremony, too. The longer she was around him, the more she realized he wasn't much of a Christian. He didn't swear or drink much and was always kind to her. He took great care of his mother, but she had never seen him read from the Bible before retiring in the evening.

He would not even lower his eyes during the blessing before they ate. In fact, he never offered to give a blessing, leaving it to Cora or herself to say it instead. The idea of being married to a Christian man had been one of her prayers and, it seemed, one that wouldn't be granted. If I don't have love or a Christian husband, what do I have? She thought, her idea of what marriage was supposed to be dissipating

Silly woman, her thoughts shot back at her. Are you letting Isaac's lack of faith help you forget that you have so much to be grateful for? She closed her eyes and focused on them, repeating them in a soft voice, creating her own kind of prayer out of them. "I have a place to live. I have new friends.

I have a mother-in-law that seems to like me. I'm not working for money to pay bills.

The smokehouse and vegetables are always available for supplies to eat. Fred Burns did not drag me to his saloon along with Birdie." She paused, a smile finally curving her lips. "I am not alone. I have people to take care of. I am needed."

She'd tried asking him about his behavior during the ceremony, trying to convey that, while she noticed, she wasn't upset by it. He'd shut that conversation down and changed the subject to the animals and whether she thought she could handle riding out to see the herd of cows in the pasture the following afternoon.

Lydia shook her head and looked over her embroidery hoop toward Cora, sleeping peacefully in her bed. Lydia put her supplies away and stood, heading toward the kitchen to start preparing dinner. They'd picked a lovely ham out of the smokehouse that morning, and Lydia had cut a few slices in it, glazed it with a cinnamon and nutmeg blend based in butter, and set it inside the cold oven.

It needed to get fired up and start warming, or they'd never get dinner ready in time. Then she needed to cut up vegetables and slice up the loaf of bread she'd baked that morning with Cora's help. By then, the oven should be warm enough to put the ham back in and let it start cooking.

She was halfway across the living area when she heard someone knock on the door. She paused, mid-step, then turned to answer it. Outside was a petite woman in a striped blue and white dress. Her face was radiant, and her eyes danced in merriment. Lydia found herself smiling back at her in greeting already.

"Hello there! I'm Essie Gray. I live in a house about five miles to the West of you!" she spoke like everything she said was so exciting she was going to burst. "I heard Sheriff Branson got married, and I wanted to come to introduce myself after you'd settled in."

"I'm Lydia... Branson," Lydia responded, stumbling a little over the name. "Apologies, that's the first time I've said it out loud."

"It feels strange, doesn't it? When I married my Jeffrey, it was the same way. Just saying my name made my smile so big that I thought my face would break. I was so happy!" Essie's face was very animated.

"I'm pleased to meet you, Mrs. Gray. I was just on my way to start cutting vegetables for dinner. Would you like to come in and talk while I do that?" Lydia held the door open a little wider and held her hand out, gesturing to the living space standing behind her.

"I would love to!" Essie nearly yelled into the living room as she entered. "I have never been inside here before. It really doesn't look this big on the outside. And please, call me Essie. We're neighbors. We don't have to be so formal."

Essie, bless her, talked almost non-stop for the next hour while Lydia prepared the meal. She shared the history of the town and the oldest families in it. She discussed her family, asked about Lydia's, asked after Cora, and then, out of the blue, Essie asked, "Are you a Christian?"

Lydia blinked at the sudden change of subject, then nodded, adding, "Of course. I attended church regularly before I moved to Franklin."

Essie's smile widened, and her giddy energy from before seemed to fill her face again. "So did I. There are a few of us around here. We meet a few nights a week for Bible study and prayer groups. We're meeting tonight, in fact. Would you like to come?"

Lydia thought about it for a few minutes. Would Isaac be alright with her attending a Christian function? Who would be available to take care of Cora? "I'm not sure," she hedged, torn between her need to commune with others who believed as she did and not knowing Isaac's thoughts on the matter. Lydia was saved from answering when Cora appeared in the doorway to the living room, announcing, "Of course, she'd love to come, Essie."

Lydia opened her mouth to argue, but Cora's look said it all. Instead, she said, "Very well, what time shall I be there, and where am I going?"

Essie beamed at them both, then told Lydia how to find their farmhouse. Then she excused herself and bustled out of the house. Lydia stared after her, her mind repeating, "how am I going to explain this to Isaac?"

Chapter Nine

It was late by the time Isaac returned from work. He'd gotten the report from the Marshal's office about Fred Burns and didn't want to take it home for the women in his life to fret over. He especially didn't want Lydia to see it, or she'd be so worried about her friend that she might go try to rescue her herself.

He was tired, and his shoulders ached from leaning over those reports all evening. He still took the time to brush his horse down and get him settled in his stall for the night before he made his way into the house. He knew he'd need to apologize for being late and do it without giving away what he'd really been doing. He wrinkled his brow as he walked toward the house, noting the lack of light coming through the windows. A soft light came from the kitchen window, but otherwise, nothing.

He walked across the porch and opened the door, all the instincts he'd honed as Sheriff on high alert. Had something happened to them? Was his mother okay? Lydia? He opened the door as quietly as possible and moved into the living room. The fire had been banked, and nothing moved but him.

He could see well enough across the room to know he was alone there. He moved into the kitchen, toward the only light available. Aside from the dinner plate covered with a linen napkin at the end of the table where he usually sat, everything was in its place. The light came from an oil lamp burning low in the center of the table.

It made him feel a little better, knowing that Lydia had left dinner on the table for him. Had she gone to bed this early?

Was he in trouble with his wife already? He scrubbed a hand over his face and crossed to the other side of the living room to knock on her door. He needed to apologize and not let this stew all night. There was no answer on the other side of the door. He cracked it open just enough to see that the room was dark, and the bed was still perfectly made.

Confused, he tried his mother's room. He found Cora curled up under her blanket, a serene smile on her lips. She's asleep, he thought, leaving the room, and closing the door behind him again. "Then where is Lydia?" he asked the living room, keeping his voice down. He didn't want to wake his mother up.

His answer came when the door opened behind him. He drew his pistol, aimed it at whoever came in through his door like that, and froze before pulling the trigger on his wife. He relaxed his shoulders and released the hammer on his pistol. He nodded toward the kitchen, and she turned to move that way without a word.

"What is going on here?" he demanded, his fingers curling around her upper arm to keep her from fleeing his anger. "I come home to a cold dinner, my mother asleep, and my wife gone! Where have you been?"

A thousand answers spun through his head, all hitting him hard. He prepared himself to hear it all: she was leaving him. She'd met someone else. She'd had secret nighttime trysts with someone else. What she did finally grind out between her clenched teeth was far from anything he'd imagined she'd say.

"I was at Bible study next door with Essie," she hissed, pulling on her arm held firm in his grasp.

"Bible study?" he asked, perplexed. "You left my mother alone to go talk about the Bible?"

A pained look crossed her face, but she didn't look away from his rage. "She told me to go, Isaac! Essie came by and invited me and–"

"And you expect me to believe that you just went to a stranger's house to talk about a book?" his voice was low and grave.

"What else would I have talked about?" she answered his anger with some of her own. "Did you think I ran away?"

He was close enough to her face to feel the heat of her breath. It triggered a totally different response in him than he'd been feeling previously, and he pushed her away from him with a thrust of his arm. He couldn't think when he could smell her scent so close when her lips were so close. When the heat of her skin so close sent his thoughts to places that no man should have about his wife. Well, not a wife he didn't intend on being a husband to, anyway.

She stumbled a step but caught herself at the edge of the dining room table. "You did? Really?"

"Well, I sure didn't think that a book club meeting would've been worth leaving my mother alone!" his voice was louder, and he heard it a beat too late.

"Isaac? Is that you?" He heard his mother's voice behind him, and he growled.

"This isn't over," he forced between the teeth clenched shut.

She was glaring at him as he turned back to the living room. As soon as he got a few feet inside the room, she flew past him, shoving open her bedroom door, storming inside, and slamming it behind her. He blinked at the ferocity of that action and shook his head. "Bible study," he muttered as he opened his mother's door. "You called for me?" he asked, no anger in his voice now.

"Come in and close the door," Cora answered. She'd lit the candle on her side table and sat in the bed, the blankets folded neatly in her lap. "I convinced Lydia to go to Essie's tonight."

"What trick did she use, Ma? Did she put on a show of tears? Did she beg to be freed from her prison, even for a night? And do you honestly expect me to believe she went next door for hours to talk about The Bible?" His tone was incredulous, and he dropped into the chair Lydia usually took in the afternoons.

"Oh, stop being a child, Isaac. She hasn't breathed a word of complaint, and you know it. I wanted her to go, so there was no need to trick me into anything. She needs to talk to people her own age who have ideals and a moral code like hers.

You are neither of those things," she waved at him slouched in the chair, and he sat up a little straighter, spluttering. She continued as if he hadn't responded. "Can you blame her for wanting to talk to mature people her age and not stick around to wait on..." She raked her eyes over him pointedly and grumbled. "No, if you're going to be angry with anyone, be angry with me. She did her best to be too late to go, creating extra work she had to finish before she left. I shooed her out the door, Isaac.

The only reason I didn't saddle the horse was that I didn't want to have an episode in the barn. No, no more arguments. I didn't give her much choice about whether to go or not."

"Ma, I asked her to look after you. She can't do that if she's off with her friends," he waved toward the window, his tone still stiff and accusatory. "She knew that, and she left you alone, anyway."

"You stop that right this minute, Isaac David Branson! How dare you expect that girl to isolate herself in this house with only me for company for the rest of her life? How dare you make me feel like I need someone to watch over me every second of the day? I can take care of myself, thank you!"

"I didn't say that you couldn't!" he shouted back at her, leaning forward. He'd never argued with his mother before, but this... This was different. "Anything could've happened to her on the drive over there or back. She didn't even know the horse!"

"She takes him an apple every morning, actually," Cora responded, taking the air out of his argument. "She was perfectly safe. So, what is your real reason for being so angry?"

She crossed her arms and pinned him with a look that reminded him of being a child and getting caught doing something he knew he would get in trouble for. It wasn't going to work this time. "What if you'd slipped and fallen?"

"Before she walked into our lives, there was the possibility of that. Why are you only worried about it now? What were you afraid of, Isaac?"

"I was afraid she had left us!" he yelled back at her. The admission took the heat out of his argument. "I am afraid she'll leave us."

"And go where?" She asked, tilting her head to the side. "She has no family, money, and no home, Isaac. She has nowhere to go."

"That doesn't always mean she couldn't have found someone to take care of her!" he felt like a petulant child in the face of his mother's anger. "She's young and pretty," he said, folding his hand over his middle. And smart and funny, with those eyes I could fall into and those lips I just want to... he pulled those thoughts up short before they went beyond a place he was able to pull them back from.

"Do you begrudge her an hour to talk to people about something they're all passionate about? Would you have talked like that to any other woman? To me? Those young people are her age and perfectly delightful. Besides, she needs friends. Every woman does." Cora's voice was wistful. He realized that she didn't have many friends, either. Before he could comment, she relaxed her arms and leaned back on the pillow. He sighed, hearing her use the last phrase as a bullseye on his argument. "Now, I need to sleep, but I think we all know what your answer will be."

He helped her pull back up her blankets, using the excuse to get closer to her. He fixed her pillow and then her sheets and dropped a small kiss on her forehead. "Alright, Ma. I will try to understand what she's doing. Maybe I'll get better when I expect it more."

"One should certainly hope so. Now, go eat and let me get back to sleep. We did a lot today, and my muscles are aching tonight." Her voice had gotten lower and drowsier, so he left her there without another word, his thoughts filled with the people around Lydia's age nearby. Alright, he finally admitted, taking the napkin from a plate filled with venison and vegetables.

His lips twitched at seeing the small fried potatoes on the side next to the spinach. It reminded him of the only conversation they'd had inside this house that first day that hadn't been an argument. He stabbed one of the potatoes with a fork and lifted it to eye level. "Think she'll forgive me for being..." he searched for a word that wouldn't have his mother howling at him and biting into the potato.

He finished the rest of his dinner in silence, his thoughts going through every second he'd been with Lydia. It seemed like yesterday and years ago, all at the same time. Was it enough?

Chapter Ten

Lydia stormed into the bedroom she'd been staying in and slammed the door behind her. She changed clothes with only one tear in a seam. She tried to sit down and stitch it back together, but she was so angry she couldn't sit still. She set the dress aside and paced. Her hands alternated between wringing and clenching at her sides as her memory looped their argument over and over.

How dare he talk to her like that! How dare he suggest she didn't care for his mother's health! How dare he make something that had made her feel so accepted into something terribly irresponsible!

Cora was perfectly capable of taking care of herself. She had been for a while. Lydia taking on most of the chores allowed Cora to reserve her energy and not overdo it trying to keep up with the woman she used to be. Why couldn't Isaac see that?

She paused halfway through a turn around the floor. What if Cora had fallen? She wasn't sure how long Isaac had been home before she'd returned from Essie's, but it might have been too late for her, even if it had been his usual time.

Lydia chewed her lip a moment, then blew out a breath. That's ridiculous. Isaac had left her to go to work every day for a year before Lydia arrived on that train. She could've fallen at any time while he was gone, and he didn't beat himself up about it!

"I'm not going to feel guilty about this," she announced to the room around her. "Cora not only encouraged me to go to Essie's, but she also practically pushed me out the door! Isaac is just being overprotective."

She sank onto the end of the bed and breathed deeply. She'd had a wonderful evening at Essie's, surrounded by people who spoke just as animatedly as she did about scriptures and the stories of the bible. They'd been working on the book of Ruth, one of her favorites. It was short, but so much lay in those four chapters, and the story always brought tears to her eyes. Tonight had been no exception, though she'd found the reasons to be completely different with this reading of the scriptures. To see others as moved by the words as she had always been made her feel... accepted. Here she was, just like Ruth, far from the places she knew.

The thought made her blink, and she chewed her lip, considering. Ruth had followed her mother-in-law back home, acted on her advice, and gained a husband who could support them both. She'd found community among people she'd never met before after the death of her husband.

The Bible study group had accepted her tonight. Cora accepted her. Could she find community with her mother-in-law in this land full of people she had never met? It certainly felt that way. She fell back on the bed, staring at the ceiling. The Bible study group may accept her, and even Cora could also accept her. Would Isaac?

***

Essie's smiling face was on the other side of the door when Lydia answered it around mid-morning the following day. She'd been settling down to do some mending in the sitting room with Cora in a chair opposite her working on an embroidery piece when she'd heard the knock. Seeing her new friend's smile reminded her of the warm feeling of being around people who understood her wish to be a good Christian wife.

"Good morning!" Lydia said, returning Essie's smile. "Please, come in." She opened the door more as she stepped back, allowing Essie inside. "We were just working on some stitching. Do you embroider?"

"Goodness me, no. I sew clothes when I must, but I make sure I hide the stitches. They're so terrible! My Jeffrey didn't marry me for my homemaking skills, that's for sure." She laughed as she loosened the ties of her broad-brimmed hat, pulled it off her head, and followed as Lydia led her into the sitting room. "I came for a visit with Mrs. Cora. I try to stop by and chat at least once per day." At least, I did until the wedding. I thought you might need some time to yourselves. Then I saw him in town the other day and heard that he's been at work every day, including the wedding day!"

Cora's delighted laughter filled the room as they entered, and Lydia smiled as she returned to her chair and her mending – the noises of happy greetings filling the space around her. A few minutes later, Cora glanced over at Lydia who snipped the last loose string from the dress she was mending. "Don't you have an errand to run in town?" she asked Lydia, pointedly raising her eyebrows.

"Do I?" Lydia asked, her eyes widening.

"You haven't had a single moment to yourself since you got off the train. Probably not even before that! Why don't you go into town and become familiar with the stores and layout? I'm sure there are very eager townsfolk who want to meet you since you married Isaac... Go on, it'll do you some good."

"But Isaac..." Lydia started. She had no intention of dealing with that man's irritation over her not being home again.

"Let me handle Isaac," Cora said sternly. "Besides, Essie is here, and she won't leave until you get back. Right, Essie?"

Essie turned her smile back to Lydia and nodded. "I plan on staying for quite a while. Mrs. Cora and I have much to discuss!"

"Very well," Lydia sighed. She had wanted to see the town more and get acquainted with the townsfolk. Besides, she hadn't heard from Birdie, and she wanted to check on her. The way Isaac talked about Fred Burns made her concern for her friend rise. "I will return by lunch," she smiled, bending to kiss Cora on both cheeks. "

Cora shooed her away and a half hour later she was riding the mare that she rode to Essie's the night before into town. The townsfolk tipped their heads and hats, smiling at her as she rode in and she found herself returning their smiles. She stopped at the Mercantile first, curiosity about supplies for sewing and embroidery work needing to be settled.

As she'd suspected, there wasn't much beyond muslin and cotton thread to stitch it together with. She talked to Mr. Hansen, who showed her the catalog he used to place orders. Since it was a Cooperative, they didn't have a lot of "fancy items," but he could probably get her some supplies from further East through mail order. He said he would check and she thanked him, promising to return the following week.

She strolled out into the street and took in the small strip of buildings that made up the town center. The sight of the saloon doors reminded her that she Had come into town with the intent of stopping to see Birdie. The Saloon owner hadn't left her with a very likable impression of him and thinking of Birdie married to him made her stomach clench.

Without a second thought, she turned toward the saloon, intent to check in on Birdie. Stepping inside the dark room, she gagged. The smell was a horrendous thing, some blend of urine, vomit, and ammonia that left the bile rising in her throat. It took her eyes a few minutes to adjust to the darkness on the inside of the saloon and, when she could see, she noticed that she'd earned more than a few sideways looks from the patrons, all men, but she ignored them.

Instead, she lifted a handkerchief to her nose, glad she'd soaked the wash water in lavender, and scanned the saloon looking for Birdie. Scattered around the floor were round tables with chairs tucked around them. Most of them had at least one man sitting at them, though not a single one of those men looked the least bit affected by the smell of the place.

The floor was very dark planked wood. Even as dark as it was, there were still spots on the floor where something had been spilled and stained the wood even darker. Given the smell, she really didn't want to know what had made any of those stains. There was a large bar that dominated the back wall, with a gilt mirror tucked behind the rows of bottles.

The bar itself was as dark as the floor, which seemed to make the brass fittings on the edges and studding the leather onto the barstools stand out. She could see herself in the mirror, but she tried not to notice how out of place she looked. It merely fit the way she felt!

Finally, Lydia found Birdie on the far side of the bar bent over a tub washing glasses. Lydia smiled and crossed the room to her. "Birdie," she said softly as she paused near the end of the bar.

Birdie jumped at the sound of her name and turned quickly to see who said it. Her shoulders relaxed a fraction before tensing back up again. Lydia took in the sight of her friend, noting with concern the dark circles under her friend's eyes and the paleness of her skin. She stepped forward, reaching a hand toward Birdie. "My goodness, are you alright?"

"I'm fine," Birdie snapped, turning away to go back to her dishes.

"Is there anything I can do to help?" Lydia asked. She did not want to press, but her concern for Birdie grew more every second.

"Help with what?" Birdie asked, turning back to her with a smile on her lips that didn't reach her eyes. "I'm happy here. I have been having some trouble sleeping, this climate isn't anything like what we're used to back East, you know?"

Lydia nodded but didn't answer right away. Birdie continued, filling the silence. "It's been so busy here, the last few days. There are so many people coming in for food and drinks. They're up at all hours of the night playing cards and keeping me awake with their noise." Her laugh sounded hollow.

Lydia nodded again and tried to smile back. "I imagine it gets really difficult to sleep with all of that."

"Birdie!" came an angry shout from the stairs on the far side of the saloon. Lydia's eyes were drawn toward the person barking across the saloon like that and, unsurprisingly, her eyes landed on Fred Burns. "Go upstairs and finish the washing there."

Birdie jumped at his order and laid the glass she'd just dried on a drying rack before shooting Lydia a tight smile and hurrying up the stairs. Lydia took a step after her only to be drawn up short by Burns. "I can help her, and she'll be done faster," she offered, nodding up the stairs behind him.

"You can leave and that'll help her even more," Burns growled at her. "Your little visit is over. Birdie has work to do. You and your husband need to leave me and mine alone."

Lydia stiffened her back and bit her lip to keep from saying anything to him that would escalate the issue. "Thank you for letting me see her," she said quietly, then left the saloon. She felt the weight of his eyes on her until she'd turned the corner to go back to the Mercantile.

***

She rubbed the horse down when she got back to the homestead, tucking her into her stall with a fresh bin of hay. Then she went to the house, her thoughts still on the interaction at the Saloon. Birdie had been acting strange, though she'd sounded a bit more like herself before Burns showed up. What did he mean that she and her husband should leave him alone? Had Isaac been checking on Birdie, too?

She'd been trying to hope for the best for her friend, but between her first impressions and Isaac's opinion of the man, coupled with today's display, she was starting to think Isaac was right. It only made her concern for Birdie grow more.

If only Isaac would talk to her about the situation. If she knew why he was concerned about Burns, it might make her more cautious of him. As it was, her lack of information about her friend made her feel like he might not be as sure of his opinions as he thought.

She paused as a shot of sadness swept through her. She closed her eyes as she paused at the door, the scene from the night before still vivid in her mind. Remembering their argument, his assumptions, and the unforgivable way he'd yelled at her stung painfully. No, she couldn't talk to him about that or anything else. It's not like they were even friendly toward each other. Not when he could so quickly jump to conclusions and attack her based on them.

She hung her hat near the door and unbuttoned her jacket. "You're back earlier than I expected," Essie's voice drew Lydia's gaze to the chairs near the fireplace. "Didn't find what you were looking for?"

Lydia sighed and dropped into the chair she'd been sitting in earlier. "Oh, I found it," she muttered. "It was not at all what I expected, though."

Essie's brow creased, and she set the book aside. "Something you need to talk about?" she asked. "Mrs. Cora is taking a nap, but I don't have to leave for a while."

Lydia chewed her lip, then leaned forward. "Something troubles me, though it's not why I went into town today. I was called out here, led to the Bride Train by a string of visions and signs. God wanted me to come here and made sure Isaac is the one who walked me off that train platform." She paused and looked around the room as if looking for a clue on how to say what would come next. "Why would He do that if Isaac isn't a man of God?"

Essie relaxed, her expression clouding. "He hasn't been the same since he came home from the war," she said quietly. "I didn't know him very well before he left, but what I did know is completely different now that he's home. I figure something happened there that made him question his faith. I've heard stories about battles from that war from a few local boys who came home. They are the stuff of nightmares, Lydia. If he's seen the things I've heard described, I can understand how that would make you question things."

"To the point that he'd be angry at me for attending Bible Study with your group?" Lydia asked, her hands curling into fists in her lap. "His mother quotes scripture, and he doesn't say anything about that. Not that I've heard, anyway. His mother acts as if this is not normal for him, or at least it wasn't normal before he went off to War."

"War does things to people, Lydia. Terrible things. Maybe you should talk to him about it?" She offered what seemed like a logical solution, and Lydia blew air through her lips.

"I doubt he'd talk to me about something so personal. He's so distant, but I can tell he's annoyed. And the way he behaved at the wedding..." Lydia shook her head and then looked up at Essie. "He didn't vow to love me, Essie. He promised to protect and honor me but refused to utter a word about love."

Essie's eyes were a little sadder as she nodded. "I heard about that," she sighed, reaching across the space between them. "I still say the best action is for you to reach out to him. Talk to him. Make sure he knows you're there if he needs or wants to talk."

Lydia sank into her chair again, slouching low and folding her hands over her stomach. "I will try. I can guarantee he won't be forthcoming about any of it. It won't hurt to try, right?"

Essie sighed and rose slowly, setting the book aside. She took the step that would bring her within arm's reach of Lydia and bent down to hug her. "I wish I could say it would be easy. That it won't hurt. But there is pain in that man, and it'll likely take more pain to get it out of him. He won't be able to find his way back to God until he clears it."

Lydia thought about that long after Essie left. She remembered her father and brother's letters, where they tried to avoid talking about what the war had done, but their tone had changed. It grew more and more tired and angry.

They wrote things, then crossed them out. She knew they were starving near the end; they'd said as much. Had Isaac experienced that, too? Cora had a daguerreotype image of Isaac in his uniform that he'd sent to her not long after he'd enlisted. He'd been fighting for the Yankees, but she didn't fault him for that. He had to know her own family had fought on the Confederate side, but he hadn't said anything about it.

If her brother and father had experienced those horrors... She sat up as she remembered Isaac's limp. Cora said he came home to recover from a wound and had stayed to take over the Sheriff's office when her husband passed. She lifted her fingers to press against her lip, and her wedding ring glinted in the sunlight.

He had been in battles. He had come home to his mother. Unlike her brother and father, he'd survived those horrors. Hadn't she seen some men who had survived the war behaving oddly before she left Maysville? Men who were kind and gentle came back surly and angry. She'd heard more wives and sisters complain that the men who had returned to them were not the men who had left. They would describe everything from fear of loud noises to fear of being left alone.

Was Isaac experiencing those things? Is that why he jumped onto his assumptions so quickly? Was it why he seemed afraid that she would find trouble? She really did need to talk to him about this! She needed to know what they were facing to help him.

"Tonight," she murmured out loud to the house around her. "I will ask him tonight after Cora goes to bed. I will break this silence, this anger, and help him. It's what a good wife would do and what I must do. God would wish it so."

Satisfied that she had a plan, she pushed herself out of the chair to begin working on dinner. He would be home soon, and he deserved the best meal she could put in front of him.

Chapter Eleven

"Well, that was useless," Jack muttered as they stepped off the porch and into the packed earth street.

Dust rose from the ground as they left the planked porch of Bishop Day's home. It wasn't far from the Bowery and was small enough for him since he wasn't married. It wasn't much to look at: a box with a porch attached outside, a two-room home inside. One room held the living area, the kitchen, and the dining area, and the other room was a small bedroom. Bishop Day had taken the time to tend a small garden out back and the plant boxes along the porch in front overflowed with fragrant blossoms.

"He didn't tell us anything we didn't already know," Isaac bit off as they strode toward the intersection ahead of them.

"If only he hadn't married her," Jack muttered, voicing what Isaac was thinking.

"Yeah, but that would've been far too easy, wouldn't it?" His words sounded like he was part of the conversation, but his tone was distracted.

"What do we do now?" Jack asked, crossing his arms, eyes scanning the streets around them.

Isaac looked over at him and smiled tightly. "We'll just have to keep poking around until we find out whether we're right about Fred Burns."

He nodded up the street toward the saloon. On the side of the building was a vacant lot where women were bent over washstands. Birdie's hair flashed brightly in the sunlight as she moved from the table on the side to the water, her movements stiff. He furrowed his brow, watching for a few minutes to see if Burns appeared. When he didn't, Isaac turned toward the saloon, Jack on his heels.

"It's a beautiful day to be outside, don't you agree?" he asked the women gathered outside. They all laughed, and one even sloshed water at him. Birdie didn't even look his way. "I came to offer my congratulations on your wedding, Mrs. Burns. Lydia will be very happy to hear you've found a home here."

Birdie flinched at the name and shot a hard look up at him but didn't answer. She lifted a clothes basket to her hip and walked to the washbasin. Isaac wrinkled his brow. Was that what it looked like on her arm? He followed a second behind her, intent on finding out. "She was worried when the last thing she saw was you being led away without even being asked about whether you wanted to go."

His eye caught her forearm again as she tipped the clothing from the basket into the water and pushed her sleeve higher to keep it from getting wet. He felt Jack tense behind him and knew he hadn't imagined the bruise up her arm.

Birdie's gaze flicked up when she realized they'd seen her arms. She pasted a smile on her lips as she turned toward them fully, pulling her sleeve down to cover her skin. "I heard you married her, Sheriff. I am very pleased she will be taken care of. Is she happy?"

"She is content," Isaac responded. It wasn't exactly a lie, was it? They weren't on speaking terms, but she wasn't lacking for anything. "Are you?"

"Why ever wouldn't I be, Sheriff?" she asked, her face a mask of innocence. His gaze flicked to her arm, and she laughed, waving him off. "She didn't tell you how clumsy I am, did she? I nearly fell down the stairs to the bar this morning. I'd probably be dead, had my husband not been there to catch my arm."

Isaac's jaw slackened, and fear raced through him as the implication in Birdie's words set in. Had Lydia been at the saloon? Had Burns seen her? As if the thought had conjured him, Fred Burns appeared out of the side door, his voice angry. "Are you not content with your own wife? You have to come and harass mine, now, Sheriff?" he sneered, putting himself forcefully, between Birdie and Isaac. "Get on inside," he ordered Birdie.

She didn't even say goodbye as she walked back into the saloon through a side door and disappeared into the shadows. His attention being on Birdie gave Isaac a moment to put thoughts of Lydia near this man out of his mind for a moment. It would be dangerous to let Burns know how badly he'd been startled and afraid for his wife at the thought of her coming here.

"No harassment, Fred. Just saw my wife's friend and came by to offer my congratulations on her wedding." Isaac fought the urge to plant his fist in Burns' face, contenting himself with keeping his distance and doing what he could to remove the skeptical look from the man's face.

"If she wanted to extend congratulations, she could've done it while she was here this morning. She didn't. Which makes you appear even more suspicious, Sheriff." He crossed his arms and fixed his glare on Isaac, not giving any attention to Jack standing a few feet away with his hand resting on the pistol at his hip. "I'll only say this once, so listen carefully. You and your wife stay away from here and mind your own business. Birdie belongs here with me, and she doesn't have time to entertain while she's helping me run the saloon. I would hate for something bad to happen to either of you, should you cross this way again."

"Are you threatening me, Mister Burns?" Isaac asked, tilting his head. "Threatening the Sheriff is a bad idea. Makes a man think you're hiding something."

"I mean it, Branson. Sheriff or no, if you continue to harass my wife, I will find a way to stop it." Burns was so mad that spittle was flying from his mouth as he spoke. Isaac was repulsed by the man, even more so now that he'd seen the bruises on Birdie's arm.

"If I find evidence that you're hurting her, Burns, I will find a way to stop that." He deliberately threw Burns' words back at him. "Good day," Isaac said stiffly, nodding his head and turning away. He stopped when he got to the street and turned back, catching Burns before he disappeared back into the saloon behind Birdie. "And congratulations on your wedding, Fred!" He said, his voice full of false cheer.

Isaac rode home as if he was being chased. His thoughts spun around all the terrible ways Lydia walking into the saloon could've gone. She was home, he hoped. Burns never said she'd left. He could be hiding something. He had to make sure she was alright. The image of the bruises on Birdie's face rang through his memory.

Before he could stop it, he pictured Lydia with the same bruise. Rage unlike anything he'd felt before surged through him, and he urged the horse to move faster. If there was a single hair on her head out of place, Burns would be having a terrible evening!

He didn't even slow his horse down until he'd entered the yard and didn't even take the time to walk him into the stable or brush him down. He slid down from the saddle as soon as his horse came to the porch, throwing himself onto the smooth boards and hurtling through the door.

"Lydia?" he called when no one was in the living room. He hurried to the kitchen and found it empty, too. As he came back into the living room, his heart thundering in his chest, he heard the sweet song of Lydia's laughter. Relief washed through him like a flood and he felt his knees shaking as his blood cooled. Trying to still his shaking hands, he moved to the door of the sitting room where his mother and Lydia were sitting, embroidery needles moving rhythmically in the afternoon sunlight streaming through the windows.

"Isaac? You're home early," Lydia said, her voice still holding that dance of laughter. "Did you forget something? Would you like me to get you something to eat?" She set her embroidery aside and rose in the same fluid movement. He couldn't do anything but watch for a moment as her graceful movements brought her to the door where he was standing.

Was she trying to distract him? The way her hips moved as she walked would suggest so, but the mixture of concern and amusement in her eyes was exactly the opposite.

"Mother," his voice came out a bit high, and he cleared his throat, turning his eyes away from the woman who was his wife to Cora, still sitting in her chair. "I need to discuss something with Lydia. Privately. Do you mind if I borrow her for a few moments?"

"Of course not, dear boy," she smiled, her eyes twinkling. He didn't want to know what she was thinking behind that knowing smile. It was a guarantee she had the wrong idea for this discussion. He kept all that to himself and nodded to her, then turned his attention back to Lydia. "May I have a word?"

Lydia stiffened as if she caught the seriousness of the situation. Her nod was just as stiff as she passed him and walked into the kitchen. He followed a few steps behind, trying to figure out how to say what he needed without starting an argument. As it was, his fear and the leftover rush from getting here so quickly made his heart thunder in his chest.

He pulled out a chair for her at the table and another for himself so that they were on either side of the corner. He was determined to keep his voice low this time.

Lydia looked at him expectantly, and he sighed, intertwining his fingers and resting them on the table. "I saw Birdie today," he started, making up the direction of his words as he went. "She seemed well enough and tried to convince me she and Burns were happy. Then Burns told me that you'd been by this morning..." he let the sentence trail off without looking up at her. When the silence stretched, he lifted his eyes to see her watching him.

"Are you asking me whether I went to the saloon this morning, or are you telling me that I went to the saloon this morning?" she asked. Nothing in her tone gave away whether she was angry or not.

"Neither," he said, looking back at his hands. "Lydia, I don't want you going there again. It's dangerous, and I don't want..." he took a breath and looked up at her again. "I just don't want you going to the saloon again."

"That's it? You're just telling me not to go, and I'm supposed to, what? Do you want me to say that I will stay away? It will be a lie, and I don't do that; I can't do that. Just like I can't stay away when I know someone needs me; when a friend needs me." She leaned back in the chair. "And I know it's dangerous. I knew it on that platform before I even knew it existed. I cannot abandon Birdie to that man, Isaac. I won't. If you forbid it, know that I will go, anyway. The only way you can keep me from it is to lock me up. Even then, I will not rest until I find a way."

Isaac blew out a hard breath. "I can't have you interfering, Lydia. Without proof, there is nothing I can do. He told me to stay away and to keep you away, too. As Sheriff, I have a right to go where I want if I have cause, but you do not. You will not go back to that saloon, do you understand?"

"How can you expect me to stay away?" her voice was breathy, her eyes watering. "How can you expect me not to help a friend who was there for me when no one else was, who comforted my nerves at coming out here? She wanted a husband and a family to take care of. Is that what she got? Can you honestly tell me that's what she has with Fred Burns?"

The tears were a kick in the gut, and he found himself getting angrier because of it. Was she trying to manipulate him? Did she think the tears would sway his position on this? He'd rather she hate him with every inch of her being than get hurt walking into that saloon, didn't she understand that? "Lydia, I've told you many times that Fred Burns is dangerous. I barely managed to save you from him the first time. I don't know if I'll get there the second time. Please don't fight me on this. Stay away from that saloon. Yes, that means you must stay away from your friend, but can you imagine her reaction if Burns hurts you because you were there trying to help her?"

Lydia gasped and slapped both hands on the table, leaning toward him. "I will not leave her, Isaac!" she yelled back at him, her tears flowing freely over her cheeks. "Don't ask me to give up on her. I never abandon anyone I care for, especially when I think they're in trouble. My gut tells me she's in a lot of trouble, and I can't leave her to it. Not when she didn't choose it for herself!"

He reached for her as he stood, pulling her into his arms. She didn't fight him, just buried her face in his shirt, too far gone to stop the tears. He held her close, a feeling he never expected to feel for this woman blossoming in his chest.

This fierce woman, cloaked in east-coast finery and Christian belief that God never let bad things happen without reason, had somehow managed to get inside the walls he'd built around his trust, friendship, and heart.

As her tears soaked through to his skin and her body shook in wracking sobs in his hands, he realized that this woman was possibly more dangerous to him than Fred Burns ever would be. Isaac had survived a bullet wound. He had barely survived losing the family he'd adopted among the ranks of his unit. After all of that, he'd survived losing his father, too. But losing this woman? He was starting to think there was no way he could survive that.

Chapter Twelve

Two days after Lydia burned the best meal she'd ever cooked because she had been so emotional about Isaac demanding that she give up on Birdie, an invitation arrived. She and Cora were in the front sitting room, doing needlework, when a horse had arrived – bearing a bright white envelope addressed to Lydia Branson.

She had accepted the envelope from Henry, a young boy who ran errands for people around town to earn money to buy supplies for his family, and watched as he disappeared back into town before she closed the door and returned to the sitting room. She popped the wax seal on the back and opened the parchment, her brow wrinkling in confusion.

"What is it, Lydia? Are you alright?" Cora had asked, setting her needlework aside in concern.

Rather than returning to her chair, Lydia sank onto the couch next to Cora and read the letter aloud.

Dearest Mrs. Branson,

In the hours after your departure, I had time to reflect on our meeting and confess that the way things were handled that day was indelicate of me. I find I must apologize on behalf of myself as well as my wife, your dear friend Birdie. I am afraid you caught us during our first quarrel and our inability to set it aside in your presence. Given the strain of making up for the recent burden of lost employees and our disagreement, I fear you found both of us at our least amiable and welcoming.

It is far from my intent to separate my wife from her dearest and only friend here in Franklin. I fear my behavior that afternoon did little to make you feel welcome in our establishment. In fact, I believe I said I did not want you to call upon my dear wife at all. Please know these words were spoken in anger and frustration, and I did not mean them beyond an ungentlemanly stab at my wife. We have since repaired our misunderstanding, and I would relish the opportunity to make it up to you.

In this vein, I humbly ask your forgiveness in the form of a visit with us for tea on Friday. I promise we will be better prepared for your visit, and I would appreciate the chance to show you the truth of our relationship and set your fears for my dear wife at ease. I will arrange for refreshments in our parlor in the upstairs apartments of the saloon. We may better know one another and perhaps become friends, if only for the shared respect of my dear wife.

We hope you choose to accept our invitation to tea. May it form a solid bond between our families for many years to come.

If you choose to separate yourself at this time, I truly understand and, though it will sadden us both greatly, we will trouble you no more. Please know that Birdie and I hope we can reconcile in the future whenever you feel comfortable allowing us to make amends.

Yours,

Fred Burns

The room was silent as she lowered the letter, though she did not take her eyes from it. She was unsure what to say to such a well-written letter, and she lifted her confused expression to Cora's equally bewildered face. She asked softly, "What do I do?"

Cora didn't answer. She just took the parchment from her hands and scanned it herself, as if scarcely believing what she was hearing. Lydia fought to align the eloquence of that letter with the man who'd threatened her the other day. The latter aligned with Isaac's opinion of the man so perfectly that she agreed with her husband about the probability of something transpiring at the saloon.

But that letter seemed like it was from a different person entirely. It sounded like a man well-bred enough in southern culture to know when he's been wrong and knows how to fix it. She had no doubt Birdie had been distraught after she'd left the saloon.

Was it possible the whole scene was simply a stress-induced lover's spat between newlyweds that she'd walked into unknowingly? It would explain the strain in Birdie's eyes and her near defiance flouncing to obey her husband when he'd ordered her upstairs. If Fred Burns saw her as an ally, someone who would thwart him against his new wife, would it be enough reason for his rude treatment of her that day?

Lydia chewed the inside of her lip. The scene at the Train Depot and her visit to the saloon made Isaac's distrust of the man seem not only reasonable but just. What reason would a man of that caliber have in offering her an apology and an invitation to tea?

Worse yet, how was she supposed to make sense of this if she didn't take him up on his offer to meet over tea? She cast a look at Cora, who handed her the parchment back quietly.

"I have to go," she said, folding the paper without looking at it.

"I know you do," Cora said softly. "But what will Isaac say?"

"I'm sure he will be angry, but he has to understand that I cannot leave Birdie to a life of unhappiness and danger. I must know for certain whether Fred Burns is a man who does hold his new wife in such regard as to concern himself with her friendships and the damage he may have caused to them. The only way to do that is to see it for myself." She wasn't asking for an opinion, not trying to justify it to anyone but herself. Her conscience simply wouldn't allow her to leave Birdie alone with a man she suspected of horrible treatment. And didn't God say that the Truth will win out? The only way to find her answers was to look for them.

Whether Isaac wanted her to or not.

When she arrived at the saloon for tea the following Friday, she'd been treated like visiting royalty. Lydia was escorted to a private sitting room, where a low coffee table was set with a porcelain tea service next to a tall pitcher of iced tea and an assortment of homemade jams artfully arranged around a plate of biscuits. Another plate rested to the side with buttermilk pie Lydia could nearly smell from the door and another plate of biscuits with sliced ham peeking out from inside them.

Fred Burns had greeted her like she was his sister, wearing a smartly tailored three-piece suit of deep gray wool that complimented his coloring, his hair was combed back in smooth lines, and his face scrubbed clean.

He'd apologized, again, claiming he had no excuse except that part of his staff had quit the previous week – leaving him and Birdie to do most of the work around the saloon. He had claimed to have an interview with a potential maid, so he couldn't stay with them for tea. "I know you'd rather have the time to catch up, anyway. I would only be in the way of that conversation."

He'd left them, pausing to give Birdie a soft kiss on the cheek that made her lips part in a tight smile. Lydia was watching carefully, thoughts of Isaac's unease about Burns in her thoughts, but Birdie didn't flinch or shy away from Burns when he got close. She didn't look comfortable by any means, but this was far from the first impression she had of their relationship. It was nothing like what Isaac had warned her of Burns, either.

Burns didn't exactly leave them alone. "This is Smiley," Birdie said. "Fred is so worried about me that he leaves a bodyguard to follow me everywhere." She waved at a tall man with a hard, chiseled face who stood behind Birdie's chair, his cold eyes surveying her. Birdie had been so lovely, her skin radiant, her dress neatly pressed and cleaned, and even wearing wrist-length gloves as they had tea, which Lydia didn't question. Birdie certainly didn't seem frightened. Not like she had that day when Lydia had first come into the saloon.

"How is life married to the Sheriff?" Birdie asked, turning her smile on Lydia.

"Not much different than I expected, honestly," Lydia answered, trying to relax. "I make his breakfast, and he goes to work. I do chores around the house and have dinner ready when he gets home. He spends time with his mother, and we all go to bed."

Birdie pursed her lips, flicking a look up at the man guarding them. Her eyes twinkled. "Are you sleeping well?"

Lydia wrinkled her brow at the question, then realized what she was talking about. "Oh," she cleared her throat and adjusted her skirts nervously. "It's not like that. He's allowing me space to get my bearings and–"

"That's very gentlemanly of him," Birdie interjected, then saved Lydia's flustered answer by changing the subject. "Say, do you know anyone who can repair clothes in town? I've worn my gowns around the saloon so much that they've got tears and cuts all over. I would really like to have them mended."

Birdie remembered what Lydia did for a living before coming west, didn't she? "I would be happy to stitch them up for you," she offered, earning a smile from her friend.

"That would be perfect! I will get them together for you the next time you come for a visit. I don't want to hear that you won't charge me for it, either. Just tell me how much it will cost, and I will make sure Fred sends you proper payment for the work," If Lydia didn't know better, she'd swear she felt rather than saw Smiley snort at that comment.

As the clock in the corner chimed, Birdie drew in a sigh. "I had best go see if Fred hired that maid or not. Do promise you'll come by again soon?" Lydia had promised, of course, having enjoyed the visit more than she'd thought.

Chapter Thirteen

Isaac rolled his shoulders and rose to his feet. He picked up the cold cup of coffee he'd poured hours ago when he'd begun reviewing the information about the disappearing livestock. It had gone missing all week around town. He was no closer to putting the pieces together as he was figuring out what Burns was up to at the Saloon on the other side of the intersection.

He strode to the window and stared out, unseeing, as the details rolled over inside his head. A few people had stopped in town since the disappearances started, most of them on their way further North or West. One pair of men had come into town, and according to the people he'd talked to during his morning patrol, they'd come to town looking for Fred Burns. Was it possible they were connected to the disappearing livestock? Or that Fred Burns was connected, somehow?

Isaac sipped his coffee and coughed, shaking his head; he'd forgotten it was cold. He sat the coffee cup on the windowsill and crossed his arms across his chest, watching the movement around town. It had been a peaceful few weeks without anything other than these missing animals to fill his mind. While he was usually perfectly fine with quiet days in town, days where his badge wasn't needed to settle arguments or chase criminals, he had an unsettled feeling in his stomach. It told him he was missing something and it was big.

His eyes focused on a richly embroidered frock coat across the street at the Mercantile, and he narrowed his eyes. Birdie

Burns was parading down the street with a parasol over her shoulder and the giant hulking mass of Mack Medina in her shadow.

She smiled at a man who held the door open for her at the Mercantile and ducked inside, Mack giving the man a nod in thanks as he took the door from him and let it close behind them.

As if he needed a reminder about the unsettled feeling in his stomach, something about how the pair made such a big show of being happy gave him the impression of the opposite. He watched Essie's husband duck into the Mercantile behind them and shook his head. The last train had brought a collection of packages and crates. Isaac didn't have to know Mister Gray to know that the new catalogs had been printed and delivered to the various Mercantile stores then, too. When nothing happened around the street, he humored himself by imagining what strange gadget Gray would order from this catalog. Since there was only one, Isaac would have to wait until he had a reason to go to the Mercantile before he could even hazard a guess.

Just as he reached for his hat to do just that, the door of the Mercantile opened, and Mack stepped out, checking the street before holding the door for Birdie. Mack carried a stack of parcels and Birdie held a letter in her hand, reading it instead of paying much attention to where she was walking. The parasol hung forgotten from her forearm, and Mack didn't try to get her attention away from the letter. He only steered her by the elbow around other people and down the stairs.

Curiosity had Isaac out the door, though he slowed his pace so it wouldn't look like he was doing anything but strolling to the Mercantile or the Post office. He was a few steps away from them when Birdie stopped dead still in the middle of the street and looked away from the letter. Tears flowed from her reddened eyes, and her lips parted. Before she could release the cry welling out of her, she pressed a gloved hand to her lips and ran to the saloon down the street. Mack followed, though he took his time and didn't run after her.

Isaac paused and watched them for a moment, dumbfounded about what could've been in the letter to upset her so much.

"Think it was from her family?" Jack's voice invaded his thoughts, and he turned a confused expression to his Deputy. "The letter. I've only known people to cry like that when they got bad news from their family. Maybe that's what's going on?"

"Perhaps," Isaac said carefully before continuing his walk to the Mercantile. Jack followed beside him and ducked into the storefront as Isaac opened the door.

"Good morning, Sheriff," came a round of welcomes, and he smiled as he gave them all a nod.

"Good morning, everyone. I trust you're out enjoying the lovely weather?" He pulled his hat from his head and turned to walk down an aisle that contained crockery and eating utensils. The back wall held ammunition and packing powders. He found the box that fit his pistols and picked up two before turning up another aisle.

"Good morning, Sheriff. Do you have a minute?" Lucy Nelson asked quietly, looking around to see if anyone else heard her. The small woman had to be older than his mother, but she got around so spryly that he doubted anyone dared to bring it up to her directly.

"I always have time for you, Mrs. Nelson." He smiled amiably. "How can I help you today?"

"I don't know if you've heard yet, but my sister is living in Wellsville, and she wrote to me, saying that they, too, were dealing with livestock going missing. Never more than one animal from a farm at a time, but every kind of animal you'd keep for food has turned up missing there, too," she whispered.

This was news to Isaac, and his eyebrows rose slightly. "The same problem in Wellsville?" Was it possible they were related? Was it possible that more than one of the settlements had the same problem?

For that matter, did that place the culprits somewhere to the South of town? He tilted his head a moment before nodding to Mrs. Nelson. "Thank you for sharing that, Mrs. Nelson. I hadn't heard. I will add it to my notes and ask in other settlements, though. Thank you very much."

She beamed with the knowledge of helping his investigation and moved on down the aisle. Isaac shook his head slowly and continued to the clerk, arriving just in time to hear Gray place an order for lye. The clerk, Mister Lee, caught sight of Isaac approaching and patted Mister Gray's arm. "You know, Sheriff Branson fought in the War. Say, Sheriff, did they supply you with anything to fight off the bugs when you were back East?"

Gray turned his eyes to Isaac expectantly, and Isaac coughed out a laugh. "I'm afraid they did not, Mr. Lee. It

116

would've been handy a few times when we got far enough south to experience those mosquitos and gnats, though."

Mister Gray beamed. "Well, you shall have to come test this new repellant when it arrives, Sheriff. We may not have mosquitos or gnats, but I'm sure we can destroy a few other insects before they become pests in the kitchen."

He seemed gleeful at the idea and bustled out of the Mercantile humming a tune. Isaac laughed after him and handed Mister Lee his purchases. "Put them on my tab, would you, Mister Lee, and hold them back there for a moment? I need to send a few telegrams, and I'll be back afterward to collect them."

With a nod from the clerk, Isaac turned and left the Mercantile, ducking into the post office next door. Within minutes, telegrams had gone out to other sheriffs in the area asking about any trouble they'd had with livestock turning up missing.

He didn't think about Birdie again until he'd picked up the ammunition and headed back to the Sheriff's office. The Saloon down the street was quiet, which wasn't unusual this early in the day. Gray was disappearing in the front doors, Isaac noted, but, again, it wasn't unheard of. Most people in town had lunch from home, the saloon, or the hotel during the day until they could get back home for a better meal.

It made him think about what awaited him at home, and he sighed. He hadn't been able to talk to Lydia since the night he'd held her in his arms while she'd cried out her worry for her friend. If it were anyone else, he'd be sure to tell his wife about a letter that her friend had received that sent her home in tears from the store. Did he dare tell her about Birdie's letter? Would she want to offer her friend some comfort? Did he trust her not to ride into town to find her?

He growled, not liking the feeling of keeping things from her but not knowing what else to do to keep her safe. He had already decided he wouldn't tell her. He didn't want his wife anywhere near Fred Burns, and he didn't dare think of what would happen if she tried to get to the man's wife again.

Maybe he would mention the frock coat to her, though. He only knew one woman in town who was talented enough to decorate a piece of clothing like that. It was the woman he didn't want anywhere near the woman wearing it. He had the rest of the day to decide whether he would believe her when she denied it.

Because he knew without a shadow of a doubt that his God-fearing wife would not tell him she'd seen her friend again so soon after their argument. She'd find ways other than lies to avoid it, of course, but she would never admit it.

Was it his imagination, or did he look forward to seeing her quick mind dance around his observation of the frock coat? Maybe, if he phrased it right, her eyes would blaze back at him, and they could stop this silly routine of stilted conversation. His jaw clenched, and he stepped into the Sheriff's office, staring at the clock. He had plenty of time to think of something else to talk about if stopping that was what he planned. Bringing up that frock coat might make his heart race when her eyes gave way to the passion of her anger, but the silence and stiffness would only deteriorate.

He didn't think he could stand another minute of her refusal to look at him as they dined. He didn't want to know what was worse than that.

Chapter Fourteen

"It's been a week," Lydia announced to the empty kitchen. "Seven days. I know it doesn't sound like a long time, but a husband and wife should be closer than this by now, shouldn't they?" There was no answer, and she took a sip of her tea, calling herself ten times an idiot for talking to no one. Since he released her from that hug a few days ago when he gave her comfort and seemed to take some from her presence, Isaac had avoided her.

Her eyes dropped to the folded invitation on the table, and she took another sip of her tea as she contemplated it.

Two days after her first tea at the saloon, another invitation appeared, inviting her to tea the following Friday. She'd accepted, hoping that any falsehood she'd seen on the first occasion would be easily identifiable with the second or that she could catch lying about their relationship.

When that Friday came, Burns met her at the door and escorted her to the sitting room, where Birdie was waiting as regal as a queen on her throne. Even her gown held the air of sophistication that had been so lacking in her first visits. Was it a show for her benefit, or had she really been that wrong about him?

Again, Burns made excuses and left them in the hands of Smiley, who never said a word. Lydia had returned home after an hour of teasing Smiley and talking about their lives before Franklin, as they had on the train. She even took an armload of mending to work on since her needlework was much more accomplished than Birdie's. She couldn't deny the nagging feeling that she was missing something when everything seemed that perfect.

She longed to ask Isaac about his feelings for Fred Burns since there didn't seem to be any weight to them. Birdie seemed content at the saloon. Fred Burns had given no hint that he was other than a doting husband on her visits. Did Isaac know something he wasn't telling her? Did she have a right to know?

"I talked to Birdie today," Lydia mentioned during dinner one evening. Isaac had stopped chewing and listened, but he hadn't responded. "She's looking well. She said that Mister Burns is spoiling her with his attention and..."

Isaac's fist had come down on the table, shocking her into silence. Even Cora had jumped and raised her napkin to her lips in surprise. Lydia's eyes shot up to meet the blazing anger in the gaze of her husband. "Do you think I'm lying about him?" he asked her.

"Of course not," she smoothed over, trying to relax. "I merely think that, perhaps, your first impression was not what their lives have become—"

He didn't let her finish, just dropped his fork on his plate, made excuses to his mother, and disappeared out the back door without a word to her. He wouldn't be back by the time she retired for the evening, but she heard him climb the stairs not long after she'd snuffed out her candle and crawled between the sheets.

For a week after that, when they did speak, Isaac's responses were stilted and emotionless. He came home late and ate in silence, not even answering his mother's questions with more than a grunt of acknowledgment. Then he disappeared to the stable or the pastures to check on the cows.

Lydia watched him from the kitchen window more often than she wanted to admit, fascinated with the shift of muscles in his arms and back as he cut firewood from the logs stacked next to the stable or herded the animals back into the barn at dusk.

Her mouth went dry every time she caught sight of his thighs straining against his horse's flanks as he rode into the stable yard. She found herself daydreaming about what their lives would be like if they didn't have all of this standing between them.

He would wrap his arms around her middle while she made breakfast and kiss her softly before he left to go into town. He would come home and kiss her again before asking about dinner, then they'd talk late into the night about whatever danced in their heads. She turned her wandering thoughts to the sound of their children playing in the yard or running up and down the stairs.

Then there were the nights when she was startled out of her sleep by his hoarse screaming or the soul-deep sobs she heard from his chest. She wondered if he held these bursts of emotion inside all day until he could get to the safety of his room and be wrapped in the blanket of night. They reminded her so much of her brother's night terrors that She'd tried talking to him after the first night.

"Something woke me up this morning. I checked the windows but didn't see anything. It sounded like crying." He hadn't responded, so she leaned in a bit more. "Perhaps you could check the lines on your way into town? I've heard that some wild animals sound like people crying to lure–"

"I'm sure it was nothing. I'll check it." Then he'd left without another word.

A few days later, she tried again, with nearly the same point, and he'd pinned her with a glare. "It was nothing, Lydia." His tone held finality. Heaven knew his posture had, too. She'd gotten the hint. He didn't want to discuss it. Not with her, at least.

But each time she'd awakened in the middle of the night since then, she'd found herself closer and closer to his door. Each time, she stopped herself from going into his room and comforting him and went back to bed, afraid her presence would only make things worse for him.

Her eyes cleared from the memories and landed on the invitation sitting next to the saucer on the table. And now, she was going behind Isaac's back, behind everyone's back, and visiting Birdie at the saloon for tea.

She had debated telling him about the invitations, and even now, she chewed her lip as she thought through the consequences that created more questions than answers. Would worry over her going to the saloon add to his nightmares? Did he really have anything to fear from Fred Burns? Would he simply ban her from going?

She growled in irritation as the conversation with herself came full circle. She gave up and tucked the invitation into the pocket of her apron, then stood and cleared the table.

Before she could get to the sink, Essie let herself inside. "Hey, where is everyone?" she called from the front door.

"In here." Lydia tried to sound cheerful. The woman had said the same thing every day since she'd stopped knocking on the door and just let herself inside. She'd just kept doing it after the first time she'd slipped up and come through the door without knocking and being admitted. Neither Lydia nor Cora was upset by her intrusion, so she'd kept the practice going.

Within seconds, Essie came through the kitchen door, her reticule and bonnet in her hand and a strangely cautious expression on her face. Lydia put her dishes in the sink and returned to the table for the tea pitcher, tilting her head at Essie. "Cora is lying down, I'm afraid. She had a headache."

"I came to talk to you, actually. Do you have a minute?" Essie's tone wasn't concerned, but Lydia could see how she wrung her hands in front of her. What could make the woman so nervous?

"Of course," Lydia responded, holding her hand up and indicating the table. "I was just clearing my tea, but I have a few sandwiches left if you want some. There's a little tea left as well."

"No, thanks, I won't take much of your time. I had an idea and wanted to talk to you about it before I forgot." Essie slid into a chair, her expression not changing, and Lydia returned to the table, sitting across from her. "I know it's a bit short notice, but I would like to hold tonight's Bible Study Group... here," Essie's voice sounded tentative, and Lydia smiled. "I thought Mrs. Cora would like to attend and, with her health..."

"I think it's a lovely idea!" Lydia smiled broadly. "She would enjoy entertaining the group, especially. Having so many people around would be good for her."

Essie chewed her lip and dropped her voice. "Do you think she will be alright with it? That she won't... you know..."

Lydia smiled softly and patted Essie's hand. "I'm sure she will be fine. She hasn't had an episode in quite a while now. She's taking a nap that will probably help, so I wouldn't worry, and we'll be here to keep our eyes on her."

Essie grinned back and pulled Lydia across the table for a hug before rising to her feet again and "Excellent! I will tell Emelda in town. She's such a gossip that everyone will know within the hour."

Lydia laughed, rising to follow Essie to the door. "Thank you for doing this, Essie. I would never have thought to move the Bible Study so Cora could join us!" Not to mention Isaac wouldn't have to worry about her leaving Cora alone to attend Bible study. He couldn't forbid her from going if it were happening in his sitting room! There was no possible way for her to lose here.

***

Hours later, Lydia was settled amidst the others of her Bible Study, immersed in a conversation about living in the eyes of the Lord and how they might commune with God most easily when they are quiet and still. People had been sharing stories of times they'd heard the voice of God in a songbird's call or the soft babbling of a stream. Lydia had to admit she'd never considered it, living in a city as she had for most of her life.

A few hours into the meeting, the door opened behind them, startling Lydia, and she looked toward it, her eyes wide, as Isaac strode through. He dusted off his jeans and removed his hat, then nodded at the assembled people and turned toward the kitchen to find dinner.

"Excuse me," Lydia murmured as the conversation started back up. "Let me see to my husband's dinner. I will return in a few minutes."

Cora was ensconced a few chairs down, wrapped in blankets and holding a Bible in front of her. She beamed at Lydia as she excused herself from the group, clearly enjoying the company.

Lydia walked into the kitchen and began putting Isaac's plate together as he washed his hands in the basin and took his place at the table. "You should come sit in with us," she said suddenly into the silence between them. "We're talking about living in the eyes of the Lord and–"

"No, thank you," Isaac said, sounding like his teeth were clenched.

She turned toward him, brow wrinkled in confusion. He wasn't looking at her at the napkin next to him on the table. She crossed the space and settled the plate in front of him. His fork was stabbing into the food almost before she'd let go of his plate. She settled into the chair next to him, and after a few minutes of silence, she continued.

"Marc Dutton said that he sits by the river near Bright Creek and just listens to the–" Lydia was cut off by Isaac.

"I said, no, thank you," he growled.

Lydia swallowed. "I really think it would do you some good with your–"

He slammed his fork down on the table and rose, knocking the chair over. "What don't you understand, Lydia? I am not interested in the Word of God. I don't care about anything He might have to sell me. I don't want to be anywhere near any group of people who spend more than a few minutes in their lifetime concerned with what comes after we leave this world. Far more terrifying things happened in it to worry about what comes next!"

With that, he turned on his heel and strode out the back door, slamming it shut behind him and leaving her speechless at the table.

Chapter Fifteen

Isaac didn't bother with the steps off the porch as he leaped to the ground. He was so angry his hands were shaking. Why, after days of muted conversations and tension, had she decided that goading him about a Bible Study group, of all things, was a good idea? Is that why she had invited them to their house? Surely she realized that he was not the man who would bend his knee to pray for anything. Not anymore.

He ducked into the shed a few feet away and returned with a bucket with tools and nails. His long strides had him standing at the fence posts his mother had been asking him to fix for a month. His temper should make that easier, at least it would if he didn't bend them all to the point that he had to spend hours straightening them out.

Once the bucket was settled by the fence post and his lips were pursed around a trio of nails, he grabbed the hammer and attacked the first post. As he'd thought, it took one hit to drive the first nail into the fence line and the post, attaching them together again. The sight gave him a tiny shred of satisfaction, and he reached for another board to repeat the action.

The feeling of pride started to slip as the sound of the hammer hitting the nails rang in his ears. An echo of gunfire rang in his head, and he shook it. He hit the nail again and once more heard the echo of gunfire. He lifted his head and looked around.

Not seeing anyone running, Isaac could only assume he was the only one hearing it. Another nail went in, and he ignored the echo. He started hammering quicker, trying to get finished and away from the annoying sounds in his head. But they only blossomed into a field of gunfire. He could smell the smoke, hear the screams....

"No," he said, shaking his head and trying to push the memories away. He continued, gritting his teeth against the pain of the memories. But before he made it a third of the way down the fence line he needed to repair, he couldn't fight them anymore. They caught him in their snare, refusing to let go.

He heard the screaming, the coordinated gunfire of the first charge, and then a random swirl of explosions that seemed to chase each other across the battlefield. Again, the air began to smell like gun smoke, and the coppery scent of blood joined it. He wiped the sweat from his brow on his shoulder like he had when he would stand in formation, awaiting orders to move.

His eyes glazed, and he no longer saw the boards and nails. He had no concept of time, no ability to see what was happening in front of him. His sight was caught in those moments at Gettysburg when he'd searched for his company and had been shot for his trouble. He did find them before the blood loss caused him to black out. The sight of their trampled bodies would never leave his thoughts, never give him peace.

He should've been there. He should be dead with them. Why had he been separated from them? When had he missed the order to turn? Every single man, from their Captain to Corporal Smith's little brother with his drum, had been slain.

The anger he'd felt then coursed through his veins. Why did his prayers fail them when they were needed most? Why did God hate them so much as to allow their deaths to be so violent?

Isaac screamed, real pain bringing him back to the present with a jolt. His vision cleared as he stared at his fingers. The nail fell harmlessly to the ground, and the hammer followed soon after as he watched blood pooling on his index finger and his thumb.

"Isaac?" came an anxious voice from the porch. He looked up as Lydia leaped off the porch and ran toward him. She caught up to him and reached for his hand, fussing about the dying sun and trying to pull him toward the house where she had better light. He pulled his hand back, trying to break her grip on him. He would not allow her to pull him around like a child!

He growled at her when she didn't let go, his voice low and mean. "I'm fine, Lydia. I just hit my fingers instead of the nail. It'll be fine in a few minutes."

"Don't be foolish," Lydia snapped, turning and pulling him even harder toward the house. He'd never heard that tone from her. It shocked him into obedience.

"Sit there." She let go of his hand as they entered the house through the back door and gestured to his chair at the table in the kitchen, her voice allowing no room for argument. Her lips had thinned into a single line, and her brow was furrowed in an expression of pure irritation. But the soft lines around her eyes gave away her concern.

Before he could protest again, his mother appeared, wrapping a towel around his bleeding hand. Lydia returned with a basin of water and a cloth. Isaac could only watch as the two women worked in smooth unity around cleaning his wound to assess the damage. Whatever motion Lydia started, his mother finished without a word passed between them. His mother held his forearm while Lydia poured water over his hand.

He hissed in pain, and Lydia's face drew up in apology, losing the sharp lines she'd been wearing on her brow just moments before. "We need to clean it so we can see where the damage is," she explained. "I need to know whether we need to send for a doctor or not."

Isaac looked down at his hand again and shook his head. "It's not that bad..." he started.

Cora interrupted him this time. "You just be quiet and let us take a look. I've bandaged you and your father up for most of my life. I think I know what I'm doing. Lydia does, too. This will be over faster if you stop talking and hold still." She didn't give him time to respond before she looked back at the hand she was holding, leaning closer to check the wound.

The blood had stopped gushing from his fingers, he noticed. Lydia leaned toward his hand at that moment, giving him a lovely view of her profile. Were her lashes always that long?

He shook his head, focusing on his hand and the throbbing pain in his finger and thumb. Where had that thought come from? He had no business... Was it flowers he smelled in her hair? She was so close that he could touch her, and the smell, a soft scent of lilacs and lavender, paired with his suddenly noticing how soft her curls looked against the creamy skin of her neck.

He flinched as Lydia moved his thumb and turned to look back at him. "I'm sorry. Can you bend it at the joints? The finger or the thumb?" She turned back to his hand, but not before he noticed the adorable, tiny freckles that danced across her cheeks.

They were almost impossible to see, but this close, he saw them all. They lit something in him that flared before he could snuff it out. He felt his smile stretch across his lips, and the urge to lean forward to see whether the freckles went across her nose or not was nearly overwhelming. He stopped himself just shy of doing just that and tried to bend his fingers like she'd asked, berating himself for getting distracted.

Pain shot up his arm, and he gasped, his mind ripped from the soft curls just a hint away from his lips and her scent. "No," he gritted out, giving up trying to move them.

"There is a lot of swelling but no more blood. We'll need to keep it up for a while. When my brother did something like this, my father kept fresh water by his bed stand and wrapped a soaked cloth around Theo's hand twice an hour.

He also kept it up on a pillow next to his side. When I took over to give him a break, he told me not to let Theo move it and to keep my eye on his fingernails. If they turned black, we needed to send for the doctor." She leaned over his fingers again, examining his fingernails.

"I will go get that set up in his room," Cora said softly and disappeared from the room. Isaac watched her go, smiling as memories from childhood injuries filled his head.

Lydia chose that moment to look up at him, and their eyes met. Her concern, so evident in those lovely eyes that never seemed to be the same color twice, struck a chord in his chest and the memories that threatened seemed to slip away. Unconsciously, he leaned toward her, not realizing his intent until he was almost close enough to touch his lips to hers. Her eyes dropped to his lips, and a completely different response made his blood thunder in his ears.

"Alright, I'm ba–" Cora stopped in the doorway, her cheeks reddening, but it was too late. Lydia gasped and leaned back, turning her attention back to his fingers. Isaac closed his eyes and gave himself a shake. Had he been about to kiss her? Truly?

"I'll find the willow bark. Go on up to your room, and I'll join you in a moment," Lydia said, her voice a little breathy as she looked anywhere but at him. Gone was the woman issuing orders with fire in her eyes. Isaac paused in the doorway and looked back at her, trying to slide a smile her way.

Her attention was on the cabinet in the corner. He turned away, but not before he caught the self-conscious swipe moving a loose strand of hair behind her ear and blowing out a slow breath. He cradled his hand against his chest but found his step a little lighter as he climbed the stairs to his room.

A few moments later, his mother came in with a small glass of whiskey, the towels, and the willow bark. He waited for Lydia to follow, but she didn't. He was disappointed and tried not to let it show, but a knowing look in Cora's eyes told him he wasn't hiding it very well.

What had he expected? They had barely spoken to each other in days. Why would that change now? His last words before leaving the house to work on the fence had been anything but kind. In fact, hadn't he been angry with her just a few hours ago?

He downed the whiskey in a gulp and handed the glass back to his mother, who passed him the willow bark and settled into a chair he'd noticed she'd pulled in earlier. Cora arranged his injured hand on the pillow she tucked under his forearm and dropped a towel into the bowl of water.

He chewed the willow bark thoughtfully, wishing he had more whiskey to dull the rest of his senses until the willow bark started working. His mother would never get him another glass, though. He'd tried that when he'd come home, depressed and angry, humbled to be asking for help after the way he'd left.

She'd refused anything more than a finger or two in the glass – only to take the edge off the pain until his medicine started working. She'd had no problem leaving him in his room if he argued, only sending his father to help him down the stairs for the next meal.

They were on the second round of cooling cloth when the pounding started outside the window. Isaac narrowed his eyes on Cora, who looked up at the window in confusion. She patted the back of his hand. Then she stood and crossed his room to look for the source of that noise and pursed her lips to suppress a smile.

"What?" he asked, shifting his eyes to the black sky outside the window and back. "What is that?"

"Your wife is repairing the fence," she said simply, returning to her seat and leaving him gaping at her. She dropped the conversation altogether. "Now, drink this and try to rest. This isn't going to get better if you keep getting your blood pumping."

She smiled and pressed another glass of whiskey into his hand. He rose his eyebrows at her, and she smiled innocently. Was she trying to assuage his bruised pride? He didn't question it further, just downed the contents and handed the glass back to her. It was rare that two glasses of whiskey were enough to faze him, but he was already exhausted. With the willow bark removing a bit of the pain, and the cold water numbing his skin, he was more than happy to let the alcohol pull him into the dark abyss of sleep.

It was the first night he hadn't had a nightmare in months.

Chapter Sixteen

Lydia put the last nail into the rail closest to the house and stepped back to check her work. She'd worked until she'd run out of light and then got up early to start that morning. Now that the rooster was crowing and the animals in the barn were waking up, Lydia had other chores to attend to. So she hoped she'd done the job well enough that the animals could go out into the pasture for breakfast and further away from the garden.

Satisfied that her work would hold, Lydia put the tools and leftover nails back into Isaac's bucket and started walking toward the back porch. She pulled up short, seeing Isaac standing there. She felt like she'd been caught doing something she shouldn't have been, but he had to realize that someone had to finish the fence. Right?

With a sniff in his direction, she gathered the tools she'd used and walked to the shed to put them away. She was unsure of how to talk to him today after his behavior while the Bible Study group had been here.

That almost kiss in the kitchen before Cora returned had kept her from sleeping all night. Her mind danced from shock to curiosity to self-consciousness and finally to denial. The sun had appeared on the horizon by then, so she gave up and took her confusion out on the nails.

"Where did you learn how to do that?" he asked, nodding to the fence behind her. Isaac walked next to her to the shed.

Lydia blew out her breath, which lifted the small wisp of hair that had come free of the thick braid down her back and fallen across her cheek. "My father was a carpenter. He taught me how to use a hammer. He'd already taught my brother, and they were building the pieces my father sold." She shrugged.

Isaac's smile broadened, and Lydia shivered at the tone of his voice when he spoke. "You are full of surprises, Lydia May."

"Lydia Branson," she corrected stiffly, though why she felt the need to remind him of her marital status, to him, she had no idea. "And I have to prepare breakfast, or we won't eat until lunch."

"Don't let me keep you," he laughed, following her as she entered the kitchen. She took off her hat and hung it by the door before moving to the washstand to clean up, pointedly not looking at him. "I am heading into town. I'll pick up something there, so don't worry about my breakfast."

His statement sent an immediate shock of shame through her, and she turned back toward him to explain. It was her duty as his wife to ensure he'd eaten before work. The townsfolk would talk if he ate anywhere but here. "Isaac, I..."

Her voice was breathy. It had to be her imagination, but Isaac seemed to lean closer to her. Her eyes dropped to his lips, the soft smile playing on them. Her lips were suddenly dry, and she darted her tongue out to fix that. He was there, as close as he had been the night before. Her pulse thudded in her chest and her breath caught, but she couldn't move.

Then the moment was broken. He straightened up, cleared his throat, and brushed past her. He had his hat in his hands as he stopped in the doorway, leaving her with a soft, "Thanks for finishing the fence, Lydia." He closed the door behind him, leaving her pulse thundering in her ears.

She stood there for a few minutes, staring at the closed door. Had it been her imagination? Had he nearly kissed her again? Her pulse raged in her ears as Cora entered the kitchen and followed her gaze to the door where Lydia's eyes were locked.

"Are you alright, Lydia? You haven't been working too hard this morning, have you? I heard the hammer earlier and saw the fence as I came downstairs, so I know you finished the fence this morning." She approached Lydia and eased her back and into a chair. "I'll get breakfast started, dear. You collect yourself for a few moments.

Lydia blinked and looked down at the ring on her hand. Was he intentionally getting her flustered now? Is that what this marriage would be for him, keeping her off balance with his almost-kisses that gave her some hope that it could be something more, just to keep her from being angry with him?

She ground her teeth and stood, straightening her skirts and taking her place at the stove, cracking eggs into a pan over the flame Cora had built. If he thought she would be cowed like that, he had another thought coming!

Chapter Seventeen

"You've got to stop smiling like that," Jack teased as he crossed the space to stand at Isaac's desk. "People might think they can rob a bank if the Sheriff walks around with that smile on his face."

Isaac scowled, and Jack clapped his hands once. "Much more like it. I'm going to take a round to check on things. Be back in an hour."

He sauntered to the door, and Isaac called out behind him, "You stay away from the receptionist at the hotel, Jack! I don't want to have to arrest you or force you to marry her if her father catches you again!"

Jack's laughter echoed down the boarded walk that connected the Sheriff's porch to the other buildings. Isaac glanced down at the handful of messages waiting for him that morning about livestock that had disappeared overnight. He laid them across his desk and tried to lose himself in Prudence Hester's disappearing chickens and George Merriweather's prize goat.

He gave up not long after, frustrated that his thoughts returned to the look in Lydia's eyes, first last night and again that morning. He simply couldn't stay focused on the issue. It was likely just some local harassment. He doubted the Natives would've had anything to do with it, and the distance between the properties that had been stolen from made it evident that it was more than one person committing the crimes. He got that much out of the messages, at least.

He rose to his feet and stretched, and a button popped off his shirt. He muttered and reached for the needle and thread on his desk, reattaching it. As he cut the string with his knife, he paused. His attention fell to the needle in his hand, and he found his thoughts heading back to Lydia.

She enjoyed sewing and embroidery. She'd brought some with her, but the small amount of luggage she'd brought west told Isaac she probably hadn't brought much. Maybe he could get her some nice thread from the Mercantile as an apology for his behavior last night. He hadn't been very husbandly, even after she'd left her group meeting and made his plate.

The look he'd seen on his mother's face at being included in the group made him feel like a heel, too. Why hadn't he thought to take her out places these last few months so she could talk to people?

He dropped the needle back in his desk, plucked his hat from the hooks by the door, and left the Sheriff's office. His pace slowed as he got to the intersection that would take him to the Mercantile, and his eyes strayed to the saloon.

A few people were moving around outside while Birdie was sweeping off the porch, head down and intent on her task. Something about her posture made him uncomfortable, but he knew confronting her about it wouldn't get him any answers. Whatever hold Fred Burns had on her, she was as tight-lipped as a child refusing medicine.

With a sigh, he continued to the mercantile, where he hoped he could find something that matched Lydia's style. He would probably have to order it since she held herself the way he imagined a debutante back east would. Would she have been one of them if the War hadn't come and ruined it for her? Would she have danced across a ballroom and met a handsome young man who would woo her and treat her like a princess?

The thought made his stomach turn and anger flare, so he discarded it. It wasn't his fault that the war had ruined her chances for a match closer to her family. Did she have more family there? He still had family in St. Louis with whom his mother exchanged correspondence, and he knew she wrote letters in the evening at the small desk in the front parlor.

There were so many things he didn't know about his wife, so many questions to ask. Would there ever be a time that he was comfortable enough to talk to her about these kinds of personal things?

He didn't have an answer for that, so he ducked into the Mercantile with a smile and ordered six skeins of silk thread from New York. He used the catalog Herald Gray, Essie's husband, was anxiously waiting to get his hands on. He ordered some flower seeds, too, and handed the catalog to Mr. Gray.

Now he just had to figure out how to apologize without mucking it up.

He also had to figure out why the urge to kiss his wife wouldn't get out of his head.

Chapter Eighteen

Lydia paused on the sidewalk before the saloon, dusted off her dress, and shook out her skirts. Then she used the window to check her hair. Her hat had done a great job of keeping most of her hair from flying everywhere, but there were small wisps that had slipped free and hung down around her face from her ride into town with the wagon. "Nothing for it," she muttered, making sure her reticule was on her wrist before stepping through the door.

As had become the custom, Fred Burns met her at the door in a neatly tailored suit, his shoes gleaming. He offered her his arm. Nothing about the man before her reminded her of the man she'd met the first day at the train platform – the man who had chased her off the first time she'd called on Birdie.

As this became the norm, she began trusting him more. And the more she trusted him, the more she wondered why Isaac felt this man was such a horrible person.

She wasn't sure but seeing this side of Fred's only deepened her confusion about Isaac. Today, Fred stayed around a little while during their tea. Birdie was unusually quiet, but every time Lydia had tried to engage her in conversation, Burns drew her attention away.

He told them stories of his life before he came to Franklin, and she didn't have to feign interest in them. He was entertaining and certainly knew how to serve tea.

She turned at one point to share a laugh over one anecdote with Birdie and nearly dropped her cup. Lydia had dismissed the style and color of Birdie's dress. She thought her position on the shady end of the couch was a coincidence.

But now, all the behaviors that seemed out of place, her forearms and collarbone typically visible in a tea dress being covered, seemed strange. Even the color of the dress was darker than usual as the skirts fell around her legs to the floor. Her face looked thinner, her cheeks more hollow, and the circles under her eyes were darker.

There was a slightly dazed expression in Birdie's eyes when she looked directly at Lydia. Then her eyes would dart between Fred and Smiley.

The confusion she felt increased as everything in the room felt different with Fred inside the room. What was going on here?

Fred left them not long after, leaning forward as if to kiss Birdie's cheek. Lydia hid her observation of their exchange in her cup as she took another sip of the tea. Once he leaned forward, his grip tightened on her arm. Flashes of pain lit her blue eyes, too, and she visibly shrunk away from him as he leaned closer. Instead of his lips brushing her cheek, they moved to her ear, and he whispered something before pulling away.

Cursing herself for an idiot, Lydia set her cup aside, picked up a biscuit, and slathered on some lemon curd, her eyes moving beyond Birdie to the man standing behind her. His posture was tense, unlike her earlier visits. Now he looked ready to rip Fred Burns apart limb by limb.

She tucked that knowledge away and pretended to enjoy the rest of her tea. The mood was always lighter between them after Fred left them, and, although today was no exception, it seemed to be lacking something. Lydia presented the mended garments to Birdie, who exclaimed over the beautiful stitches. Then they sank back into their usual banter.

Soon, it was time for her to leave, and she hugged Birdie tight, biting her lip as Birdie stiffened when Lydia touched her shoulders and back. She pasted a smile on her face and left, deciding to check in on Isaac before she stopped by the mercantile for her supplies.

"Mrs. Branson!" Jack welcomed her as she opened the door to the Sheriff's office. "How are you this fine day? I hope it wasn't you that broke our Sheriff's fingers. I'd hate to have to put you in jail!"

Lydia laughed softly and shook her head. "Blasphemy. I would never do such a thing. And if Isaac told anyone differently, I'll be happy to tell them the truth!"

"Which is?" Jack suggested, leaning forward as if being told a secret.

"I will not besmirch my husband's name!" she added with mock indignation to her voice. "How dare you assume I would!"

Jack clutched his heart, his smile never wavering. "Oh, you got me," he coughed and pretended to collapse in his chair.

"You are really something, Jack, you know that?" she asked, her voice shifting in laughter.

"Yeah, that's what my mama says," he said with mock solemnity.

"I understand the sentiment." Lydia tried for severity and ruined it with laughter. "Where is Isaac?"

"He's out looking for people who will tell him what's going on at the saloon," he answered, his voice dropping to a whisper. For once, his expression was dead serious.

She nodded and chewed her lip, debating whether she could tell him what she had witnessed. In the end, she decided to tell Jack about the visit, hoping that maybe someone without the feud that seemed to loom between Burns and Isaac would see something they didn't.

She explained all about the invitations. How they'd started, how Burns had treated her each time, how wonderful the conversations had been between her and Birdie. Then she told him about today's visit and how Birdie had become withdrawn and looked so haggard.

Jack, surprisingly, was a good listener. He sat in his chair with his hands folded across his belly the whole time she talked. When she finished, he nodded, then cast his eyes down to his fingers. "I agree. Something's going on there. But I don't have to tell you that mistreating your wife isn't illegal, Mrs. Branson. It ain't right, but it ain't illegal. There's gotta be more."

Lydia stiffened but nodded. "Isaac believes there's more?"

Jack nodded. "It ain't for a lady's ears, Mrs. Branson."

"Lydia. Please call me Lydia," she asked.

Jack nodded. "Alright, Lydia. But on the street, you'll still be Mrs. Branson. My Ma would tan my hide if she heard me call anyone but my wife by her given name. I don't aim to have my hide ready for a saddle any time soon if it's all the same."

Lydia shook her head, a smile stretching her lips at his humor. "You needn't tell Isaac I stopped by. I will pick up our supplies and head home. I would appreciate it if you refrained from telling him about my latest visits to the saloon. He got upset when I mentioned going to check on Birdie" Lydia's voice sounded hopeful as she rose and walked to the door.

"I don't lie to the Sheriff," he answered, his shoulders stiff. "But since it's you, I will try to find a way to bring your concerns up without giving away the part about the visits."

"That's understandable and fair. I appreciate it, Jack." She nodded her goodbye and left the Sheriff's office. Her order was ready and already loaded in the wagon at the general store, including five spindles of silk thread she hadn't ordered. Lydia was on her way home within the hour. "How did he know which ones I wanted?" She wondered aloud, knowing it had been Isaac who paid for the thread.

Before she was even out of the old fort district of Franklin, she was whispering prayers to God for the protection of Birdie, while she and Isaac tried to find some way to get her free.

Chapter Nineteen

"What's eating you?" Jack asked as Isaac entered the Sheriff's office the following afternoon. Isaac pinned him with a look across the room, then moved to take his seat behind his desk.

"I just spent my morning trying to find anyone who's been in Fred Burns' saloon and might know anything about what's going on there with Birdie. Not a single person admitted to knowing a thing, even the ones I know I've seen in that saloon in the last week." Isaac dropped into his chair and crossed his arms over his chest. "So, I can only guess that Burns offered or threatened them with something if they said anything to anyone. I can't prove that, though, because no one is talking."

"Seriously, no one talked?" Jack asked.

He didn't answer, so Jack continued. "I talked to Lydia earlier. She came by to talk to you while you were at the mine. Said she came in town to pick up supplies from the mercantile." Isaac nodded. He remembered her saying something about that this morning.

"And?" Isaac prompted, his tone belying his impatience.

"She's very concerned about Birdie," Jack shrugged. "Said she saw her, but the whole thing was strained and uncomfortable. She was asking about Mack Medina and why he doesn't seem to be very far from Birdie's side lately."

Isaac's eyebrows rose. "Medina was with Birdie, and they were away from the saloon?"

Jack shrugged. "I guess Lydia saw them while she was shopping and stopped to talk to Birdie. Either way, the interaction with Birdie didn't seem to bother her nearly as much as Mack standing guard over her all the time. She asked me if I knew why the wife of a saloon owner needed a giant of a man as an escort when she went to the Mercantile for soap."

"Why, indeed," Isaac's smile stretched for the first time in a while. He may be able to use that at some point. Every little piece he could put together would help him bring Burns down. That man was everything that was wrong with the world, and Isaac had felt the need to get him as far away from the people he took care of as possible the second he'd met him.

Unbidden, the memory of Burns' hand curled around Lydia's arm leaped into his head, and he curled his hand into a fist on the desktop. Lydia would say that God had sent him to rescue her, to save her from whatever fate Burns had in store for her. God was good and kind in her world.

What proof did Lydia have that God would keep her safe? Why had she trusted Him so strongly to travel across the country to marry a man she'd never met?

"Does she see something I'm missing?" he murmured aloud, earning a brow-wrinkled look from Jack.

A few minutes later, Jack stuffed the papers he was looking at back into his desk drawer and stood with a stretch. "I think I'm going to call in on Ma, then call it a day. It's near quitting time, anyway, and I've heard and read enough about men going against God's laws for one day."

His mother's laughter was something Isaac hadn't heard in a while. The most he'd heard since he'd returned home was a chuckle, which was nowhere near what he was used to from her. He leaned on the wall next to the door and enjoyed the sound for a few more minutes, unwilling to disturb the unguarded time of the women in the sitting room.

Guilt gnawed at him, and he tried his best to shove it aside. Lydia, his wife, for Heaven's sake, was more relaxed with his mother than with him! He straightened his back and stepped into the doorway of the sitting room.

His mother's face lit up as he walked through the door, and she stood to meet him, moving faster than he'd seen her move in months. Her face glowed, and she wrapped him in her arms as if he'd given her a gift. "What are you doing home so early?" she asked, pulling back. "Is everything alright?"

"It couldn't be better." He smiled. Over his shoulder, he noticed Lydia had been embroidering and, if he wasn't mistaken, she was using the silk thread he'd ordered from the Mercantile. "I just wanted to come home and spend time with you."

With a smile as bright as the sun, Cora pulled him to the couch and gestured for him to sit while she poured him a glass of lemonade. Once they were all seated, the room became quiet.

Then his mother broke the silence. "I was just telling Lydia about the time you and your father fell into the creek behind our house in St. Louis. Do you remember that?" she turned to include him in the conversation. Her eyebrows rose as if she hadn't just brought up one of the most embarrassing days of his life.

Lydia grinned at him, and it was his turn for red cheeks as he stammered. "Actually," she interrupted. "I was about to tell you about that time my brother fell into the river on the edge of our property and had to swim back before Pa caught him." Her smile instantly made him relax, and he sent her a grateful look.

"Right," Cora laughed. "You said your Pa sent him to town to get... what was it?"

"Soap," Lydia grinned. "He had to cut through the woods to get to town, but it wasn't anything Theo hadn't already done, hunting for squirrels."

"Squirrels?" he asked, a laugh in his voice.

"Squirrels!" She laughed. "He was pretty good at it, too. He became a sharpshooter for their regiment within weeks of joining them in Virginia." She shook her head slightly, a hint of sadness turning the corners of her lips down. "But those squirrels didn't stand a chance! If he couldn't shoot them from the ground, he'd climb the tree after them!" Cora laughed at the image, and Isaac felt himself smiling, too. "One time, he'd slipped about halfway out a branch! When he didn't come home at a reasonable time, Pa and I went looking for him. We found him, his suspenders stretched to the limit as they held him up in the tree, caught on a broken branch under where he'd fallen! He looked miserable, and Pa ribbed him about it for ages afterward."

They all laughed at that, and Isaac relaxed even more. Was this what it could always be like? The three sitting around telling stories as the sun set out the window? Did he dare hope?

***

"I am glad you're still here," Lydia said softly.

After dinner, Cora bid them goodnight, and Lydia rose to start working on the dishes. Isaac stood nearby, drying them. Before he could ask where else he'd be, she continued. "There's something I need to talk to you about."

She dunked another dish into the soapy water and then continued. "I saw Birdie today." The way she hesitated made him suspicious, but he didn't press her for the details.

"Oh?" he said, stacking a plate onto the shelf above the sink.

"I'm worried, Isaac," she said, pausing her hands and lowering them to the sink. She looked up at him. "She puts on a good show, but she's thin. She always has that man, Smiley, she calls him, following her. She wears long-sleeved dresses in the heat of the summer," she said flatly. "Something is going on there, and I want to help you find out what it is."

"Lydia, I have a deputy to help me. This line of work isn't fitting for a woman. It could be far too dangerous for you. Besides, Ma needs you here." He felt like a bit of a heel using his mother as a reason to keep her close to home, but the thought of Lydia getting too close to Fred Burns made his skin crawl.

She pressed. "He won't suspect me of looking for anything, though, because it's precisely not a woman's place." Her voice sounded hopeful, but Isaac couldn't let her get tangled up in this. Not as dangerous as he suspected Fred Burns was.

"I can't let you do that, Lydia," he set the plate he had been drying down on the counter, tossed his towel on top of it, and then turned and curled his hands around her upper arms. "I couldn't bear it if something happened to you. Please don't ask me to put you in danger when we all need you so much here."

She opened her mouth to argue, or maybe it was shock at his admission, but he continued before she got a sound out. "I promise I will tell you everything I find out, and if I can find a way for you to help without putting yourself directly into the line of fire, I will let you know."

Her head jerked in a nod as she accepted that it was the best she was going to get, then softened the motion with a smile. "I would appreciate that," she murmured.

His eyes dropped to her lips. He forced his hands to let go of her and grab the plate again. "It'd be my pleasure," he murmured as he started rubbing so hard at the water drops on the plate he nearly took the finish off the ceramic. My pleasure, indeed...

Chapter Twenty

Lydia hummed to herself as she added a forget-me-not to the handkerchief she was embroidering. The silk of the thread Isaac had ordered for her slid through the fabric smoothly. Her mood had improved significantly as the tension between her and Isaac had lessened. He smiled more, she laughed more, and Cora smiled that knowing smile more. In general, things seemed much happier.

A sudden knock at the door drew her out of her happy thoughts. She set her embroidery aside to answer it, pleased to see a familiar place behind it. "Bishop Day, it is lovely to see you. Please, come in," she stepped back, allowing the Bishop to enter the house. He removed his hat as he crossed the threshold, and she took it from him, hanging it on a hook by the door. "What brings you out this morning?"

He followed her gesture to the sitting room and eased into a chair by the window before he answered. "I came to call on Mrs. Cora. I was out this way, and I do enjoy our visits."

Lydia smiled and nodded, settling into her usual chair and folding her hands in her lap. "I hope no one is ill, though I know Cora is always happy to see you. She is resting presently. We had a busy morning, and she wanted to nap before dinner. I know she will be so happy to walk you through the garden when she wakes. The seeds you sent her are growing splendidly. I will have to make regular trips to trim and dry them soon."

He returned her smile and cast a look at the door. "I do hope they continue to do well."

Lydia's smile warmed as she caught the direction of his gaze. "Will you stay for tea, Bishop? I'm sure she will be awake and ready to show off her new prized herbs very soon."

Bishop Day seemed to relax as he turned back to her with a smile – much warmer than his previous one. His voice seemed warmer, too. "I would like that very much."

"We can take it in the kitchen if you like. Or I can bring it in here. I try to keep a pot ready for warming on the stove since you never know when friends will stop by for a visit," Lydia said as she rose.

"I would like that very much, Mrs. Branson. I find taking tea in the sitting room tends to make discussions more formal, even between friends," he nodded in her direction, and she laughed merrily.

"If I may, Mrs. Branson, I wanted to ask after your husband. How is he these days?" Bishop Day's question could've been taken a few different ways, and Lydia found herself wrinkling her brow in confusion. "You see, war does things to people, Mrs. Branson. Forgive me for saying so, but I've heard many times from those who survived the war that the lucky ones are the ones who died and didn't have to live to see the aftermath. Sheriff Branson had some traumatic experiences while fighting in the war. I just wanted to inquire about how well he's really doing. He's very good at putting other people's needs before his own. I feel he's been using his mother's situation as a shield to keep from thinking about what he's experienced."

Lydia frowned, but the tea kettle whistled. She returned to the table a moment later with a trivet and the kettle, which she settled on the table. "I'm afraid I don't understand,

Bishop. How could anyone who died in battle be considered lucky?"

Bishop Day sighed, his eyes leaving her face and focusing on her hands as she measured out tea and dropped it into the kettle. "War is brutal, and having to adapt to that causes men to confront things about themselves that they didn't know before they experienced it at its worst. Some men are drawn even more to God, accepting that their lives are given in service to Him, and if it is His will that they die that day, then they will go with the love for Him in their hearts. Other men, however, see the vile acts of battle as the opposite of anything Godly. They blame Him for the wrongs that put them there. For the horrors they've witnessed. For the lives they were forced to take to survive. No one makes it through a war unscathed. Seeing so much death and destruction changes them." He paused and looked back up at her for a moment. "Sheriff Branson is a good man. When he left for the war, he did so with a Bible in his pocket and his mother's prayers on his soul. When he came home, however..."

Lydia nodded, understanding. "He doesn't want anything to do with God," she finished for him, her voice resigned. "I don't know how to help him, Bishop. I would love nothing more than to share this part of my life with him. He just pushes me, and even his mother, away. I don't know what to do."

She poured the tea into the cups through a strainer, and they both sipped quietly. "It won't be anything we can force on him, unfortunately. Free will is a part of His gift to us, after all. I will think about how to help him more. It could be that he just needs time. He's lost a lot in the last four years. Then he came home and lost his father, too. And his mother is almost unrecognizable from the woman who moved here with her family five years ago." He took a sip of his tea, his expression thoughtful. "Having you near with your steadfast faith will help, I think. Between you and Mrs. Cora, he will see the good in the Lord again."

"No man can stand in the dark so long that he cannot find the light, again, my dear," he said softly, patting her hand.

"I hope you are right, Bishop," she murmured.

They sipped their tea in companionable silence, Lydia's mind replaying what he'd said. Each time, it was chased by one of her favorite scriptures. Anyone who follows Me will not walk in darkness. He will have the Light of Life.

"Bishop Day, it's so good to see you?" Cora announced her arrival by walking through the door with a broad smile on her lips. "Why are you both so glum? Is everything alright?"

Lydia's smile stretched across her lips. Cora was one person she didn't have to fake her smile with. "We are fine, just thinking, that's all. Bishop Day is here to see you." She turned to him as he rose, leaving the empty teacup on the table. "It's always a pleasure to see you, Bishop. I hope we can catch up again soon."

"Indeed, always a pleasure, Mrs. Branson," he was genuine when he said it. "Mrs. Branson was just telling me about your garden. Are you feeling up to showing me around?"

Cora laughed and nodded. "You will be so surprised at how fast my herb bed has recovered!" her excited chatter faded as the pair of them walked out the door and off the porch on their way to the garden.

Lydia removed the tea set from the table, cleaning and refilling the kettle with water and settling it back on the now-closed grate. Once the teacups were cleaned and put away, she settled into the task of chopping vegetables to go with dinner and let her mind wander over her discussion with Bishop Day.

While Lydia hadn't seen battle, she had been scarred by the War. She hadn't realized it at the time, but she'd been one of the survivors to get closer to God, understanding her luck in still being here. Could she help Isaac see that he was lucky to still be here, too? She was fortunate that he was there. Cora was, as well. The town was, for they knew their Sheriff was a good man, the son of another good man. What would it take to make Isaac see that?

She paused, easing the knife to the tabletop as a question flitted across her thoughts. Lydia knew helping Isaac find his way back to God would ease his suffering. But would he ever let her help him with that?

Chapter Twenty-One

Isaac felt the white-hot pain of the bullet piercing his leg, heard the hoarse scream as it was ripped from his throat, and smelled the stench of burned sulfur from the rifle of the man who had shot him.

As if time had slowed, he saw his arm swing around, a cocked pistol in his hand. He pulled the trigger, saw the flash, and smelled the sulfur of his pistol's discharge, followed by the lightning-fast shock of the man across from him as the bullet hit him square in the chest.

The recoil from the pistol knocked him off balance, now that his thigh was on fire, and he felt the earth reaching for him. Then, it seemed, the very trees were reaching for him. He struggled to get free of those limbs, but they curled tight fists around his arms and yelled...

"...Isaac!"

Isaac opened his eyes, and the vision from the dream faded into the sight of Lydia, so close he could feel her breath on his face. He blinked, trying to decide if this was heaven or hell, giving Lydia the chance to pull herself out of his arms. In his struggle against what he now realized had been her hands on his shoulders trying to wake him from the nightmare, he had toppled her. It wasn't the ground trying to pull him under or the trees trying to pull him up into their branches. It had been Lydia. And he had pulled her back hard enough to drag her down on his chest.

The emotions warred within him, the ones lingering from the dream, the ones he tried very hard not to feel for this woman he'd married, the ones that teased him whenever his guard was down. The cool midnight air met his sweat-covered torso, and he shivered involuntarily. The bed dipped at his hip, and she was there.

This time, she was pulling the blanket over him, whispering soothing words and brushing her fingertips over his forehead. Her touch was a soft whisper on his damp brow. The more Lydia whispered to him, the more he settled, secure in the knowledge that it had been a dream and that he was not back in the years of never-ending battles.

He was at home, in Franklin, in his own bed. The familiar smell of the lavender his mother grew in the garden outside the window drifted in on the breeze. The cotton sheets clung to his sweaty body, the linen curtain that floated with grace from the window as the breeze whispered into his room. Yes, he was home.

"Lydia?"

Her name felt like a prayer on his lips, and her answering smile brought warmth to his soul. "Yes, Isaac. It's me. It's all going to be alright. I'm here to help you." She continued stroking his brow, and he felt his heart rate calming in response. He didn't want her to stop. He wanted to feel this calm, this comfortable, forever. "I will go get you some water. It will help."

Her weight shifted, and she stood, turning away to go to the door for the water. Isaac's hand curled around hers, though, and her eyes met his in confusion. "Isaac, I promise, I will be right back. I'm just going to get you a glass of–"

"Please don't go," he whispered, interrupting her with a voice that sounded a little desperate in his ears. He couldn't deny that the ache he'd felt since that day in Gettysburg seemed to ease when she was this close, though, and Isaac didn't think he could handle its return just yet.

She seemed to pick up on that and smiled at him. With a nod, she sank into the chair next to his bed, still holding his hand. That's where his eyes went next, their hands curled around each other on the side of the bed. He hadn't noticed how small her hand was in his on their wedding day. He'd been distracted, then.

He wasn't distracted now. His free hand traced the lines of the back of her hand, learning the curves and the graceful length of her fingers. Then, his eyes traveled from their hands curled together next to his side to meet hers. "I apologize for waking you," he murmured, not willing to break the comforting silence of the room with a louder voice.

She seemed to think the same thing. When she answered, her voice was equally as low. "There's nothing to apologize for, Isaac." She smiled, her head falling to the side, sending a cascade of hair over her shoulder. He realized she was wearing a sleeveless linen chemise that left her throat, the curve of her shoulder, and her arms bare. It was hardly proper, but he wasn't going to complain. She was his wife, after all. Didn't he have a right to see her this way? Besides, her skin was lovely all the time, but here in the moonlight, it seemed to glow.

"Will you tell me about it?" Lydia asked softly, leaning over their joined hands. "About the nightmare?" Her voice was full of concern and tenderness, and he wanted to respond to that, to tell her anything she wanted to know. Her eyes were searching his as if she would see it all if she found the right spot in his gaze.

If she'd wanted to know his entire life story, he'd have been too happy to hand her every minute of the life he'd led that brought him into this room with her. Every foolish stunt he'd pulled, every book he'd read, every tutor that had rolled their eyes at his antics.

He knew deep down in his soul he could trust her with his most bizarre secrets, and she would never betray him. He could tell her everything – even the details about the fight with his father that had led him to war. Anything, all of it.

But not this. Isaac couldn't burden her with the things that stalked his nightmares each night. Lydia would remain pure and safe from these horrors. She should not share his fear nor take on the burden off him. He would make sure she stayed free of them. He, at least, deserved them. He'd sent many men to their deaths during the War, so it was only fitting that they visit their horrors in his nightmares. But he wouldn't, couldn't, allow them to get anywhere near hers. She was too good.

Isaac opened his mouth to tell her as much, but he simply couldn't find the words. His lips moved, but no sound came out. No words formed. Unsure of why they seemed lodged in his throat, he shook his head at her. While he could see the sadness in her eyes, she chased it with understanding.

Then her features softened even more. She leaned closer, leaning over their joined hands as if they were the bridge between the island of misery he lay upon and the mainland of hope she called home. Lydia's voice wasn't a whisper now, but it was still low, gentle, and soothing. "'When you lie down, you will be not afraid. When you lie down, your sleep will be sweet.'"

"Proverbs?" he asked, his voice a low murmur. He wasn't surprised at finding comfort in them, but he wasn't sure he deserved the comfort she offered so freely. Her smile was serene as she nodded, though he saw the dazzling bit of joy surging through her eyes even as his e grew heavy. Sleep pulled on his senses, the reassurance of her presence lulling him into a state of calm he hadn't felt since he was a child.

***

Isaac wasn't sure what woke him up the following morning, but the sun was streaming through his window. The chair was in its usual place next to his bed, and Lydia was gone. Lydia. Had he dreamed that she had come to him, soothed his nightmare away, and eased his soul into a more restful sleep? Had he dreamed her up, imagining the moonlight on her creamy shoulder? Imagining the warmth of her hand in his?

He ran his hand over the sheet under where his hand had been and felt the warmth there. He could trace that warmth to the edge of the bed and even see a small indention where Lydia must've fallen asleep beside him. He pictured her head on the bed pressing into the straw mattress.

Even the air smelled of her rose soap, a scent Isaac had caught a few times as she'd passed him in the time she'd been in his home. He was sure his smile was full of pride and probably looked downright foolish as he curled his hand against his chest. Lydia, his wife, had stayed with him all night. She'd come when he'd needed comfort and had not left him when he fell asleep.

Whether he deserved it or not.

Whether he had earned it or not.

He had a wife who cared enough about him to ensure he was comforted in the worst moments. While Isaac was no longer a man of God, even he had to admit it was a blessing.

Chapter Twenty-Two

Lydia rolled her shoulders back and then forward again, trying to stretch the knot of discomfort she felt between them. She'd jolted awake when she heard Isaac scream, memories of her brother's night terrors pulling her from her bed.

She was out the door before she even thought about getting a wrap to cover her chemise. When Theo would scream, she'd crawl into his bed to hug him, and he'd quieten. They'd stay that way for hours until he went back to sleep. She'd return to her room, then.

But she hadn't returned to her room last night. Isaac had asked her to stay, and she couldn't bear to leave him when he was so vulnerable. Not after how he'd reacted to her touch. Not after she had soothed his fears, and his breathing had returned to normal. Most certainly not after she'd been unable to focus on anything but being crushed against his chest, his hand curled in hers, clinging to her like she was his connection to peace. And when he knew the scripture she quoted?

Hearing footsteps coming down the stairs, she gave herself a mental shake, collected the bacon from the pantry, then started slicing thick pieces to fry for breakfast. She dreaded facing Isaac this morning. She'd been worried about how to react to keep him from being uncomfortable.

Should she ask if he was alright? Should she pretend nothing was different between them? Would he get angry at his weakness not being his alone to bear, any longer? Would he be angry if she pretended it hadn't happened?

Her mind was foggy, and she nearly cut her finger twice as she felt the panic rising. The footsteps grew closer, and Lydia inhaled softly. They were too small and light to be Isaac's. His boots sounded different coming down the stairs, she reminded herself. It couldn't be her husband coming down the stairs.

Cora entered the kitchen with a cheerful, "Good morning, dear," and crossed the space to kiss her on the cheek in greeting. She followed it up with her usual, "How did you sleep?"

Lydia was glad her back was to the woman. The pan was finally hot as she dropped bacon into it, and it started hissing. It would explain the sudden redness of her cheeks as she tempered her emotions. "Good morning, Cora. I slept well enough. And you?" she asked, deferring the conversation to her mother-in-law. She did not want to lie, but she did not want to tell Cora where she'd spent most of the night either.

She wasn't up for questions about it this morning, and she knew Cora's curiosity would get the better of her. Lydia wasn't sure what the answers were, anyway.

"I slept very well and woke with a smile on my lips," Cora replied. That was far different from her usual answer of 'just fine, thank you.' Lydia turned and looked at her, her head tilted to the side. There was something a bit different in her smile as if she knew a secret.

"Good dreams?" Lydia asked, adding eggs to the pan after the bacon was finished.

"The best," Cora answered vaguely, her lips still pressed into that knowing smile.

Lydia felt her cheeks reddening again and turned back to the eggs. "I am glad to hear it," she answered. "I was thinking about taking the drapes down today and giving them a good beating and cleaning. Do you think you're up for it?"

Cora didn't answer for a moment, and when she did, Lydia realized she was hiding her laughter. "We'll see what we can do. Have a lot of energy today?"

Lydia didn't answer that one. She just shook her head and flipped the eggs in the pan. There was no way she could say a word without referencing her sleep. Anything she said about that, Cora seemed to want to take a far different path from the one she and Isaac had traveled the night before.

Isaac walked through the door to the kitchen with a sunny 'Good morning' to them both as she settled the serving dishes on the table a few minutes later. Lydia couldn't stop the smile from stretching across her lips at seeing him, and the heat in her cheeks erupted as Isaac's eyes met hers over the space between the table and the door.

He sauntered into the room, bent, and placed his usual good morning kiss on his mother's cheek before continuing toward his chair. Lydia held her breath as he approached her and then felt her cheeks redden again as he brushed a quick kiss on her cheek and whispered a soft, "Thank you for last night," before sinking into his chair at the head of the table.

Cora started coughing, and he cast a look up at her, reaching across to pat her back a bit. "You okay, there, Ma?"

"Yes," she coughed, reaching for a glass of water that rested next to her plate. "I'm fine."

Lydia couldn't eat a bite until he'd left for the day, whether from the embarrassment of Cora misreading the situation or Isaac's soft smile that seemed to peek at her every time she looked up from her plate. Cora's smile said she knew something had changed. She had helped her with the dishes and excused herself to tend her garden, leaving Lydia to gather the drapes. She was far from efficient in taking them down as her thoughts swirled in confusion around the last twelve hours of her life and the crazy turn it had taken.

She and Cora were in the sitting room, working on embroidery as they usually were when Essie arrived and brought welcome distraction with her – as always.

"The Town Fair is this Saturday," she announced, her voice high and frantic, as she dropped onto the couch next to Cora. "Do you think you could help me with the decorations and things around the Bowery on Friday?"

"Good afternoon, Essie. I don't see why not," Lydia smiled. "When would you like me to be there?"

"What about me?" Cora asked, feigning indignance and bringing her lips to a pout.

"You both are welcome to join me, silly goose," Essie laughed, relaxing. "Around ten, I think. I am heading into town to talk to Bishop Day about it when I leave here. He said something about the school children using it to rehearse something earlier that morning, so I need to make sure we avoid interrupting them but still have time to get everything done before Saturday morning."

She paused, bent over the tray of small cakes Cora had made that morning and brought in for them to share in the parlor while they did needlework. She chose a slightly larger one in the center of the tray and took a bite. Her eyes closed in bliss, and she sighed. "I wish I could put such delicious things on the table, Miss Cora. You simply must teach me everything you know so my guests will tell everyone how wonderful a cook I am."

Cora chuckled. "You're always welcome to visit earlier when we're doing the day's cooking, Essie. I'll be happy to teach you anything you'd like to know."

"How much earlier?" Essie asked cautiously, her chin dipping toward her chest.

"We usually bake before lunch, then everything has a chance to cool so it can be finished up with any decorating we want. Perhaps around seven or eight?" Cora's eyebrows rose, and she tilted her head innocently. The whole town knew Essie Gray wasn't a morning person. If the maid she hired to help with her household duties was any reliable gossip, it took quite a while for Essie to be ready to leave her bed chamber when she woke up.

This seemed to be reinforced as Essie's face flashed a sour expression before she looked away. "Yes, well, maybe we can make something work later." Lydia and Cora burst into laughter, and Essie joined in, not at all ashamed to admit she was not one for rising with the chickens in the morning.

When they'd calmed their laughter and Essie had swiped another cake from the tray, she got back to the festival. "The whole town is pitching in. Even Fred Burns, from the saloon! He has offered to help set up tables. He even offered some extra seating from the saloon since he'll be closed until the festival is over.

She talked right over the look of disbelief spiking in both Cora and Lydia's faces, more intent on selecting another of the small cakes on the table in front of the couch. "Maybe you can ask Isaac if he'd be willing to help, too? You can never have too many tall men to reach the tops of posts."

Lydia laughed and held up her hands. "I will do my best, but I make no promises!" she shook her head at Essie's initial pout, which broke into a huge grin.

"I'll stop by and work on him, too then." She grinned.

"I almost want to dare you to try," Lydia laughed back. Even Cora laughed about that one. "If it were happening anywhere but the Bowery, Isaac would be all over it. As it is, though..." She let the sentence trail off and shrugged. "I will do my best, as I said."

"Well, that's all we can ask," Essie grinned. "Maybe we'll get lucky and he'll drag that deputy of his along with him! We're going to need all the tall people we can get!"

Chapter Twenty-Three

Isaac turned the key in the lock, feeling he was being watched. Birdie stood a few feet away from the Sheriff's office front, her lips parted as if she was going to say something.

"Birdie, what brings you by today?" He asked.

She opened her mouth to speak but snapped it shut again and hurried down the walk toward the saloon. Isaac frowned, tempted to follow her back and confront Fred Burns about whatever was bothering Birdie so much. With a sigh, he shook his head. He didn't have any more of a reason now than he had five minutes ago. Charging into the saloon now might undo any chance he had of catching Burns.

He continued on his way to get his horse and go home. He had to be smart about this. Watch his step, his words, and, especially, watch his actions.

***

Walking through his front door a little while later, he found the house empty.

"Lydia?" he asked, walking through the kitchen to the back door, where he could see the small backyard and the fence that Lydia had repaired. A movement to the right drew his attention, and he opened the door to get a better view of the garden.

He made his way to the garden fence, where he propped his forearms on the top rail and watched, unnoticed by the women focused on their work. His mother was kneeling to the right of a large rosemary bush pulling small weeds from the bed next to it.

She looked across the garden at Lydia, who was tying vines of squash to a rail behind the bed they were growing in as she stepped back to survey her work. Cora's laughter filled the air between them. Isaac felt the air suck out of his chest as Lydia doubled over in her laughter. The sounds were mesmerizing and Isaac realized, he looked forward to coming home to hear them every day.

He was entranced by Lydia's laughter.

His eyes slid to the vines, and the twisting greenery seemed to smile back at them. His smile widened upon seeing the face Lydia had created from the vines of the squash. His gaze slid to Cora, and he felt a happy warmth suffuse him. She'd smiled more since Lydia had come to stay with them. Lydia was someone she could talk to, who understood her maladies as well as Isaac.

"Need any help?" he asked, stepping into the garden.

Cora, still laughing at the face among the vines, waved him deeper into the garden. Then she set him to work on the deepening of the irrigation trench.

Isaac arched his eyebrow at her, then looked over his shoulder at Lydia, who held her hand over her mouth to stifle her laughter. "I hope you have a big meal planned. I'm going to be hungry enough to eat the shovel after this!"

"As long as you don't eat the spinach finally getting some height on them near the back fence, I will be happy to add an extra potato to your plate this evening," she grinned back at him. He enjoyed her sense of humor as much as the fire in her eyes when she stood up to him.

Once he was working, Cora started up their conversation again. "You were telling me about how Theo flooded your father's garden, weren't you, Lydia?"

Lydia's laughter filled the garden once more. "Right. Well, father told him to dig a trench from the river that bordered our property to the back of the main garden. It didn't have to be very deep, so he was pretty sure Theo could handle it. Father started working on the trenches inside the garden since those would have to be dug around existing plantings and he didn't trust Theo not to destroy those."

"Because of the incident with the corn?" his mother asked, her voice dancing in remembered hilarity. He'd have to ask Lydia about that one later if it made his mother laugh.

"Well, that and the time he was supposed to be weeding the herb bed and pulled all of the plants, instead!" She laughed, then. "So, Theo started the trench at the back of the garden, then made his way to the river. I was weeding the herb garden because my father said I was much better at it than Theo.

Theo was gone a long time after Father finished the trenches inside the garden, so he left me in the garden to look for Theo. I was nearly finished when I heard what sounded like a train thundering down the tracks. Except there isn't a railroad line anywhere near the house. I looked up from the other side of the gate to see a wave of water rushing toward the garden! I was hoping the gate would stop the force of that water when it hit. It turns out the slope of the yard on the other side of the garden was higher than the bed of the garden, and the water never got that high. When the wave hit the back of the fence, though, it sprayed straight up in the air and landed with a splatter right in the middle of father's bean trellis."

The images played in his mind, and he found himself laughing at what must've been a hilarious disaster.

"The wave crashed through the garden and destroyed the climbing trellis he built for the beans and the rail lines he'd run the squash down. When Pa finally got the trench closed off, the garden was a few feet underwater, and the land between us and the forest was flooding too! I don't think Theo ever recovered from that thrashing!"

"Why did the water rush in?" Isaac asked, pausing to lean on his shovel. "Theo couldn't have dug a trench that deep that quickly."

"Oh, he didn't!" Lydia gasped in between her laughs. "He found the dam the neighbor had built on the river to keep that section of the land from being flooded and pulled the logs free! Our neighbors threatened to thrash him, too!"

"What happened to the garden?" Cora asked, a touch of concern lighting her voice.

"It turns out we had a drought that year that lasted about three months. Theo had diverted so much of the river he saved all of the gardens in that area." Lydia shook her head and dusted her hands off, the bed she'd been wedding now free of intruders. "He was the savior of the gardens in town, too. Halfway through rebuilding the dam, the three landowners got together and decided to build a bridge instead. They named it something no one ever remembered. Everyone just called it Theo's River Bridge!"

Isaac found himself laughing along with them, and before long, Lydia excused herself to begin dinner preparations. Isaac finished the trench and started gathering the garden tools so he could put them away. When Lydia called out that dinner was ready, he escorted his mother inside and cleaned up before he sat at the table to eat.

***

"Isaac?" Lydia's voice called softly from the other side of his bedroom door. "Can I talk to you for a moment?"

He'd retreated here after spending time with his mother, as he usually did. He had a book open in his lap, but he couldn't help but think whatever Lydia needed was better than anything within the pages of Moby Dick. "Of course," he answered, setting the book aside and crossing the room to pull open his door.

"What do you need to talk about?"

"Essie came by today," she started, then paused as if searching for the words to tell him what was on her mind. "She said she needs help setting up for the Fair at the Bowery tomorrow. I told her I would love to help, and she asked if I would talk to you about helping out, too.

The whole community will be there helping decorate it, and I know you like to ensure the townsfolk see you as part of their community, even if you don't attend their services. She said even Fred Burns will be there, helping set up tables and bringing over seating from the saloon. I'm sure Bishop Day will have a team of women..."

The rest of what she said drifted out as his mind focused on what she'd said about Fred Burns. Maybe if he was there working on a project and happened to be near Birdie, or anyone who could give him information about what Burns was doing in that saloon when the townsfolk weren't looking, it would be worth every second he spent hanging bunting from the rafters. Lydia was still rattling on about everything Essie had told her about the Fair. He held up a hand to stop her mid-sentence.

"I would be happy to help." He smiled in apology for interrupting her speech.

Lydia's eyes bulged a bit, and she stammered into a smile. "Th…. Thanks!" She let out a relieved breath.

He felt guilty upon seeing the happiness bloom in her eyes. He'd agreed to help, though, and so help he would. "We'll talk more about it over breakfast. How does that sound?" he asked, stepping back to shut the door before he wrapped his arms around her and pulled her into his room.

She stepped forward and reached for his hand, and he flinched. She tilted her head but curled her fingers around the wounded and bruised digits he'd pounded a few days ago. He didn't want her to see the blood blisters that had come up under his nails on the sides, but her warm hands felt good against his callouses – as if they were soothing away the wariness in his shoulders. As she examined his nails and the sides of his fingers, he had to admit a surprising fact.

He didn't want her to let go and walk away tonight.

Chapter Twenty-Four

"I'm so glad we can spend the day together," Lydia said as she passed one end of the bunting to Isaac and started to climb a ladder to reach the frame above her head. Isaac smiled and nodded, though his eyes strayed from her toward something behind her.

She pinned the bunting to the edge of the frame and moved down the ladder. Isaac was still standing there, the other end of the bunting in his hand. He made no move toward the ladder or to reach up and attach it to the frame.

"Isaac?" she asked, drawing his attention back to her. She shifted her eyes the way he'd been looking. She saw Birdie and Fred had entered the Bowery ahead of a pair of tall men carrying stacks of chairs like they weighed no more than a box of linens. She sighed and pulled on the bunting from his hand.

He looked down at her then, his brows knitting together in confusion. "I was going to get it, Lydia," he said, turning toward the frame over his head. He pulled the ladder a little closer – only used the bottom step to attach the end of the bunting to the opposite corner of the frame they'd hung it from. "See? Done!"

She shook her head and pulled another bunting from the box. "Not even close, Sheriff," she smirked. He laughed and moved the ladder to the next frame, then held his hand out for the end to attach.

Two frames further down the line, his eyes strayed again. Once again, they were landing on Birdie across the Bowery. Jealousy uncurled in her chest, and she fought to tamp it down, urging him to pay attention as they worked on the bunting. She grew tired of fighting for his attention three more frames around the outside of the Bowery. "I need to get something to drink," she murmured without breaking his attention from the woman on the other end, stringing together multi-colored paper fans and creating streamers from ribbons. He hadn't even noticed she stepped away.

She grumbled as she headed to the refreshment table where, true to form, the older women of the town were manning a drink and snack station. They happily handed her a glass of water as she came close enough to reach and urged her to sit for a while and rest. She sank next to Cora, who was sitting under a tree behind the Bowery, watching what was going on underneath it.

"He's not making it easy, is he?" Cora asked, a smile on her lips that didn't quite reach her eyes.

"I was hoping we could make today the first day of working together on something. Like the garden and the sitting room, I was hoping he'd see that the people of the community adore him, and he doesn't have to separate himself from them." She sighed and took a drink from the water glass before lowering it to her lap. "Instead, he can't seem to keep his eyes off Birdie."

They watched as Isaac realized he was standing alone, holding the bunting, and looked around as if trying to find her. He set the bunting back in the box on the nearest bench and walked away, the opposite direction from the refreshment stand. Cora patted her hand gently. "He has something on his mind today," she said softly.

Lydia wanted to ask why spending time with her wasn't on his mind, but she kept it to herself "You're right. A Sheriff is always on duty."

Cora echoed her sigh but confirmed it. "Indeed. His father never took a day off. Not in twelve years. The only time he wasn't at work was when we loaded up the wagon and moved to Idaho. Once our things were in the house, he was back at work again."

Her voice sounded a little sad, and it was Lydia's turn to comfort Cora. A few minutes later, she had emptied her glass, rose, and returned to her assigned task. She climbed the ladder, pinned the bunting, moved the ladder, climbed the ladder, pinned the bunting, and moved the ladder... over and over again. At one point, Jack Sharpe arrived and volunteered to help her out. She didn't see Isaac again for a while.

He appeared as she pinned the last bunting in place – acting as if nothing was wrong. Jack tipped his hat to them both, and Lydia thanked him for his help. "Never a problem to help out the lovely Mrs. Branson," he said warmly, shooting a look at Isaac that the man didn't even catch. Again, his eyes were tracking Birdie across the room.

Lydia couldn't take it another moment. "If you're going to eye her in public, can you please not do it when I'm around? I don't expect you to care for my feelings, but I am growing weary of the pitying looks sent my way, Isaac."

That snapped him out of tracking Birdie, and he turned, his lips parting. "It's not... I wasn't... I'm sorry, Lydia. I was hoping to catch Birdie away from Fred. She came to see me the other day, and it seemed like she was going to tell me something, but she changed her mind and left. I know she was going to say something about Fred that would give me the evidence I need, but..." he closed his eyes and shook his head. "It's no excuse. I wasn't being subtle at all, and not only I've ignored you, but I've also ignored my duties and left you to put the bunting up all by yourself."

"Your mother is enjoying herself," Lydia said, nodding toward Cora, who seemed to be holding court under the massive oak tree. Her face was alight with humor and the women around her matched her laugh for laugh.

"I'm glad," he answered, smiling. He dropped his eyes to her. "How can I make it up to you, Lydia?"

Lydia chewed her lip and looked up, only to see his face arranged in a sorrowful pout. "Let's start by putting these boxes along the back wall with the rest and putting up the ladder. Then we'll find Bishop Day to see if there's anything else he needs for us to do."

He nodded sharply, again snapping a military-grade salute at her, which left her laughing even more. She scooped up a box as he snapped the ladder closed. "Tag!" he shouted, tapping her on the shoulder and darting to the back of the Bowery, the ladder gripped in his hand sideways. Lydia laughed and chased him, holding a box in one hand and lifting her skirt out of the way with the other.

She had to give it to him, he was fast! She caught up with him when he slowed to put the ladder against the wall with the others, and he wrapped his arms around her to keep her steady as the box in her hand tilted and slipped from her fingers, nearly taking her with it.

"I got you!" She laughed, and his smile seemed a little more predatory as he leaned closer to her and growled. "It looks more like I got you," he said.

Her face flushed, and she struggled to her feet, brushing her hands down her front. "Yes, well," she looked everywhere but at him. "I think the box goes over here." She pulled away from him and scooped the box off the floor before depositing it on the opposite wall a few steps later. She returned to find his grin on her and his eyes darker than she'd ever seen them. The sight of it sent a chill down her spine, and she had to look away before embarrassing herself.

"We should find Bishop Day," she reminded him, and he held out a hand, offering her the chance to go first.

"After you, my dear." He bowed, and Lydia couldn't help but shake her head at the false tone of primness that filled his voice.

Shaking her head, she started walking to the side of the Bowery closest to the road out front. "I think I saw him out here," she murmured, stumbling to a halt before passing beyond the linen sheets hung to hide the prep space on that side of the Bowery.

"What did you say to her?" She clapped a hand over her mouth to stop the startled squeak as Fred's voice barked a demand on the other side. "Answer me, woman, or I'll…" He bit off the rest and Lydia felt her heart stop in her chest. "You're the most ignorant fast trick I've ever met!" His voice grew louder the angrier he seemed to become. "Have I not warned you against talking to people, you sniveling gallinipper?"

Birdie never said a word, and Lydia pressed her fingers to her lips to keep from confronting him, glad the pair couldn't see them on this side of the cloth wall. He'd been so proper during their tea times – always escorting her with the grace of a man managing a business and pampering his wife. But this? Lydia cast wide eyes at Isaac, whose jaw was clenched as tight as his hands were at his sides.

They both flinched as the linen sheet was roughly pulled to the side, and they were almost run over by a thunderous Burns. "Why can't you stay out of our business?" He shouted at them. Lydia opened her mouth to say they were searching for Bishop Day, but Isaac snarled an insult at him instead.

"Useless guttersnipe. Why are you treating that woman like that?" Isaac hissed between his teeth.

"I tell you what, how about the next time this one comes over for tea, I'll send Birdie home in her place and keep her, instead. Maybe she'll be better at following directions!" Burns shoved past them and stormed out of the Bowery on the other side. His stride didn't falter. Lydia turned back to Birdie and rushed over, seeing a fresh red mark on her cheek.

"Did he hit you?" she asked, reaching up to touch the mark. Birdie flinched away, and Lydia's fingers curled onto themselves. "Do you need help, Birdie? Please, let me help you! I can't bear to see you this way?"

"Guilty, are we?" Birdie snarled at her. "This could've been you, you know? Then I could have the Sheriff, and you'd be the one..."

She trailed off. "I'm fine, Lydia." Her eyes are saying anything, but Lydia curled her hands into fists again. "Stay out of it."

Then Birdie walked the same path Fred had, though with much more dignity. Not even the blow to her cheek would cause her chin to dip. Lydia hoped her pride didn't get her killed.

For the first time in a few minutes, Lydia turned to Isaac. She'd honestly forgotten he was there in her need to check on Birdie. He stood, his body rigid, his jaw clenched tight, and his hands curled into fists at his side as he watched Birdie disappear into the saloon. Lydia felt the anger rolling off of him and bit her lip. "Isaac, I can explain..."

Chapter Twenty-Five

Isaac turned to look down at Lydia as she spoke, his clenched jaw keeping him from letting loose his fear for her. That she'd gone to the saloon after he'd told her not to irk him, but he wasn't going to say anything about it, here. He was no Fred Burns to make his arguments with his wife public.

Lydia didn't apologize for going against his will, and he had to admit that she'd told him she had no intention of avoiding Birdie. The fact that she'd been visiting the saloon without his knowledge said as much.

He really should've expected her to do exactly what she had done. "Let's see if we can find Bishop Day," he said, taking her hand. He saw that her face was pale and her expression drawn, as if afraid he would start in on her as Fred had on Birdie. "You don't have anything to worry about from me, Lydia. I understand. We'll talk about it later, alright? We're here to help set up for this Fair. So that's what we're going to do. Let's go find the Bishop and see what else we can do to help."

She tried a weak smile but nodded. He took that as consent to more decorating and gently pulled her away from the linen. "I think we can agree he's not back there, right?"

Her smile was a little more genuine then, and she even managed a single bark of laughter. "I wouldn't think so," she agreed, and they set off to find the Bishop.

***

It was late by the time they'd finished helping Essie and the Bishop decorate the Bowery for the festival the following day. Cora nearly fell asleep on the wagon ride back to their house, and Lydia held herself tightly against Isaac as he drove. The air was unseasonably cool that evening, so he understood why she was clinging to him. Besides, he enjoyed feeling her pressed so close.

It had been a day that reminded him what it was like attending services in St. Louis before they moved out here. The fellowship, the camaraderie, the feeling of being part of something so much bigger than he was alone, all swirled around in his head around a single idea. Every single person, Burns aside, of course, had welcomed him into their space with smiles and kindness. They'd offered him food and drink, and had even insisted on feeding them dinner since it had run so late before they'd been close to finished.

Sitting at the table with these people that made up his town was a blessing he didn't know if he was worthy of. They fed him with food prepared by their own hands and he had nothing to offer him but his thanks. Any time he'd mentioned even that, they'd waved his thanks away, saying, "You put your life on the line every day for us, Sheriff. And, even if you didn't, you're a member of this town and we take care of our own, here."

The meal and the company had filled him with a warmth he hadn't thought he'd ever feel again. Lydia had leaned over and reminded him that it was God's will to provide for others. "You provide them with safety," she pointed out. "They supplied you with food. It seems like everyone got what they needed."

As he watched her interacting with the townspeople around her at the table, he had to admit that he had, indeed, gotten what he needed. He just hoped he didn't let her down!

Neither Fred nor Birdie had reappeared that evening and Isaac was more than a little glad for that. It had given him a night to be a part of this community, instead of an outsider keeping watch over the sheep he'd been hired to tend.

Cora bid them goodnight as he came into the house after releasing the horse to his stall and storing the wagon in the barn again. Lydia was sitting at the table, a cup of tea in front of her, waiting on him when he walked into the kitchen.

"Did you see enough of the upper floors of the saloon to be able to navigate your way around? Would you be able to find that room again if you went in?" he asked.

Lydia's eyes widened, and her lips parted. He took her silence as the opportunity to sink into a chair next to her and curl his fingers around hers on the table. "We have to do something, Lydia. Right now, you're the best source of information we've got. Were you able to learn anything?"

Lydia closed her mouth, and he could see she was trying to focus on the details she'd learned during her visits. "He never stayed very long. Always had a meeting to attend. But he also never left Birdie and me alone. That mountain of a man they call Smiley always stood behind Birdie's shoulder. I could tell he made Birdie nervous. Smiley would walk me to the door of the saloon, 'to make sure I remembered the way out,' he'd always say." She shook her head. "I could find the room, again, sure. But it wasn't her room. And it wasn't anywhere near Burns' office or meeting room where he disappeared to after leaving the tearoom each time."

Isaac mulled that over silently, not releasing her hand. "I don't know how we can get her out of there. I've been trying to find something I can pin on him, but nothing sticks. The men I've seen going into the saloon from the mine all claim they've never met the owner or his wife personally. They refused to talk to me." He rubbed his free hand over his face. "She's his wife. How he treats her is none of my business, either as a citizen of this town or its Sheriff. There's nothing I can do."

"There has to be something," Lydia whispered, her eyes pinned on their joined hands on the table. "There has to be somewhere that he's slipped up!"

"I feel horrible letting her go with him," he admitted. "I should've demanded that he release you both and not supplied him with an out to take even one of you." He was staring at the lines on the table and not looking at her, he knew. Truth be told, he didn't even see the table. Then his eyes lifted to see Lydia's resting on his face.

"I should've told you I'm not a good man, Lydia. I didn't even try to save your friend. I had a rather heated argument with my father and ran off to join the war. I stood next to men who died while I lived and it made me feel good that I survived. At least until my unit was destroyed. Believe me when I say that no amount of prayers I sent up spared them that day." He shuddered, trying not to remember what he'd found when he went searching for them.

Lydia murmured something softly, lifting her free hand to his forehead and brushing over his hair like she had when he'd been pulled out of his nightmare. "You couldn't have known what would happen, Isaac. Whether it was her or me, one of us would be in this predicament, right now, and it would fall upon you to find a way to free us from it. That doesn't make you a bad person, Isaac."

She leaned close, lifting their joined hands and brushing a soft kiss against the back of his hand. "Fear not, for I am with you," she murmured against his skin, the scripture coming easily from her lips and the mixture of her soft lips and the words she breathed over the hand she held sending shivers up and down his spine. "...be not dismayed, for I am your God. I will strengthen you. I will help you. I will uphold you with my righteous right hand."

Isaac laughed softly, drawing her eyes up to his quizzically. "You have a verse for everything, don't you?" he grinned at her, taking the sting out of the words.

Just as she opened her mouth, no doubt to throw another at him, there was a knock on the back door. They both jerked toward it, dropping hands and rising to their feet. Isaac held up a hand, telling her to stay where she was, and moved toward the door, pulling it open cautiously.

Mack "Smiley" Medina, Fred Burn's right-hand man and Birdie's erstwhile shadow, stood on the other side, now bathed in the flickering candlelight of the kitchen.

"Mack," Isaac acknowledged the man with a nod. "What brings you out tonight? And why the back door?"

"I didn't want anyone to see me," Mack answered directly, his voice a deep baritone that seemed to make the air vibrate. Mack was not a small man, not by any means. His voice was the only warning you got about his nature. "I need to talk to you about Fred Burns," he said, leveling his gaze on Isaac for a moment before it slipped past him to rest on Lydia "... and Birdie."

Chapter Twenty-Six

Of all the things she may have expected Mack Medina to say, what came out of his mouth was not among them. Lydia fought the urge to gape as Isaac took a step back and pulled the door open with him, allowing room for the giant of a man to enter the kitchen.

He took his hat off as he stepped across the threshold and held it against his chest in a gesture of respect to the lady of the house. Lydia nodded in acceptance but didn't take her eyes off of him.

During their tea visits, Medina, who Birdie called Smiley, hadn't seemed to loom so large, but here in the kitchen of her home, he seemed to tower over everything. His scowl was the most frequent of his expressions – if the deep creases on his forehead and around his lips were any indication.

There were no tell-tale laugh lines at the corners of his eyes to suggest that this man had much experience with anything close to joy. His broad shoulders strained the seams of the wool coat he wore over a linen vest and shirt, and the dark brown pants completing the look were also wool if she had to guess.

Lydia felt sweat beading on her forehead as Isaac closed the door behind him and gestured Medina to a chair.

"I believe you've met my wife, Lydia," Isaac drew her into the conversation, and she shook herself out of her thoughts. Medina's expression held none of the intensity that it had during her visits with Birdie. Something was going on here.

"It is nice to see you, Mister Medina," she said softly, taking her seat once more.

Medina sank into the chair Isaac indicated, putting him at the head of the table, and he slid into the chair across from Lydia. It gave the air an even more relaxed feeling, with everyone being on eye level and Isaac's choice of seating communicating that he didn't see Medina as a threat.

"You said something about Birdie?" she asked, filling the quiet at the table with the part she was most concerned about.

Medina nodded and took a deep breath, then looked from Lydia to Isaac a few times before he spoke. When he did, his voice had a low gravelly tone that sounded like the rumble of thunder that always followed a particularly nasty bolt of lightning. She could swear she felt the table trembling under her hands in fear.

"Yes, ma'am, I did. I came here because you seem to be the only folks who are trying to look out for her and..." he paused and shifted his gaze back to Isaac, where he left it. "I can't stomach what Fred Burns is doing another minute. He seemed to become worse with her every day and I am afraid of what will happen soon if no one intervenes."

Lydia leaned forward, but Medina didn't turn her way. Isaac spoke before she did. "What do you mean worse? What is going on in that saloon, Mack?"

Medina swallowed and shot a quick look at Lydia as if he wasn't comfortable discussing this in front of her. Her eyes drifted to Isaac, begging him not to send her away. If Birdie was experiencing it, then Lydia needed to know about it. She couldn't help her friend without knowing what the dangers were. "Lydia can handle it, Mack," Isaac said smoothly, not even looking back at Lydia. The surety in his tone warmed her heart.

It was short-lived.

"He uses her like a slave, Sheriff," Mack said, his voice softening and lowering to just above a whisper. "She forces her to clean at all hours of the day and if she's not moving fast enough, he hits her with whatever he has handy. At first, it would be a slap. That ain't illegal, so I turned the other cheek. She can be mouthy, ya know." The last was accompanied by a shake of his head as he lowered his eyes to the table. Had she caught a bit of admiration, there?

Lydia's hands curled into fists, but she remained silent. Isaac didn't respond either, so Mack continued. "I should start at the beginning so you'll understand," he said, laying his hat on the table and curling his fingers in the brim. Lydia couldn't stop the part of her mind that noted that the inky black hat was, much like everything else Mack wore, made of wool. Even the band around the hat was of braided wool, instead of the leather straps she'd seen more often since moving here. "Burns comes from a wealthy family in Alabama. He hasn't said much about it, but I've heard him mutter about his idiot father cutting down on cotton production. I don't know much about farming, Sheriff, so most of what he said was beyond my understanding."

Isaac nodded, urging Medina to go on. "The war started and Burns refused to go. His father was shunned by the other plantation owners in the area, first for adopting the smaller crop sizes, but then because their sons all went to war to defend their way of life, but Fred Burns did not.

When the draft came, Burns paid a farmer from the northern hill country to take his place. He's tight-lipped about where he got the money for that, but it was the last straw for his father. Burns said he forced him to leave and so he started moving west. I met him in Oklahoma City where he hired me as his assistant. He claimed he had a mine that was going to hit it big soon, but the mine never panned out.

We left Oklahoma before the people he owed money could come after us – he didn't make enough money and his debts mounted. When we were in Silver City, he heard about the towns built in the Utah territory and got the idea to open a saloon and make enough money that the men hunting him for debts would be paid off if they ever came to visit. That's what brought us here."

He paused and looked down at the table. "At first, the saloon was an honest place. Burns sold beer and whiskey, I did the heavy lifting and made sure the patrons were civil. Then a man showed up, saying Burns owed him money. Burns offered him a room for the night, and when I didn't see him the next morning, I figured left early to get back to wherever he came from.

Then a couple more showed up claiming Burns owed them money and turned up missing the next morning. The third time it happened..." Medina stopped and cast a pleading look up at Lydia, whose jaw was clenched so tight, she felt like her face would break any second.

"What happened the third time, Mack?" Isaac asked, trying to get Mack to focus on him and not Lydia. She appreciated the gesture, but she was starting to think she should've left for this.

Medina took a deep breath and closed his eyes. "I found them attacking Burns in the alley behind the saloon. Since he was my employer, I defended him. When I'd pulled them off of him, Burns drew a pistol and shot them."

Lydia pressed her fingers to her lips, and her eyes widened. She didn't make a sound, though, and Isaac kept Medina's attention on him. "He killed them?" Isaac's voice wasn't shocked. This was the Sheriff asking questions now.

"Burns convinced me that I had to help him hide the bodies, or your Pa would've arrested me along with him. I know it was wrong, but I helped him bury the bodies outside the town." He dropped his head with that admission, and Isaac clasped his hand around Medina's forearm in support.

"I understand, Mack," he said softly. "What happened after that?"

Medina sat a little straighter. "Burns heard about Bishop Day's train idea and hired a few men to help him. He said that having a few women around would liven the place up a bit, and that would make him more money.

Then he could pay those debts and not worry about people coming for him or getting arrested for killing them when he was only defending himself. I allowed him to convince me that having barmaids would be a good idea. He made it my job to keep watch over the women, to make sure they weren't mistreated."

"But it was a bride train," Lydia interrupted. "Women weren't coming here for a job. They were coming for a husband."

"Burns thought he could sneak a few off before anyone noticed," Medina wasn't looking at her when he answered, nor when he continued. "I didn't go to the station with him. He got a few men from the saloon to help. When he brought Birdie home, I thought he had hired her to run the drinks out or clean up the bar after hours."

He shook his head, his shame starting to ooze out of him. "Then he married her, but I thought she'd be more inclined to help since the place was hers too. I saw him slapping her a few times, but the bruises grew worse, and I knew there was more to it. Then, when Mrs. Branson started coming for tea, Burns had to be more careful about hurting Birdie.

He didn't want her... you–" he swung his heavy brown eyes in her direction, and she flinched from the weight of shame in them. "He didn't want you to get suspicious. Not any more than you already were. He worked hard to ensure that all you saw when you came was a happy Birdie and him in a different light. Having the Sheriff's wife approve of her friend's situation would go a long way to increasing business, too."

His expression seemed apologetic, but Lydia was beyond hearing it. She had the horrible sense that it was only going to get worse. He turned his gaze back to Isaac, and he paused, his eyes flying to Lydia for a brief second. Whatever he was about to say was what he didn't want her to hear. "Mack, just tell me," Isaac urged, his grip on the man's arm tightening.

"He's been selling her," he said in a rush. "Selling her to men who come to the saloon after the rest of the town is closed up. I didn't know about it until recently when I saw him drag her up the stairs to where I'd seen him escort a man not ten minutes earlier. I don't want to contemplate what happened after that, but the sight of her eyes, big and round and full of fright haunts me.

Lydia lurched to her feet and half-ran the few steps to the sink, where she emptied her stomach. The men behind her were silent while she cleaned and dumped the water bucket into the sink basin, saving a bit on a rag of linen to press against her face and lips.

Lydia turned to find them both watching her, and her stomach rolled again. Isaac raised his brows at her in silent question, and she nodded back but didn't move away from the sink or lower the cool cloth from her lips.

The implication of what Fred had been offering other men made Lydia's stomach roll again. His abuse was enough to turn Lydia's stomach, but that went far beyond anything she'd imagined he would do. Even as she tried to put it out of her mind, her stomach threatened to heave up the rest of her dinner. She curled her hand around the cloth on her mouth and leaned on the counter next to the sink. She lowered both arms to curl around herself as if she could keep her stomach from revolting again.

With her nod, Isaac turned his attention back to Medina. "Why are you telling me this, Mack? Why now?"

"Because I can't..." he breathed and closed his eyes. "Because no one should have to suffer the way that woman is suffering. I cannot respect a man who doesn't respect the woman he promised to love, honor, and cherish before God. I want to help her get away from him."

"Do you realize how dangerous that will be?" Isaac asked, his voice dropping low. Medina nodded but didn't give any other reaction.

Medina's growling voice broke the silence as the weight of what they had to face to get Birdie free filled the air. "I will do whatever it takes, Sheriff, including killing Burns."

Lydia hadn't realized the prayer that had begun a cadence in her head until then. She gave her voice to it, though. "Surely goodness and mercy shall follow me all the days of my life, and I will dwell in the house of the Lord forever," she said softly.

"Amen," Medina murmured back.

Chapter Twenty-Seven

"We have to get her out of there. Burns' violence toward her gets worse every day. I don't know how much time she has left." Mack's deep voice sounded strangely vulnerable, and that made Isaac more than a little uncomfortable.

"But how?" Lydia asked. Her tone suggested she was quickly losing control of her emotions, and Isaac knew someone at this table had to remain calm and in control of themselves. They wouldn't do Birdie any good otherwise.

"We have to find a way for her to slip out of the saloon without Burns being suspicious," he turned his thoughts around, hunting. "Any time I've been in the saloon, Burns has always shown up pretty quickly thereafter so I can't go in after her."

"I won't have tea with her again until next week. Burns always escorts me in but is usually too busy to escort me out." She was thinking out loud, and Isaac could see the thoughts in her eyes before she spoke to them. Her eyelids dropped a bit as she found a problem with her idea. "I think he'd notice if Birdie went with me, though."

Isaac nodded, having dismissed the whole idea anyway. He didn't want Lydia anywhere near that saloon when this happened. If it didn't go to plan, she would be in more danger than he could stomach. The room fell silent, each of them lost in their thoughts, trying to find a hole in the security Burns kept around his wife.

"Tomorrow is her market day," Mack broke the silence with that, and Lydia's head snapped up. "I accompany her to the mercantile every Wednesday at midday. The saloon isn't usually busy until the miners get off work in the next county, and Wednesday is always a light evening, anyway. If I can get her out and get back before dinner, he might not notice that she's not there for a while."

"How would you hide Birdie's whereabouts from him when he starts asking?" Isaac asked, his mind turning over this plan. Mack had the best accessibility to Birdie, so he'd have to be the person to get her out of the saloon.

"I'll do what I always do," Isaac saw the man's lip inch up on one side under the thick beard covering the lower half of his face. "Shrug and grunt."

Lydia's lips twitched, but she managed to keep her expression neutral. Isaac knew Mack's reputation for being the quiet type usually in charge of the security of the place, so he wasn't surprised to hear this from him. "For how long will that work?"

"If he starts drinking, all night," Mack responded. "He's usually sloppy by dinner time on Wednesdays, having spent the slow day drinking his way through a few bottles of whiskey. Most of the time, he doesn't even make it back to his bed before he passes out."

Lydia's expression was full of revulsion so Isaac spoke up to keep her from getting distracted. "Perfect. I'll have my Deputy on duty in the alley beside the mercantile. Just find him when you get to the mercantile, and you can arrange the drop-off with him. He'll bring Birdie here in the wagon, and we'll house her until we can get her on a train."

"Where will she go?" Lydia asked, her voice a frightened whisper.

"I have family in St. Louis that will be happy to take her in and help her find honest work. I'll send a telegraph once she's on the train heading East, so they'll know to expect her on the other end." Isaac kept his voice level, forcing the tone to be calm and sure. He was rewarded by Medina's posture relaxing.

No one moved for what felt like an hour, lost in their thoughts. If Isaac had to guess, they were all trying to find the holes in their plan. What would happen if Burns figured them out? At any of those steps, it would mean disaster, not only for Birdie but also for whoever was helping her.

Then Mack rose to his feet, and Isaac followed suit, his eyes straying to Lydia leaning back in her chair, her arms crossed over her chest and her eyes a bit dazed. She looked up as they rose, but her expression didn't clear, nor did her body posture change. Isaac's jaw clenched, but he walked Mack to the door, shook his hand, and watched him ride off under the moonlight outside.

Once he was out of sight, Isaac shut the door and returned to the table. Lydia was watching him, her expression unreadable. He eased into the chair that Mack had vacated, right next to her. His anger, which had been seething beneath the surface as Mack spoke, had little resistance now that Mack was gone. "If they get caught..." he started, then stopped and speared his hands through his hair.

Lydia's hand curled on top of his where it rested on the table, drawing his mind away from the issue of Mack and Birdie. "It's the only way to get her out of there," her voice curled through his senses and his eyes met hers. It wasn't the bolt of shock he'd been expecting, given the way his pulse leaped at her touch. Instead, he felt a soft click, as if everything fell perfectly in place at that very moment.

"It's not fair," he whispered. "Why does God allow men like Fred Burns to hurt people and live, but good men die over an illness or in a war they didn't get a choice to fight in? Why does He let men like Fred Burns exist – to hurt innocent people?"

Her eyes softened, tears gathering at the edges. "Revelations says that although evil walks the Earth, it is only temporary. It will eventually be destroyed by those who believe in goodness. It's meant to give the believer hope that He will create a way to be free of the evil."

Her words wound themselves in his mind, and he felt a quiet rush of... hope? Understanding? He wasn't sure, but it was warm and comforting in a heart that had grown cold and hard.

"Paradise lost will be paradise regained. God will right every wrong and put away evil once and for all, in His time." She recited the verse from Revelations, and instead of growing angry at her use of scripture, it gave him some comfort. Hope that there was an end to the misery he'd witnessed and continued to see every day.

"I just wish His time wasn't so secretive," he snorted, lightening the mood. "There seems to be more evil surfacing every day and far too little to suppress it."

Her smile deepened, and she leaned closer, her hand curling tighter around his hand and drawing his eyes back up to her. "He brought you home," she said. "He got you here before your father passed, put you in a place where you can fight it. He even sent you away to get experience – to see the horrors that come with evil gone rampant, only to bring you home and put you in a place to keep it from happening here. I can't help but be glad it's you, Isaac, holding the reigns and representing the good. You are well respected, and everyone in town knows they can trust you to be there and protect them from the evil that threatens their daily lives."

"Thank you," he murmured, covering the hand and clasping it with his other hand. Her hand was delicately-boned, which seemed the opposite of the strong-willed woman who stood up to him with fire in her eyes or held him when the nightmares started. "Thank you for being there the night I had..."

She dropped her head but looked up at him through her lashes. It did things to his pulse he wasn't completely sure were in his wedding vows, and he cleared his throat, adjusting his place in the chair. "I am glad I could help you," she murmured.

"The War had so many horrors, and some of them followed me home," he admitted, looking down at their joined hands on the table. "I keep them at bay during the day, most of the time, but I can't control my dreams."

"You're a strong man, Isaac. But even strong men have weaknesses. I appreciated you allowing me to help you, to see you so vulnerable. While it wasn't my most comfortable night's sleep I've gotten, lately, it was at least helpful." She smiled a little ruefully and squeezed his hand. "I promised before God and the assembly in the Bowery that I would love, honor, and keep you protected from all harm. I meant it then, and I mean it now. If I have to protect you from yourself, so be it."

Without thinking, Isaac lifted his free hand and touched her cheek, his fingers sliding to cup it in his hand. Surprisingly, it fit the contours of his palm nearly perfectly. He smiled, looking at the stark difference between the ruddy tan of his hand and the porcelain white of her cheek. He was almost lost when she tilted her head to lay her face in his hand and raised her free hand to stroke the back of his hand against her cheek. He wanted little more than to kiss her, right there in their kitchen.

The warmth in her eyes that seemed to lure him closer made him pause. Realization about how close he was to making this marriage more than he'd intended it to be slammed into him, sending his heart thudding. He knew where that heat would take them, but he had no idea how to handle that along with the marriage they'd agreed to, and he pulled away as politely as he could. "We have a long day ahead of us. Let's get to bed and see what the morning has in store for us."

Lydia blushed but said nothing. She followed him up the stairs. He paused by her door and looked over his shoulder. "Pleasant dreams, Lydia," he murmured, looking back at her over his shoulder. Her eyes widened a fraction, but she made no move to follow him as he walked down to his door. He doubted he had a nightmare to worry about that night. He would be thinking about how soft her skin had been and the fire he'd seen in her eyes when she stood toe-to-toe with him.

Nightmares don't stand a chance against the perfection that was his wife. Could he bear to tarnish the glory of that perfection when all he'd ever known was death and fighting? Could he live with himself if he did?

Chapter Twenty-Eight

Lydia was awake long before Isaac started moving around. Still, she could tell by the tired expression in his eyes that he hadn't slept any better than she had. He was dressed all the way to the boots when he entered the kitchen, but his usually cheerful demeanor was bogged down by the slump of his shoulders and the disarray of his hair.

She waited until he was in his chair before she settled a plate of food in front of him and sank into the chair around the corner from his.

"I put the coffee on," she said softly, curling a hand around the free hand he rested on the table. He grunted his appreciation as he lifted a fork full of eggs to his lips. "We need to do something about your hair," she tried to move his mind off of the nagging worry that seemed to haunt him. "Can't have our Sheriff looking scruffy now."

"Scruffy?" He asked. His fork paused halfway to his mouth, and his eyebrow quirked up. The first twinkle of humor entered his eyes, and it helped her relax a little.

"You didn't shave. Your hair looks like you just lost a fight with an alley cat, and..." She paused, her lips twitching. If she was honest, she thought he looked a lot like he did the morning after his nightmare had sent her running to help him. The image rose from her memory, rarely far out of reach these days: Isaac lying on the bed before her, bedclothes down to his hips baring his chest, his face in relaxed slumber, a slight stubble shading his strong jaw line, and his hair in complete disarray.

She couldn't tell him how difficult it had been to walk away from him that morning after seeing him so vulnerable. She cleared her throat and looked away before he could see how her face bloomed red just remembering it.

"Are you saying I should shave and comb my hair?" he questioned, trading the fork for a slice of bacon and snapping his teeth around the end.

"I'm saying that if you look even the least bit different than you usually do, people will wonder. It will draw attention," she tried to be casual as she rose and moved back to the stove, where the coffee finally looked ready to drink. She poured him a cup, then returned to the table, sitting it down, but not taking the seat again. "We need to work hard to not give anything away or we will draw too much attention to things we don't want anyone to see. Besides, with the festival today, everyone is going to town dressed for a celebration. It would be shameful for the Sheriff to arrive with anything less than a clean-shaven jaw and..." she trailed off because she was about to say much more.

"You have a point," he smiled. She didn't have to see him to know he was smiling either. She could hear it in his voice. She busied herself with putting Cora a plate together from the food left in the pans and settling it in the warm stove to stay hot until she came down to breakfast. She poured herself a cup of coffee. Although she couldn't stand the taste of it, she may need it to get through the day without collapsing.

Twenty minutes later, he paused by the kitchen door, his jawline freshly shaven and his fresh button-up shirt open a few buttons at his throat, and gave her a look that made her heart skip a beat. "Better?"

She nodded and smiled, trying to cover the way her stomach fluttered. "Indeed," was her breathless reply. Why was he so beautiful? Those eyes glimmering in humor and those perfect lips drawing her eyes down to them.

She blinked herself away from that thought to see that he was still standing in the doorway as if there was something else he wanted to say. His mother arrived and took the option away, though.

"I am so excited about the festival today! It's been so long since I've felt like celebrating much of anything, and it looked like Essie was putting on quite a thing yesterday while we were helping," she bustled around the kitchen, gathering honey for tea and a small jar of jam she kept in a stash she'd hidden in the pantry. She didn't look at either of them as she slathered it on a warm biscuit and scooped eggs onto her plate.

"Yes, well, Now that you're here, I will get myself ready." Lydia kept her voice level, her mind already dancing through her meager wardrobe. She wondered if she had anything that would catch his attention like Isaac seemed to be catching hers. She felt his eyes on her as she climbed the stairs, though, and bit her lip to keep from turning around and smiling back at him in the kitchen doorway where she'd left him.

In the end, she'd chosen a shawl she'd been embroidering in the evenings before she retired. She'd used the silk thread he'd purchased for her to add roses in bunches and long vines over the entire thing. She had to admit, with the little glass beads she'd saved from a broken bracelet in Maysville, they would be lovely when the candles were lit in the Bowery that night.

She clipped little silver rose barrettes on each side of her head to anchor a snood embellished with similar glass beads that covered the braided bun she'd tied into her hair. She gave herself one more look in the mirror and nodded. It was the best she could do to dress up the more matronly dresses she'd brought for this journey.

Maybe, once the harvest was in, she'd buy herself some fabric for a few new frocks. Come to think of it, Cora would probably like a few of her own.

Smiling, she left her room and descended the stairs. Cora had finished eating and returned to her room to finish her day's look. Soon, she was standing with Isaac at the foot of the stairs waiting for her. Lydia felt a bit like a princess entering a ball as she descended, barely seeing the large smile stretching across Cora's lips as her eyes met Isaac's.

He reached for her hand and brushed a kiss over her knuckles, earning himself a blush as she dipped her head. Lydia looked for anything to distract herself from throwing her arms around her husband.

Cora had chosen a deep blue gown with a square neckline. Her hair was styled similarly to Lydia's, with the addition of a single ringlet that fell from the top of the bun to lay on her shoulder. She wore a short navy coat with elaborate silver embroidery along the cuffs and neckline. The color may have made her seem pale, but her eyes were dancing with humor, and her smile was bright, so Lydia couldn't resist smiling back at her.

"Shall we, then, ladies? It's time I showed off the loveliness hiding at my farm!" Isaac stepped between the two women and crooked an elbow at them. With a short laugh and a loving swat from his mother, they left the house and made their way into the wagon for the journey into town.

The festival was getting started as they arrived and they were ushered into the Bowery to watch the children singing hymns and reciting poetry for a while before the various stalls lining the sidewalks in front of the existing businesses were open. Cora found a few of her old friends settled into a seating area. It had been supplied with tables and chairs from the saloon covered in linens and ribbons. She shooed them away.

Isaac held her arm as they strolled along the various vendors nearby selling all sorts of marvelous-smelling delights. "I'm afraid Ma believes something is going on that we're keeping from her," Isaac said. Lydia's eyes darted to his, but he wasn't looking at her. He was focused on a game down the street.

"Is there?" she asked quietly, trying to pretend the same nonchalance as he seemed to hold.

Isaac stopped and turned toward her. As close as they were, their bodies nearly brushed down the front, and her hand didn't leave the crook of his arm. "I wish I knew," he answered, his voice a bit husky. "I only know that I'm more confused about what's happening every day."

Lydia breathed out the air she'd been holding and smiled. "Then it's settled. We're not hiding anything." She cast a look over his shoulder and grinned. "I believe your deputy is trying to become Franklin's next strong man."

She nodded and he turned to follow her gaze. She knew the second his eyes landed on Jack, with his hands curled around an ax, trying to muster up enough strength to split a large tree trunk in a single blow. He covered his laugh with a cough and looked back at her, a raised eyebrow and a look that did wonderful things to her stomach coming just before, "I should show him how to do it properly, don't you think?"

Without waiting for an answer, he pulled her towards the booth with a line of thick tree trunks and axes with varying handle lengths standing behind them. He pulled her hand free and slid his coat off his shoulders. He passed it to her and grinned, then dashed away to snag an ax and a spot next to Jack. Lydia wrapped her arms around his coat and walked closer, unable to keep from smiling as the men lined up there bantered before the order to hit was given.

The crowd cheered as Jack, Isaac, and one other man split their trunks in the first strike. "Since it's a tie, we need a tie-breaker!"

The crowd's 'ooh' dissolved into giggles when three even bigger trunks were rolled into place in front of the three contestants. "Are you sure these should've been cut down? What were you building with them? The whole schoolhouse? You can cut down more than one for timber, you know that, right? We ain't gonna arrest ya!" Jack's voice seemed to match the wide eyes on his face, and even the men next to him had to laugh.

This round was done one at a time, and the man she didn't know swung first. It took him two strikes to split the trunk, and the crowd cheered. Then it was Jack's turn. He swung once at his and laughed, then started hacking at it as if the tree were a drum.

He thumped out a rhythm until the judge lost track of the strikes, and he took his leave with a salute to the still unsplit trunk. Whether it was her imagination or not, the crowd fell quiet as Isaac rolled his shoulders and hefted his ax. He didn't look at her this time before he swung it in a smooth arch and the tree trunk in front of him split like he was cutting butter with a hot knife.

Loud applause rose, and Isaac's gaze finally met hers, triumph and laughter lighting his eyes as he stood straight. The announcer clapped Isaac on the back and handed him an envelope and a stuffed bear.

Then one of the older women brought him a satin sash that she dropped over his shoulder. When she kissed his cheek, the crowd erupted in laughter again, and Lydia found herself clapping along with everyone else.

Chapter Twenty-Nine

Isaac caught up to her as the crowd dispersed and proffered the stuffed bear to her as if it were the golden fleece of legend. She laughed and dipped him a curtsy, with a giggle. "My thanks, good sir!"

His heart thudded in his chest at the easy smile on her face and had to remind himself where they were before he did something unacceptable. He'd watched her as the contest had progressed and the way she clutched his coat against her chest made him wish for her to hold the rest of him like that.

He cleared his throat as she passed the coat back to him and helped him slip it on, but he noticed the coat had been replaced by the teddy bear she now held tightly to her chest.

The rest of the day was a blur as they played games and ate food she said she'd never heard of before. They rested in the shade of an oak tree and had a small picnic with his mother, then listened as groups of their neighbors sat around the Bowery and played instruments or told stories from the time before they came to settle Franklin.

It reminded him of the time before the War, before he had clashed with his father. His father would lay his head in his mother's lap, and she would comb her fingers through his hair and feed him pieces of fruit.

As a young man, he hadn't been comfortable with his parents showing that kind of affection for each other in front of his friends. He'd parted ways with them to run about with friends and play the games until it was time to return home. But even he couldn't deny that there hadn't been a day that she hadn't looked at his father with that soft smile on her lips.

He wondered, as they laughed and smiled with their neighbors and sought the shelter of the shade of the same trees his parents had picnicked under so long ago if Lydia would ever look at him that way. As he laced his fingers together under his head and watched the clouds move in the sky, he wished it was her lap he was resting in and her fingers combing through his hair instead of the grass of the park next to the Bowery.

He allowed himself a bit of nostalgia, and it amazed him how very well Lydia fit into that daydream.

The Bowery floor was cleared and tables were moved along the far edges as night fell. Townsfolk moved inside as the booths closed up and the candles were lit. As he remembered from those younger days, the feel of the space completely changed. A band set up one end and music once again filled the air. Refreshment tables lined the opposite side of the Bowery, leaving the other two sides open to the night air and the sound of frogs and crickets who wanted to play along with the band.

Younger people, including Jack, danced around the space in between with fervor, and older couples joined them in country dances Lydia said she remembered from before the war. She smiled, seemingly happy. "Amazingly, things between the sides involved in the war hadn't been completely different," she said as the band announced a reel and couples lined up. "At least they had dance in common!"

An entertaining hour later, Isaac rose from his seat next to her and offered his hand as the band announced a waltz.

Lydia's expression was one of pure surprise, but he didn't question whether it was the announcement of a waltz in this company or that he knew it. He smiled warmly and tilted his head, "Would you care to dance?"

Lydia slid her hand into his wordlessly, and he escorted her to the floor. He felt more than saw the number of eyes that swung their way. "I didn't know you knew how to dance," she said, the surprise evident in her tone.

"There are many things, Mrs. Branson, that you do not know about me," he smiled and tucked her into the curve of one arm. The warmth of her body against his was the same curious mix of pleasure and torture he'd heard his tutors laughing about when teaching English history and the culture of the Ton. Carefully, he curled his hand in hers on the other side. "I may be out of practice, but I'm sure I remember enough not to embarrass myself or you."

She grinned, and the opening notes played. She snorted as she stifled a giggle, and he realized it was because their position didn't allow them the proper introduction to this dance. She couldn't bow to him, or him to her, because he was already holding her so closely. Then the music swirled, and he swept her across the floor, letting the music and the memory of the steps remove the awkwardness of the beginning.

There weren't many couples dancing the waltz, but he couldn't see the faces of those in the crowd as they moved past them. He focused on Lydia – on the way her eyes sparkled in the candlelight, and her cheeks became rosy as the exertion of the dance increased. Their bodies brushed against each other as they moved, stepping in and out of the swirling circles of the dance steps.

As the music ended, Lydia panted beside him, and he had to admit a bit of trouble slowing his heart back down, though he couldn't tell whether it was from the speed of the steps or the crazy way the blood rushed in his head. He kept his arm around her back as he escorted them back to their table, then excused himself to get them fresh drinks.

When he returned, women had surrounded her, their faces full of smiles and the air full of their chatter. He paused and watched as she kept her smile pinned on her lips and nodded the whole time, but he could tell by her eyes that she wasn't listening to anything they said. He could only hope they weren't asking her to head one committee or another around town without her being aware.

"May I have my wife, please? There's something I'd like to show her." Isaac's voice cut through the chatter, and Lydia looked where he stood behind her with a cup of punch in each hand and an apologetic smile on his lips. The other women tittered but moved away, leaving them sitting alone again. He sat next to her and set the cup of punch down on the table. "I guess Ma isn't alone thinking we're hiding something, now, is she?"

She laughed and reached for the punch. When the cup froze part way to her lips, he followed the line of her gaze. Fred Burns and Birdie were sitting a few tables away. Birdie had her back to them, and Fred was drunk. Lydia laid the cup against her lip and watched, but Isaac noticed she never tipped the cup up to take a drink.

She nodded their way and Isaac turned his gaze back to them before he realized that Mack Medina stood just outside the light cast by the candles in the Bowery, his glittering eyes never leaving Birdie.

"Would you like to find some cool air?" he asked softly. "If the smell of this punch is any indication, one of those young folks has dropped a bottle of something rather heady, and I'm only getting warmer sitting here drinking it."

She turned and smiled at him, and he almost laughed at the less than graceful way she moved. "Is that what this is? I never took so much as a drink of Pa's liquor, but it did taste a bit off."

He grinned and slipped the cup from her fingers, setting it on the table and helping her rise. "Let's find Ma and head home. We can find something cooler without worrying about who emptied their Pa's stash in the punchbowl."

He took her hand in theirs, and they strode from the Bowery while the dancing continued. They found Cora with her friends along the edge of the Bowery, fans swinging quickly back and forth. Without another word about the punch, Isaac and Lydia helped her into the wagon, and they returned home.

Isaac was far from surprised when his mother said, "Goodnight, children. Sweet dreams!" and headed upstairs as soon as they were inside the door. Lydia went upstairs to change into her casual attire, leaving him alone in the kitchen. He lit a candle and settled in his mother's usual chair to watch the back door. Time stretched a bit, and he tried to relax as he waited for the visitors that were supposed to arrive within the hour.

As wonderful as the night had been, and he vowed to tell his wife how wonderful it had been when she returned to the kitchen, he couldn't shake the feeling he'd been fighting all day. Something was not going right. With that thought in mind, he left the kitchen and checked the gun belt hanging by the door, sliding one of his father's revolvers free and returning to the table. It didn't hurt to be prepared. Besides, his gut had never been wrong in knowing when something was going wrong before.

His thigh ached, and he clenched his jaw again. Even the day he'd gotten the wound, he'd known something was wrong. It was one of the reasons he'd been praying so hard all day before and during the battle. He dreaded finding out what was coming this time. Still, he would not get caught unprepared to defend his family the way he'd been unable to protect his regiment.

Isaac wouldn't lose them due to his blind faith in God. That had failed him last time. It would not fail him again.

Chapter Thirty

Lydia returned to the kitchen, greeted by a single candle flickering on the table, and watched the light dance in his coppery hair. He didn't move when she entered the kitchen – he did not even turn his head and acknowledge she was there.

"This doesn't feel right," Isaac said as she took her seat across from him. He sat in his mother's chair at the table, his eyes on the door to the farm behind the house, revolver in hand. "I need to go find out what's keeping them."

"No," Lydia rushed to put in. "You'll tip them off. We just arrived home, and they were all still at the dance. They will be here. We just have to give them more time."

He nodded in understanding and continued tapping the toe of his boot against the back of the chair. He didn't say anything for a while after that. He just sat in the chair, his feet propped up on the one next to him, arms crossed, and the fingers of his right hand pinching his lower lip.

When someone finally knocked on the back door, it startled them both into action. Lydia turned toward the back door, the frying pan she'd been cleaning clasped tightly in her hand, soap dripping on the floor. Isaac crossed the space between his chair and the door in three strides and pulled it open to reveal Medina and Birdie standing on the back porch in the low light of the last quarter moon.

Relief surged through Lydia, and she set the pan on the counter before rushing to the door to pull Birdie into her arms as she entered the kitchen. Medina took off his hat as he entered, his posture tight and his eyes hooded. Birdie's eyes were shadowed by dark half-circles, and her luxurious golden hair appeared to have been hacked off. She nodded to her a second before he turned to Isaac. "Things didn't go the way we expected. I think you've got a few hours before he knows anything, though. Half a day, at least."

"What happened?" Isaac asked, gesturing to the table for Medina to sit as he followed and took one for himself. Mack's gaze turned to Isaac as he nodded, then stretched a hand to Birdie to allow her to enter before him. The tightness around the man's eyes said he was aware of the trouble he was in and was concerned that it would affect more than just him now.

"Fred didn't let her go to the mercantile today," Medina said simply. "Whether he could sense something was up, I don't know. We were nearly walking out the door to be on our way when he stopped us and redirected Birdie to some menial tasks.

It felt as if he knew what we were doing and was trying to stop us, but when Birdie disappeared into the kitchen, Burns started drinking. He must be watering down the whiskey again because it took him much longer to pass out this time." Medina scrubbed his hands over his face. "He'll be out for a few hours. I need to get back before he wakes."

"Thank you, Smiley," Birdie said softly, turning from Lydia's embrace to smile at him. "I owe you one."

"No, Miss Birdie, you don't. I should've done this much sooner. It would've saved you so much pain and suffering." Medina looked repentant, and it made Birdie wince. "As I said, I should get back to the saloon before I'm missed. I'll tell him you took ill, Miss Birdie, and that you're abed. That should give you a few more hours before he knows you're missing."

"Let's get you settled and resting," Lydia said softly to Birdie. She paused and fixed Medina with a soft smile. "I can't thank you enough for this, Mister Medina. I shall be in your debt for a long time to come."

Medina closed his arms around Lydia and returned the hug. "You're taking care of her. That's all I could ask for. And the name's Mack." His eyes strayed to Birdie standing in the doorway, a hint of a smile on his lips. "Or Smiley, if you'd rather."

"Smiley?" Lydia laughed softly. "I've been meaning to ask this and never found a good time. Where did you pick up that nickname? I don't think I've ever seen you smile once while Birdie and I did our best during our tea visits. "

"Because I never smile. Most people use it sarcastically, but she keeps hoping that calling me that would make me smile more." He nodded his head in Birdie's direction, and the woman had the nerve to giggle at the reference. Lydia shook her head at them both.

"Goodnight, Mister... Smiley," Lydia corrected herself with a warm smile, rejoined Birdie, and pulled her up the stairs to the room she'd set aside for her.

Smiley turned to Isaac as they left the room, and she heard him ask Isaac, "You know this will be the first place he goes to find her, right?"

Lydia saw Isaac nod sagely, but his answer was lost in the distance between them as she and Birdie reached the top of the stairs.

***

She returned downstairs a little while later, leaving Birdie in the bedroom she'd been sleeping in. Birdie had been tearing up with the knowledge that, for the first time since stepping off the train in town, she'd be able to sleep without fear. The admission brought tears to Lydia's eyes. She was wiping at them as she descended the stairs to Isaac, who was sitting alone at the kitchen table, his hand curled around a cold cup of coffee.

He looked up as she entered, his lips stretching into a tired smile that sank at the corners when he noticed her tears. "Everything settled?"

Lydia nodded and stopped next to the chair he was in. "Thank you for this," Lydia said softly. "For caring enough to get her out of that saloon."

"I could hardly leave her to fend for herself with a man capable of such heinous acts." He rose as he finished, reaching for her. "But if it brings you peace, too... Well, that will make doing this my pleasure."

Her shoulders shaking in a mix of quiet relief and fear for what might happen between that moment and the one that saw Birdie back on that train, she stepped into his embrace and relished the warmth of his body as he closed his arms around her.

As a rush of love for this man ran through her, she bit her lip. He never promised to love her, but he'd more than shown he was worthy of her love. Could she live the rest of her life loving this man, knowing he'd never return it?

She tipped her head up, taking in the way the lamplights danced in his eyes. A jolt of emotion shot through her as those enigmatic eyes met hers. He leaned closer and closer until his warm lips brushed hers, tentatively asking all of the questions she'd not been able to answer.

Her lips parted in surprise and answer, and her thoughts rushed clear of her head as he tilted his head just enough to mold their lips together. The soft pressure of his kiss and the warmth that spread through her warred for attention – she could focus on none of them for longer than a blink.

The kiss lasted forever, and yet it still wasn't long enough. They parted, her heart thundering in her chest and her breathing erratic. His smile wasn't as steady as it had been. That gave her hope that he might feel the same about her as she was beginning to feel for him. She had to know before this went much further, but there were more important problems at hand. She reluctantly pulled out of his embrace and whispered, "Goodnight, Isaac."

She looked down at him as she reached the top of the stairs and saw that his eyes were still on her. If her heart had contemplated slowing down, his softly spoken, "Goodnight, Lydia. Sweet dreams," ensured that her dreams would never be able to match the reality that was her husband.

As she slipped into bed beside the sleeping Birdie, she touched her lips, wondering if that kiss had been a dream. "I'll have to find out tomorrow," she murmured to the ceiling, a smile stretching over her lips as she imagined ways to get him to kiss her again.

Chapter Thirty-One

Isaac blinked awake as the beams of early morning sunlight filtered through the window. He sat up, swinging his legs off the edge of the bed and staring at the thigh bared from the sheet. It looked as it had since the war – it was the scar of the bullet wound still a bit pink and puckered in the center of his thigh.

It didn't hurt, though, and he wondered at that. The lack of pain made him realize that he'd slept a restful, dreamless sleep all night. He felt relaxed, energetic, even. As he went through his morning routine, he had to acknowledge what he knew had changed.

Lydia.

She'd soothed his demons that night and had taken the time each night before they parted to draw his attention away from them. He hadn't realized that's what she was doing, but he couldn't deny that she had, and it had been effective. Last night, his need to comfort her, to assure her that everything would be fine, had been a distraction, whether it was what she'd intended or not.

The kiss had been the most distracting thing he'd ever experienced, so much so that he'd gone to bed with thoughts of how she felt in his arms. How the heat of her snuggling into his embrace felt until he had difficulty figuring out where she ended and where he began. How perfectly she seemed to fit there, how the touch of her lips had sent fire through his veins, and the need to soothe and protect had become something else entirely. Sleep had been elusive, but those last-minute thoughts before sleeping weren't filled with dread or fear for the first time in a very long time.

"I am not falling in love with her," he whispered. Then he looked at the door, hoping she wasn't close enough to hear him. When no sound came through it, he turned back to his reflection and glared. "She will never accept that God and I parted ways years ago. She won't be able to stomach that in a husband.

Getting any closer to her than we are now will only give her permission to force me to pretend that I can forgive Him for the way he ignored my prayers." His hands slowed as they knotted the tie at his neck, and he met his gaze again. Do I really expect God to forgive ME? He blinked at the realization and looked away from the mirror, finishing the knot in his tie without looking. Even he had to admit that it was a ridiculous idea.

"Sometimes," his mother's voice filtered through memories of things he'd prayed for and never received as a child. "Sometimes, Isaac, God's best answer to a prayer is not answering at all. He knows what plans are coming and has to weigh those plans against the things you may want at the moment, but won't help you reach the place He wants you to reach. You just have to accept that God's plan is not to hurt you and that sometimes bad things happen. He will always be there to comfort you when you need it and to help you find your way, though."

He had difficulty accepting that as easily as he had when his favorite chicken died. But he had to wonder if God had planned for Lydia to be in his life all along. Hadn't he wondered at the wedding if she was supposed to be his salvation?

With a final shake of the head, he left the room and headed to the kitchen for breakfast. When he came through the door, all three women were sitting at the table, including his mother, who had gone to bed early, blissfully unaware of their plot to rescue Birdie. Her expression was unreadable, which tightened his stomach. He hadn't discussed this with her. Had Lydia?

They'd saved his seat, and Lydia rose to get his plate from the oven when she saw him. "Good morning, ladies," he said cheerfully. "How did I get so lucky to have three of the most beautiful women in the world sitting at my table this morning?"

Cora gave him a look that made his smile fall before she chuckled, swatting his arm as he sank into his chair. "It would've been nice not to come down in my dressing gown this morning to find we had company, but we fixed that while you were lazing around in bed."

Her face seemed to say she knew more than the situation with Birdie, which brought a blush to his cheeks. He looked up at Lydia's grinning face as she slid the plate and a mug of hot coffee onto the table in front of him and took her seat next to him.

His gaze moved to Birdie, who had stopped eating and pinned him with a worried look. "I shouldn't be here," she answered him softly. "Fred will come here looking for me as soon as he realizes I'm gone this morning, and I don't want to put any of you in harm's way. He's such a dangerous man."

"We've already thought about that," Isaac inserted, doing his best to look and sound like he wasn't concerned at all. "Mack will tell him that he saw you leave with a man who stopped at the saloon last night and left early this morning from the hotel, headed South. He'll tell Fred that he overheard the man promise you a life of luxury, and it seemed to be all it took to convince you to leave."

That didn't seem to make Birdie feel any better, but she didn't argue. They finished their breakfast in relative silence, broken only by conversations about the weather and how long it would take to move the cows to another pasture in a few weeks.

Afterward, the women helped Lydia clear the table, and Isaac finished his coffee. He had the distinct urge to stay, to protect them himself. But he had to appear not to know anything about Birdie's disappearance or give anyone any hint that he was involved in it.

As he was leaving, he turned to see them all gathered in the doorway between the living room and the kitchen, holding on to each other. He put on his best smile but told them to be careful and keep Birdie away from the windows and inside the house. "The train will be here tomorrow at noon. We just have to keep her out of sight until then."

They each gave him a stiff nod, and only Lydia's demeanor gave any hint of being sure of their success. He didn't have to ask to know she'd prayed for this plan to go smoothly. He didn't have it in him to tell her that. God had no time for answering prayers, no matter how worthy the cause. Instead, Isaac nodded, put on his hat, and strode out the door.

***

"Jack," Isaac started his sentence before he'd even opened the door. Jack was waiting for him. The man was leaning on the edge of the desk, pistols in their holsters, and arms crossed over his chest as he watched the door. He visibly relaxed when he saw that it was Isaac who opened it. "Is everything okay?"

"Perfect," Jack shot back without his usual smile.

Isaac narrowed his eyes, then closed the door behind him and crossed to stand closer to Jack so they wouldn't be overheard. "I was hoping I could avoid including you in this, but Mack Medina snuck Birdie out of the saloon and out to my place last night. We need to…"

"Oh, I knew she's gone. Fred Burns has been storming around town this morning. He blew through the door before the sun rose and cursed because you weren't here. He demanded I ride out to get you, or he would get you himself." Jack puffed up his chest and blustered for his impression of Fred Burns, but Isaac felt as if he'd punched him in the gut. "'I have biz-niss with the Sheriff, Boy. Urgent Bizniss. You get on out there and fetch him like a good boy, so's I can discuss it with him.'"

Isaac's blood ran cold at the thought. He clamped his hands around Jack's shoulders. "What did you tell him?"

"I told him you were a married man and if he wanted anything from you, he should remember that dragging a married man from his bed so soon after the wedding was not a good recipe for said married man doing what you wanted him to do," Jack said with a smile and a shrug. It wasn't his usually toothy grin, but it was better than the scowl Isaac had seen just moments earlier. "He said he'd be back before the saloon opened if Birdie wasn't back and you'd best be ready to do your job."

Isaac snorted, then strode to his desk. He scratched out a note and handed it to Jack. "Take this to the telegraph office and send it to the Marshal's office in Colorado Springs, then send it to the Marshal in Tuscan, as well. If my hunch is correct," he pointed to the wanted posters on the other side of the office.

The one from Colorado Springs was a man vaguely fitting Burns' description accused of murder and theft by taking. The Tuscan poster had a hand-drawn picture of a man that looked somewhat like Burns, this time wanted for evasion. "They will get here with the train tomorrow if the telegrams got to them in time to make arrangements for it."

Jack nodded and strode from the office with the note tucked into his vest pocket. Isaac watched him leave, then opened his desk drawer for his pistol belt. He buckled it, then slid the matching pistols he'd inherited from his father into their holsters. Better to be safe than sorry.

He was halfway back to his desk when the door to the sheriff's office burst open, and Fred Burns rushed inside. "My wife is missing, Sheriff. I demand we send a search party out after her."

Isaac raised his eyebrows and turned to face the ruddy-faced man that stopped barely a foot away from him, fighting the urge to wave his hand in front of his face. The smell of the previous night's overindulgence still emanated from the man. His clothes looked like he hadn't changed since they had seen him at the Festival, much less taken a bath. "Good morning, Fred. It looks like you've had a good night but a terrible morning. How can I help?"

Fred's expression darkened, and Isaac mused his anger about the sheriff being late had just been compounded by his lack of taking his concern seriously.

He took a calming breath that had Jack clapping his hand over his mouth to keep from laughing out loud behind the man's back. He cleared his throat, schooling his features into a concerned expression. "When was she last seen at the saloon?" he asked, following his usual procedure for investigating what occurred before acting on the demands of those seeking his help.

"Last night. Medina said he saw a man talking to her. Medina believes he left town this morning. He believes the man took my Birdie with him. I fear for her safety." His tone didn't sound like he feared for her safety, at all, but Isaac didn't say anything about that.

"I understand," Isaac said, lifting his hand to his chin in a gesture of deep thought. "May I talk to Mister Medina? I need a description and..."

"He said they went South this morning. You don't need to talk to anyone, and we've already wasted far too many hours waiting on you to do your job. Get after her and bring my wife back." Fred was starting to shout and turn even redder in the face, and Isaac bit back the urge to kick him out of his office.

"I have a procedure I must follow, Mister Burns. We can't base an entire search party on one person's testimony. We need to make sure we know all of the facts, so we know, for sure, which direction to send a search party and what to tell them to look for. Jack will be back in a few minutes. Do you think you can describe..." he paused and narrowed his eyes on Burns. "No, you didn't see the man. Where were you when she disappeared, Mister Burns? Is it possible Medina is lying to cover you harming your wife? Is it possible Medina didn't say anything of the sort? That you're just making it up to send us on a wild goose chase?"

Fred gaped like a fish, so Isaac didn't give him the chance to speak again. "You see, I need to speak to Medina to verify his story and get all the facts straight."

"Just go get her!" Burns was close to shrieking by the time that squeaked out of him.

Isaac tried not to smile back at him. "I'm afraid I can't mobilize a search party without facts, Mister Burns. I have something to take care of here, then I'll be 'round the saloon to talk to Medina. It might be an hour or so, though. Make sure he's there when I get there so we can conduct our investigation. Once we have the facts, we'll get that search party organized."

"I'll do it, myself!" Burns barked at him, red-faced and spitting with each word. He stormed across the office and threw the door back only to be drawn up short by Jack, who stood on the other side.

"Ah, good, Jack, you're back. Let's work on that missing pig issue, so we can help Mister Burns with his missing wife. Is it strange that both show up missing the same day?" Burns made a noise like a strangled mule. "Oh, and Burns? Perhaps, if you'd taken better care of your wife, she wouldn't have run away less than a month after your wedding."

Burns knocked Jack over while getting out of the doorway, and they watched him storm down the street, each silently stroking the pistol grip on their right hips.

Chapter Thirty-Two

"I can't do this," Birdie announced, flouncing onto the couch next to Lydia and tossing the linen shirt she'd been trying to mend on the floor at her feet. "I've never sewn a thing in my life! "How am I supposed to fix this?"

Lydia smiled and set her embroidery aside. "It's a lot easier than you think," murmured, lifting the shirt from Birdie's hands. "This tear is an easy thing to fix. Since it's right along the seam, you just have to–"

"It's not easy," Birdie moaned. "I have stabbed my finger three times in the last four minutes. The thread knotted up at least that many times, too. How am I supposed to–" Lydia's chuckle interrupted her, and she handed the shirt back with three stitches already in place. "How did you–"

"As I said." Lydia smiled. "It's easy. Here, let me show you." She pulled the needle from her embroidery and threaded it, then lifted the hem of her overskirt and flipped it upside down, showing the inside hem. She inserted the needle and moved it through the fabric, shifting her fingers so she could see both ends of the needle when the sharp end came out.

"You want to see both ends so you can judge your stitch length and make sure it's straight. I used this part of my fingernail to make sure I'm measuring it correctly." Lydia showed her the side of her thumb and the edge of the fingernail. "I go into the fabric where the curve is at the bottom and back out where my nail ends. Since I keep my nails short, it's a handy measuring tool. Since your fingernail is longer, you just have to measure to the spot where the nail turns white, then angle the needle back up toward you."

The sharp end of the needle appeared at her finger where the nail stopped and where Birdie's nail showed white. "Once it's showing in the spot you want, just pull it through, move the fabric so that the end of that stitch lines up with your knuckle, then do it again."

She demonstrated the stitch and Birdie watched, her eyes wide. Lydia watched her practice a few stitches. Birdie was fussing at how slow and uneven her stitches were. "Speed and precision are something you get with repetition. I'm sure you'll have it down in no time if you keep working at it."

Birdie smiled half-heartedly, as if she didn't believe her. Cora chimed in, showing her uneven stitches on a pillow beside her. "I stitched this when I was carrying Isaac," she rubbed her stomach and smiled. "My mother called it nesting, but I just wanted to get this pillow together so I could put it behind my back for some support!"

Birdie's laugh was loud and shrill, and she clapped a hand over her mouth. "I'm so sorry," she said quickly.

Lydia and Cora laughed, shaking their heads. "For laughing? That was such a sound!" And they all dissolved into laughter.

"Don't we need to be peeling potatoes for dinner?" Cora asked Lydia with her eyebrows raised.

Lydia checked the clock and nodded, setting her embroidery aside. "I will get them from the porch if you gather the knives and bowls?"

Birdie smiled, glad to get away from the stitching if Lydia had to guess. "Can I help?" she asked, already rising to join them.

"Absolutely," Cora laughed. "Come help me reach the bowls. I'm not tall enough to do it without a chair, and I'm too old for climbing these days."

Lydia smiled as she heard Birdie repeatedly telling Cora that she was far from old and shouldn't talk like that. Chuckling a bit to herself, glad to see the pair of them getting along so well. She wasn't sure how Cora would take Birdie's presence, given the situation. She pulled her apron off a hook in the kitchen and stepped onto the back porch to grab the basket of potatoes they'd dug out yesterday. She thought she heard something as she came back into the kitchen, but it wasn't until she saw Essie shaking Birdie's hand that she realized what the sound was.

She stopped dead in her tracks and dropped the basket, her hands moving to her lips before she could stop the reaction. Cora looked back at her, eyes wide, and gave her a stiff shake of her head. Essie turned toward her at the sound of the potatoes rolling across the floor.

Playing it off as an accident, she limped a step and hopped to a chair, rubbing the toe of her boot. "Essie, how great to see you! We were just starting to work on the potatoes for dinner," She cast a look back at Cora. "Remind me to take a hammer to that threshold when we're finished? I keep tripping on it, and I'm afraid it's getting worse waiting on Isaac to take care of it."

"Of course, dear. I was just telling Essie about Mrs. Burns finally coming for a visit. I was just about to ask if Essie would like to stay for dinner, as well," Cora sent her a wide-eyed look, the message clear. Keeping Essie here would lessen the chance that word would spread about Birdie being here. It didn't stop the knot of fear that dropped into her stomach at the thought of trying to keep up the charade that Birdie was here for a friendly visit through dinner. "She could invite Mister Gray. We'll make it a formal dinner. I haven't had one of those in years!"

Lydia smiled at the sly workings of her mother-in-law's mind, then turned back to Essie. "If you do, you have to peel the potatoes, just like Birdie, here, is going to do."

Birdie dipped her head and sat at the table, picking up a knife as Lydia tipped the large basket and the rest of the potatoes rolled onto the table before them. Essie shuddered and settled into a chair at the table, setting her reticule on top. "Potatoes were in the dirt," she reminded them. "I only eat food that was on top of the ground. Thanks for the offer. Maybe some other time? I was hoping to get a recipe from you, Mrs. Cora. My husband loved the dill sandwiches you sent him yesterday when I left. He ate the entire plate while I was here at Bible Study last night. You said your mother taught you how to make them before you were married?"

Cora launched into a story about her mother teaching her how to make the dill cream sauce she served on the bread Lydia had baked the day before. Essie scribbled notes on a paper she'd folded up in her reticule. "I will head into town and pick up the things I need when I visit Mr. Gray," she laughed. "He asked me to lunch with him today. He asked me to bring the wagon, so I hope it's not to pick up some strange thing he saw in the Mercantile catalog. He's always ordering the strangest things! Last month, it was a barrel roller."

Lydia laughed, and Cora gasped, her fingers going to her lips. "Whatever would he need a barrel roller for?"

"He saw it in the catalog," Essie said with a dramatic flair. "'It is the latest thing!' he said, so he just had to have it."

"How many barrels do you need to roll, Essie?" Lydia laughed. "Is it such a time-saver for you?"

"Two!" Essie laughed. "We have one in the pantry that holds grains and one in the shed that holds chicken feed. Since he doesn't move either of them and just refills them from the bags we purchase or the crops when they're harvested, they don't even need moving! But, he wasn't about to say he wasted money buying the thing, so he bought another barrel of corn, just to roll it out to the wagon and then into the pantry!"

The women dissolved into laughter, and the conversation continued until Essie rose, saying, "It's getting late. I must be off if I'm to meet Mister Gray for lunch and find out what he has purchased this time." The women all laughed at the exasperated expression on her face. Lydia rinsed her hands off, then walked with Essie to the front door while the others finished scraping the potato peels off the table.

Lydia pulled open the front door, allowing Essie to sweep out onto the porch. You will have to tell us what it was Mr. Gray purchased this month." She smiled. "Now I'm curious."

"And how he liked those sandwiches!" Cora chimed in from the kitchen door, drying her hands on her apron. "Ma will be terribly upset if it's not made correctly," she said in a rich, clipped tone. Lydia was sure she was imitating her mother, but she had no idea. It was entertaining, either way.

"Oh, I will," she laughed. "Maybe I'll save you a few so you can rave about my cooking skills! I'll bring them for book club tomorrow!" Essie grinned, swinging onto the porch and pulling the reins free on her horse's bridle.

"There's not any cooking involved," Cora said, the hint of a question in her tone.

"Exactly," Essie laughed. Then she climbed on the wagon seat and turned to wave to them. "Until later, ladies!"

Lydia sagged on the railing to the porch, and Birdie groaned from the doorway behind them. She'd kept her composure throughout the visit, and the confidence she pretended around Essie seemed to dissolve like sugar in the water now that she was gone. "She saw me," she yelled. "She's going to go into town and–"

"She won't," Lydia said softly. "There's no need to fret. Things will be fine."

She tried to sound sure of herself and even more sure in her bluff. She was worried, too, but she wasn't going to say so in front of Birdie. They should've considered Essie's visit, especially since the woman had stopped knocking on the door and just let herself inside these days. She closed her eyes and whispered a prayer, then opened them and lifted them to the sky. "Keep us safe so we may continue our good work," she said softly. Cora was busy urging Birdie back into the house behind her, saying something about finishing the potatoes before they browned on the table.

"They'll be ruined if we don't get them in a pan soon," Cora was saying as they disappeared inside behind her.

"And we'll be ruined if Essie Gray opens her mouth while she's in town," Lydia murmured, still watching the cloud of dust behind Essie's wagon. "Please, just let her stay quiet, just this once?"

Chapter Thirty-Three

Isaac rubbed his hand over his face and shifted his eyes to the clock. It was about time he went home. But when the telegram came in from the Marshal's office a few towns over to inform him that former soldiers were riding around the area stealing cattle, he'd had to start working on it immediately.

Jack had volunteered to go out to the farms along the Western borders of the county to ask after their cattle. Isaac had started asking questions around town about whether anyone had heard anything about this gang of ex-soldiers or missing cattle.

He'd kept his word and gone to the saloon, acting like he was doing an actual investigation and pulling out all the stops to find Birdie. He was actually just wasting as much of Burns' time as possible.

Rather than waste his time, he also asked about the cattle and the soldiers. Most of the men in the saloon had ridden in from the outskirts of town at this time of day and might have information to help him protect Franklin.

When he overheard Isaac's line of questioning, Burns grabbed Isaac's shoulder and pulled him around, a balled fist flying in anger and his voice a gravely howl. "Cattle will not get my wife back!"

Isaac caught Burns' fist an inch from his cheek as he turned with the pull. He tilted his head to the side and smiled. "Now, I know you're upset, but do you really want to sit in jail while you're waiting for us to find Birdie? Striking an officer is a serious offense."

"You have everything you need, Sheriff," he'd growled at him, jerking his hand back. "Go find my wife."

"Yes, yes. I will stop by the hotel on my way back to the office and find the name of the man we're looking for. Then I'll have Jack send a telegram to see if he's wanted anywhere else. Meanwhile, collecting as much information as possible during my visit seems prudent to cover the bases of everything I need. Especially since these fine gentlemen will be heading North soon and I won't get a chance to talk to them. They may run into trouble moving a full herd North, so they'll probably appreciate the information as well." Isaac nodded to the cattlemen, tipping his hat in thanks, before he walked toward the door, his little wad of scrap bits of paper creased in his hands. "I should be able to get the townsfolk together tomorrow at first light for that hunting party you're after."

An idea formed in Isaac's head, and a plan started to take shape. He could get Jack to lead a hunting party of men South as Burns demanded, which would get Burns away from town for a few days. It would give them plenty of time to get Birdie on the train and give the train time to get as far from town as possible before Burns suspected she'd been on it.

Burns had yelled, "Why is it taking so long for you to do your job and find my wife, Sheriff? She gets further away every hour of your shoddy handling of her disappearance!"

"Did you not tell me she left of her own volition? That changes the urgency a bit, Mister Burns. Besides, if I don't follow the procedure and the disappearance has a less voluntary beginning, the man won't be arrested or held. You'll get your wife back, but no justice for her tarnished reputation? Besides, if I even attempt to send a hunting party out in the dark, no one will volunteer to help out. You want as many men on this as possible, right? Let them get a good meal and a good night's sleep, and you'll find they're much more likely to find what you're looking for." He raised his eyebrows at Fred, whose grumbling lowered to a mutter.

Isaac had sauntered out of the saloon not much later, looking like a man with all the time in the world on his hands. He could hear Burns breaking things inside the saloon for almost half a block as he left. Serves him right, Isaac thought to himself.

What if it were Lydia who was missing? His mind tossed out at him, making his stride hitch a bit. He'd be frantic, much like Burns. Pacing and irritable, chomping at the bit to get her back. Frightened for her, ready to deal punishment to the man who took her. The realization left a sour taste in his mouth, and he almost felt bad for Burns. Almost.

He then stopped at the hotel and asked for the man who stole Birdie away, but only so the clerk didn't have to lie and say he didn't, should Burns think to ask.

When he'd returned to the Sheriff's office, he'd picked up the collection of telegrams and pony-delivered wanted posters that had been dropped on his desk and laid the notes he'd taken from around town on top of them. He then lost himself in the details, looking for patterns and clues between the scattered information and finding very little. The notes Jack had taken along the county's borders were more telling than anything he'd gathered that day. Incorporating them into the bigger picture of these former soldiers turned cattle thieves took longer than he expected.

He leaned backward, his hand moving to his temples as the headache settled there, and he saw how dark it had become. A quick check of his pocket watch made him curse and gather the collection of information into a folded Wanted poster and slide it into his desk drawer. He'd deal with them tomorrow. He was tired and hungry, and the thought of seeing Lydia's smiling face was filling him with a distinct need to go home.

Just as he was putting his gun belt back in the drawer, the door to the Sheriff's office burst open, and Mack Medina lurched inside. He was sweating profusely and had lost his hat somewhere on the way to the Sheriff's office. His face was red, and he had trouble catching enough air to speak.

"Calm down and breathe, Mack," he turned toward the man, gun belt still clutched in his hands. "Tell me what happened."

"Fred left the saloon," Medina said between gasps. "I don't know when. One of the men Burns hired said they saw Mr. Gray come in and talk to him. Gray left, then Fred told the man to get me. He sent me back to get a crate of whiskey three crates deep in the far corner, and when I came back, he was gone. No one saw him leave or knows where he went."

Gray? Isaac felt his face fall.

Essie.

She was always going over to talk to his mother and Lydia. Had she gone today and seen Birdie? Her husband was a regular at the saloon, though she would never know that. If she told him that she'd seen Fred's wife, even conversationally, Gray would've shared that the next time he was in the saloon. That hadn't been very long after Isaac had left, which meant he'd wasted a lot of time that he couldn't afford to waste.

Isaac felt his stomach tense and twist, his hands clenching around his gun belt even tighter. "Jack is checking on the mercantile before heading home for the night. Tell him to get to my place as fast as he can." He buckled his belt back on and headed for the door, seconds after Medina nodded and darted back out to find Jack.

Isaac rode out of town like the devil was on his heels. The only thought in his head was, "I've got to get to Lydia before Burns does. Please, let me get home before Burns does." The words rolled over, and his horse's gallop seemed to echo her name as they raced home. "Lydia, Lydia, Lydia..."

Chapter Thirty-Four

Cora, Birdie, and Lydia lingered around the dinner table after eating. Cora and Birdie had helped clear off the table and washed the dishes. Now they just sat around the table with glasses of water, recounting fun anecdotes about the last month or their past, long before coming to Franklin.

"How long did he court you?" Birdie asked Cora, her eyes wide as Cora related the story of falling in love with Isaac's father.

"Two years," Cora answered with a little smile. "At first, I was too young for him to court openly. Then I was playing too hard to get!"

"If you liked him and he liked you, why would you not just agree to marry him?" Birdie's voice was breathless, hanging on Cora's every word.

"I wanted to make sure it was me he wanted," Cora responded, her eyes a little distant. "There were so many other girls in St. Louis that were prettier and wealthier than I was. Why would such a nice man want to settle for me?"

"Because he knew you were the one that would make him the happiest and fill his days with laughter and love," Lydia responded, her smile a bit envious. "He could hardly let you go once he realized how much you meant to him already."

Cora laughed and clapped her hands. "That's almost exactly what he said!"

They were all laughing when the first loud BANG hit the front door.

Shock froze them in place as the silence outside was split by Fred Burns' angry voice.

"Birdie, I know you're in there! Get out here, now, and I won't have to hurt your friends!"

Birdie's face paled, the blood draining right out of it until she was as white as a sheet.

"Don't you even think about it," Lydia warned, narrowing her eyes. "We're not giving in to him. Not now, and not ever."

"Not ever, again," Birdie nodded, her hands wringing and her eyes darting around them.

The banging continued, violent cracks that seemed to threaten the integrity of the door. Each strike on the wood made them all flinch. But Lydia kept her face stubbornly set in defiance and refusal to give in to the bully at the door. He hadn't promised he wouldn't hurt Birdie, just not to hurt them. Lydia was done allowing her friend to be mistreated that way.

Then, just as suddenly as the banging had begun, it stopped. Silence fell again, and Birdie seemed to relax a little. The sudden silence made Lydia even more uneasy. Cora seemed to feel the same since her eyes darted around with every creak of the house. Lydia kept the woman in the corner of her eye. Cora had been much better lately, but her hands were shaking. How much could she take before the seizures caught her in their grip again?

Then Birdie's scream pierced the night a second before the glass in the kitchen door shattered, and a large stone landed a foot from Cora's chair. They all scrambled to their feet as Burns' angry countenance appeared in the broken window, growling as his eyes landed on Birdie.

"How dare you...?" he growled out, pushing his torso through the window frame around the broken glass. Lydia could see the edges of the glass cutting into his chest and arm as he tried getting through. "You ran from me. I warned you what would happen if you ran from me!"

Birdie shouted something unintelligible, and Lydia pushed her and Cora out of the kitchen toward the stairs. "Go, I'll slow him down."

"Don't be daft," Cora muttered, grabbing Lydia's arm as they rushed to the stairs on the other side of the living room. "You're coming with us."

The kitchen door groaned as Burns climbed in the window, the broken glass drawing blood. Lydia didn't bother wasting time arguing as she urged them all upstairs and into Cora's bedroom. It was the farthest from the stairs, so it should give them plenty of time to hear what was coming before it got to them. And Cora had a large oak tree with a conveniently sturdy branch outside her window.

Lydia slammed the door shut behind her, ordering the other two to move the heavy armoire in front of it. They leaned on the door to keep it from coming open as Burns crashed into it. He fought to open the door, and she fought to keep it closed. Her head smacked the door each time he lifted his hand to strike again, and she hoped they'd be faster with that armoire.

When they were finally close enough to get it wedged in front of the door, Lydia moved to help them and released her hold on the door. As if she'd written an invitation, Burns pushed the door open and lurched through the doorway. Before anyone could react to his presence, Burns darted to Birdie, who turned to run. His hand curled into the hair at the back of her head as she turned away. His whip-quick jerk had her careening back toward him.

"Let her go!" Lydia screamed at him, lurching forward to pull him away.

His grip on Birdie's hair tightened, and Birdie screamed, making them all tense. "Don't anyone move," Burns hissed.

Lydia's pulse stammered to a stop at the same time her feet did, her eyes fixed on the pistol against Birdie's temple. The smear of blood on his arms and face from climbing over broken glass to get in was terrifying. His voice was low, a menacing hiss that parted air suddenly thick with tension. "No one takes what's mine."

There was no way Cora could climb down the tree outside the window behind Fred Burns. But seeing Birdie in his arms only deepened the intense feeling of helplessness in Lydia's heart.

Chapter Thirty-Five

Jack caught up with Isaac within minutes, his horse having been at the post outside the Mercantile when Mack found him. Isaac sent him a grateful look, taking in his deputy's stern expression. The smile he usually wore was gone, leaving only grim determination in its place.

Mack was there a few minutes later, his large horse eating up the space between the saloon and them. Isaac didn't have to look at the man to know his face wore an expression that would frighten the cruelest criminals.

Isaac had a suspicion that there was more to Mack looking out for Birdie than her treatment going against his principles, though. If he were right and Mack cared for Birdie more than he let on, there may be worse problems if he got to Burns first.

The sight of his house chased any thought but the safety of his wife and mother from his mind. There weren't many lights on, which was typical at this time of night. Lydia often left an oil lamp burning in the window just off the porch for him, so she'd known he was going to be late.

The rest of the house was dark, including the window that would be Lydia's room on the second floor over the sitting room. Was she asleep, or had she not even gone to her room yet? The unknown gnawed on his gut, and he swung out of the saddle before the horse had stopped, rushing onto the porch and grabbing the door handle.

It was locked, making Isaac proud and even more frightened all at the same time. They'd kept the door locked just like he'd wanted. All the curtains were drawn too, allowing no sight into the rooms on the other side. All except the window by the door where the lamp burned, waiting for him to get home.

He heard his name from the side of the house and glanced over. Jack stood at the corner, waving at him frantically. Fear rose in Isaac's chest, and he vaulted over the porch rail to the ground to follow Jack to the rear of the house. Mack stood by the back door, his expression thunderous, as he looked into the kitchen.

Isaac could see the lights from multiple lamps burning in the kitchen, and his unease grew. He leaped onto the edge of the porch, and the glistening light dancing off broken glass around the door made his stomach flip. Mack took his expression as permission and tore off the edge of the door with one hand. He reached in and flicked open the lock. Isaac stormed through it with Jack hot on his heels.

The sight of blood on the floor, the handprint on the table, and another on the doorframe confirmed his worst fear. Isaac followed the droplets across his living room and up the stairs to the second floor, pulling one pistol from his gunbelt and pulling the hammer back.

He held it aimed at the ceiling, his finger laying across the trigger guard to keep from accidentally firing it and giving them away. He'd learned much about sneaking up on the enemy in the last few years. The carpet runner that covered the center of the floor disguised any further stains. But the scream coming from his mother's room was unmistakable.

Mack took a step in that direction, and Isaac held up his hand, urging them to move slowly to the door that was pushed open wide enough for one person to get through.

"You may as well come in, Sheriff. I know it's you," Burns called. Another moan of pain followed this sentence, and Isaac waved Jack back as he pushed the door open and walked through it. Mack wasn't going to be left out, so he walked in behind Isaac, shoulders tense and eyes narrowed.

His years of scouting for the Army came back, and he took in the scene before him, his gaze checking on the people inside. Lydia appeared fine where she stood a few feet away from Burns as if she'd been about to attack him. His mother stood to the opposite side, her hands wrapped around the tall post at the end of her bed. Burns stood between the two, Birdie clutched to his chest by the hair and a pistol aimed at her temple.

The only people who seemed to be wearing blood were Birdie and Burns. How much of that blood is Birdie's? he wondered as he stopped a few feet away with his left hand held away from the pistol stills on his hip and his right loosening its grip on the pistol he'd drawn on his way up the stairs.

"You can just put that pistol right on down, Sheriff, and kick it over here to my dear wife," Burns sneered, knowing he had all the power in this situation. They would not move while he held Birdie's life in the balance.

"No, I don't think I will," Isaac said, earning a warning sound from Lydia's throat and a cry from Birdie as Burns pulled her hair even tighter. He pressed the gun deeper into her temple.

"I don't think you understand, Sheriff. I will kill her rather than let her free. She's mine, and no one takes what is mine." Burns pulled back the hammer on his pistol, the click echoing in the otherwise silent room.

"Just put the gun down, Fred," Isaac returned, his voice smooth like talking to a frantic horse. "No one has to get hurt here."

"Do you not understand?" Burns shouted, his arms tightening, earning fright noises from Birdie. Isaac noticed his finger tightened on the trigger, too. "If you weren't such a busy body, getting into a business that has nothing to do with you, we could've avoided this."

His eyes shifted to Mack standing at Isaac's shoulder, and anger twisted up his face even more. "And you. What was her pet name for you? Ah, yes, Smiley. I don't see you smiling too much now, traitor!"

Isaac shifted the weight on his feet, bringing Burns' attention back to him. "Now, why don't you just put that pistol on the floor like I told you? The other one from your holster, too. Nice and slow."

Without much of an option, Isaac did as he asked, nudging them across the room with the tip of his boot. When he stood again, Burns pushed Birdie forward by her hair. "Why don't you pick those up for me, sweetheart? We'll see how our hero likes being shot with his own Pa's pistols."

Birdie cried out at the shove, but Burns wasn't done. He pushed her to the floor with his hand still curled in her hair. She did as he instructed, and he jerked her back upright against his chest once she held both pistols in her hands.

He grabbed one of the pistols and cocked it, turning the barrel up to press under Birdie's chin, then released the hammer on his other pistol and tucked it back into his pants. With his free hand, he snatched the last pistol and cocked it, leveling it on Lydia. Isaac looked for a break in his attention during the exchange but there didn't seem to be one. Even Mack shifted his weight as if looking for the chance to leap for Burns.

"Would you like to know what it feels like to not know whether your wife's alive or dead, Sheriff?" Burn's voice, low and menacing, was louder than a rifle shot.

Chapter Thirty-Six

Lydia had never had a gun pointed at her before and after this experience, she would be perfectly fine if she never did again.

The situation had been grim before, but now? Burns held all of the cards. Whether Isaac loved her or not, he wouldn't put her life at risk by pressing the wild man with the pistol pointed at her now. He wouldn't jeopardize Birdie or Cora's life either, for that matter.

Her eyes were pinned on Burns – or rather, on that gun barrel pointed at her. Even while his crazed eyes danced around the room at them all, the barrel never wavered. Birdie was squirming against Burns, trying to get free of the pistol that was jammed into the soft tissue under her chin, now, her hair still wrapped around the fingers that held it.

Even if she could move the pistol before he fired, she wouldn't get far enough and would probably pull the gun in her direction with the way her hair was trapped. Lydia felt despair curl in her gut. She had no idea how to help them get out of this!

"Just let me take my wife home," Burns shouted. "That's all I wanted when I came here. I knew she was here, and I came to get her back. She's mine. You saw to that."

Isaac didn't answer, just held Burns' gaze and inched forward.

"It's your fault, you know? You made me marry her. If you'd just stayed out of my business, I'd have been able to spread the work between the two of them, and neither of them would be..." Isaac made a sound of disgust but didn't make any other noise.

"If you come one step closer, I will kill her," Burns was close to screaming at Isaac now. The gun moved even higher into Birdie's neck, and she strained up on her toes to keep it from burying too far into her skin.

"You're going to kill her, anyway," Isaac answered, his voice level. "I can't allow that, Fred."

He didn't address the rest of the accusation, but Lydia knew one thing for sure. Isaac was never going to let Burns leave the room with Birdie. She wasn't sure what he'd do to keep it from happening – but he couldn't imagine a scenario in which Isaac or Mack would allow her friend to be at this man's mercy again.

"I'm warning you!" Burns shouted as Isaac eased closer. Lydia focused all of her intent on the barrel of that gun and the twitching finger dancing on the trigger beyond it.

When she heard the hallway floor creak, she nearly turned her head toward it. She caught herself before giving away anyone who could be lingering outside to help them and noted that Isaac's body posture changed.

Burns' did, too, and Birdie stopped squirming as he held her closer to his chest with the gun.

"Show yourself!" he shouted at the door, the gun in Birdie's throat inching up into her skin a bit more and a strangled sound coming from Birdie's throat as she strained to keep that gun from digging in further. When nothing moved, he screamed his demand louder, adding, "I will shoot them both, right now, if you don't show yourself!"

Burns' attention was wholly taken by the appearance of Isaac's Deputy in the doorway, looking like a hero on a penny novel cover. Lydia didn't have time to smile at him, but she did notice the devilish grin and sparkling eyes that pinned Burns across the room as if he was the angel of Death come to take him to his maker. Burns spouted a bit, backing up a few steps, his eyes riveted on Jack, though the pistols never moved.

Seeing his distraction, Mack took the opportunity to lunge for Burns, aiming to get Burns away from Birdie and drop the guns pointed at both women. Lydia watched in horror as the gun pointed at her swung around, and the shot was fired right into Mack's hulking form.

The blast was so close it knocked Mack backward and time seemed to slow around Lydia, her ears ringing from the discharge.

"NO! MACK!" shrieked Birdie, struggling again in Burns' arm and shoving at the pistol buried in her neck. Isaac jumped for Mack as the gun moved, and Lydia's lips parted in a scream as he curled his hands around Mack and swung him to the ground. They landed with a thud, muffled by the rug around Cora's bed. Isaac pulled Mack's body around the back of the bed frame, out of the line of fire.

From the blood she saw as the shot landed, she wasn't sure who had been hit or where. As they'd rolled out of sight, the memory of Isaac's nightmare crashed through her, and she stared at the pistol in Burns' hand. Even if he wasn't hit by that bullet, would the sound and the blood cause him to sink into that despair that haunted him? Her hands were shaking with the need to go to him and see if he was alright.

Her eyes darted to the side of the bed, away from the pistol and Burns, but she couldn't see Isaac. His mother dropped to the floor next to them, her voice frantic as she joined in the search for Mack's injury. She couldn't hear Isaac's voice and her heart started pounding a painful refrain in her chest. Was he hurt? Had the nightmares claimed him again?

She took a step in their direction, needing confirmation that he was alright, that he was still clear-headed and able to handle this situation. Lord knew it was far out of her control! It had been ever since Burns pulled out his pistol.

As if the thought reminded him that she was still there, Burns' voice slithered through the air to her. "Not so fast, Mrs. Branson."

She froze again, her eyes leaping to see the pistol swung back at her, the round chamber having loaded another round as Burns cocked the hammer back. Silence fell around her, and the glimmer in his eyes was the only thing she could see as her mind repeated, "Yea, though I walk through the valley of the shadow of death…"

She lifted her chin, her fear and anger blending in one fervent prayer. "I will fear no evil."

Chapter Thirty-Seven

Looking around the end of the footboard, Isaac saw that Burns was pointing his father's gun at Lydia again. He closed his eyes, forcing his mind to focus and his hands to still. He prayed for the strength to get past this and for protection. He prayed for his wife, Birdie, his mother, Mack, and even Jack. His deputy hid behind the chair next to the bookcase on the other side of his mother's bedroom.

He felt a peace settle over him, one he hadn't felt in a very long time. As if he were stepping out of the rain and into a shelter, his eyes cleared, his heart slowed, and his mind started assessing the danger again. His hands steadied, and his resolve solidified as the knowledge of what he needed to do settled on his shoulders. He needed to get them all out alive.

All of them.

He caught Jack's gaze and signaled him to toss over one of his pistols. Jack's face reddened, and he looked down before sending Isaac an apologetic look.

"I don't have them," he mouthed, and Isaac groaned inwardly. Of all the times for his deputy to forget his pistols, this was by far the worst. Isaac had made sure Jack had his pistols when he left the Office to go on his rounds earlier. He raised his hands in a questioning gesture, and Jack's face reddened even darker. "They're on my saddle..." he answered in a hoarse whisper that had Isaac closing his eyes and breathing a few seconds to calm his irritation.

He called to Burns, "You know you can't win this. Let's talk about this and handle it like gentlemen. Just put the guns down, and no one else gets hurt."

When no response came, Isaac eased onto his feet, his hands up, and walked around the edge of the bed. "There's no reason for this to get worse than it is, Fred." His tone was back to the one he used to calm his horse, and he saw Lydia relax a bit out of the corner of his eye. She trusted him to...

The thought was cut short as Burns, a wicked gleam in his eyes, shoved Birdie at him and crossed the few steps to latch onto Lydia, the gun still pointed directly at her face. "I tell ya what! Since you're so keen on rescuing dear Birdie, I'll make you a trade. You can have her! The boys will be glad to have a new woman to entertain them. She's still fresh and pretty, while Birdie doesn't get them excited the way she did when she was new. Mrs. Branson, though, with that fire in her eyes, will fetch a much nicer price. I should be able to rebuild my place in another town and use her to amass a fortune!"

Isaac caught Birdie by reflex, his horror-filled eyes not leaving Burns. Isaac felt his stomach drop to his feet but didn't dare take a step toward Lydia with those guns pointed at her. Nothing in his life had punched him in the gut like seeing the fear on her face shift to repulsion and determination. He knew his wife well enough to know she would never allow him to use her for anything. She'd die first.

The thought did nothing to quell the fear coursing through him as he gently pushed Birdie to the side of the bed near Mack and faced Burns squarely.

Burns shifted, twisting Lydia under his arm and holding the gun to her temple while aiming the other at Isaac. "We're either going to walk out of here together, or I'm walking out alone, Sheriff. As you said, no one else needs to get hurt."

Isaac's jaw clenched as he read the expression in Lydia's eyes. Her eyes were calm and cool now. The rage was gone. "Let me go, save the others," her eyes looked around the room at the people he loved, and her lips turned into a small smile as they returned to him. There was an emotion in them that he never thought to see from her, hadn't realized he wanted to see from her.

Love.

Isaac's jaw clenched as he watched Burns drag his wife through the bedroom door past him. He didn't so much as breathe as he counted their steps; the hard clip of Burns' shoes on the floor to the door, the slight squeak in the hinge he hadn't fixed, and then the few barely audible steps across the porch. He'd let them get out the door. There were too many other people Burns could hurt here. He wouldn't get far, though. Especially not with that look in Lydia's eyes.

He closed his eyes and counted to four. He'd intended to wait until he got to ten before he moved, but he heard the horse whinnying out front, the rustling of Lydia's skirts, and none of that sounded like she was going along with Burns' plans to get her off the property. He grinned and ducked into the hallway, all thoughts of waiting forgotten, as he rushed down the stairs and to the open front door.

He cursed as he saw the cloud of dust the horse had kicked up behind it as Burns' kicked it into a run away from the house. He growled in irritation and dashed back into the house to grab whatever he had to get his wife back home safely. He was in his room within seconds with the trunk at the end of his bed flipped open. His army colt laid against the deep blue uniform inside the trunk, and he took a deep breath, his hands curling around the grips.

He'd forced himself to take these pistols apart, clean each piece, give them a good oil rub, and put them back together over the last few months, and each time, the pain was the same. Each time the cold steel made his hands ache as he remembered clutching them in a desperate need to fire before the Rebel soldier had.

Fear, pain, and grief had slammed into him. Memories flooded him: finding his regiment wiped out, his fear as he heard the rifle shot and felt the blistering pain in his leg, and even the smell of blood mixed with the mud. He'd cleaned them so well each time that there wasn't even a trace of dust the next time he did it. He owed it to the men who had died, destroyed by their patriotism and the belief that their cause was right, that God was on their side. He'd done it as penance, as an apology for not dying with them, for not protecting them, for believing that his prayers were enough to continue shielding them from the horrors that befell so many other regiments.

But now?

His lips thinned to a single line as he shut out the sounds of people moving around the house. He stared at the shiny barrel that felt nothing like the heavy weapons he'd dreaded even looking at since he'd come home. They weren't heavy in his hands anymore. The steel didn't seem as cold. It was as if they knew this wasn't about guilt or questioning his place in the world and why he'd been spared. This had nothing to do with anything but protecting his family and wife from danger. What he should have done sooner.

The thought of her in Fred's hands made his long fingers curl around the grip of the pistols in each hand. His jaw shifted as he clenched his teeth tightly in determination. With the practiced hand that had cleaned these guns for months and loaded them for years, he set one pistol down and reached for the leather satchel tucked in the side of the trunk. He arranged the instruments inside the satchel across the uniform jacket and, with not a bit of fear or guilt, started loading the pistols he'd hated for so long.

As he worked, he heard his father droning on and on about how useless guns were if they weren't taken proper care of. Isaac had to admit that if he hadn't spent so much time instilling respect for the firearms into Isaac, he might've avoided so much as looking at them since his return.

He'd always said that if he had no intention of using one, he shouldn't keep it around. But his father hadn't said a word about them when he'd come home and locked them away in this trunk. He hadn't said anything when he caught Isaac cleaning them, either. He nodded, a sad expression of understanding in his eyes, and turned away.

That look floated in his thoughts but was quickly replaced by the look of stubborn determination and love his wife had sent him as she'd been pushed through the bedroom door. The muscles in his jaw clenched again, and he counted rounds as he thumbed them into the first revolver.

Gone was the fear of killing someone he loved, paying the price for him killing someone, or even for fear that he'd freeze up and not be able to shoot, too haunted by the ghosts from that long ago battlefield. Gone was the sad look in his father's eyes as he nodded his understanding of the pain Isaac was feeling.

Now, all he felt was the focus of a man who knew what he had to do and exactly what was at stake. He wasn't the boy he'd been on that battlefield. Not anymore. He rolled the revolver down his sleeve, checking that he'd loaded all the bullet packs and that the cylinder was rolling smoothly.

He set the first revolver down and started loading the second, a familiar metallic click sounding as each bullet pack slid home. "You saved my life back then. You saved my life when I wanted to die. Now, I don't want to die. I have far too much to live for. But the woman who holds my heart is in danger. Even if you don't save my life, I need you to be ready to save hers."

All six rounds nestled in, he clicked it back into line along the barrel of the gun, then rolled the cylinder down his sleeve like he had done with the first, making sure it spun freely and that the bullet housings were settled. He pulled the gun belt around his hips and slid the revolvers back into their holsters once it was buckled on. Their weight felt more comforting than frightening for the first time since before Gettysburg.

Only after he swung into his saddle did he understand what he'd said. Whether he wanted it or not, Lydia had become his very air. He pulled the star off his shirt and looked up as his mother stepped onto the porch. He dropped it in the dirt and rode off after Burns. He wasn't the Sheriff chasing a fugitive or an officer riding down a rebel. No, his thoughts growled. He was a man riding to rescue the woman he loved from a sadistic monster.

And he had no intention of losing her.

Chapter Thirty-Eight

Lydia's skirts were still tangled from the awkward way Fred had tossed her into the saddle when she'd started wrestling to get free at the house. He was much stronger than she was and her determination and fear didn't give her any advantage as he used the bulk of her petticoat to trap her and then toss her into the saddle.

He had climbed up behind her, barely getting settled before the horse lurched forward. She had no choice but to hold onto the pommel as they'd thundered away from the people she'd come to love and any hope of help coming from the house.

She didn't fight to get free again until they were well away from the house. If he was going to wave the gun in her face, she wouldn't chance anyone getting hurt. She watched the land rush by and felt the muscles in the shoulders of the horse under her legs stretch and bunch as it ran. When sweat began coating the animal's sides, she tried to use it to slip free.

She tried everything – tossing her weight to one side then the other, rocking her head back to bash into his nose, even balling her hands into fists and punching his legs on either side of her. He cursed and yelled, "Do you think I won't pull this trigger?" The barrel of the gun pressed harder into her temple. "I will kill you before I let him have you back, Mrs. Branson. You have both ruined my life, and it's time I had a little payback for it."

Lydia didn't respond, only continued to struggle. At one point, she'd managed to get both legs on one side of the horse and wrestled with him to slide down the side of the horse. She'd take her chances at being hurt when she landed, as long as she was free to do something.

"Isaac will come for me," she repeated inwardly, the words giving her strength to keep fighting. "God won't let this horrible man win again." She'd seen the wealth of emotion in Isaac's eyes when they met hers as Burns pushed her out of the room. There was no resignation or loss in that expression. She knew he would be after them as quickly as possible once they were free of the house. God would see to it.

"Good God, woman, stop! You won't get away from me. I won't let him win!" his rage was still very apparent. How long she struggled, she had no idea. Burns cursed every time her hands connected with his face or neck as she tried to scratch her way clear. The horse, whose balance was being disturbed by the shifting weight on its back, had slowed but hadn't stopped, and she still had her legs on one side of the horse while she fought him, hoping that she could topple herself, if not both of them, off the horse.

Then, suddenly, she slid free! She hit the ground and rolled to keep herself out of the horse's way. Getting free just to get trampled wouldn't do her any good. Once free of the horse's stride, she took a deep breath.

She'd torn the skin off her hands when she'd braced her fall, but they weren't broken. She did a quick check of her legs and torso. Aside from some bruising from the corset against her ribs, she didn't detect any major injuries. She felt a rush of giddy pleasure and her lips spread into a smile.

She'd done it! She'd gotten free of Fred Burns! She didn't need to be rescued! She looked up and thanked God for giving her the strength and determination to get free from what she had no doubt was a hellish future.

She promised to spend more time expressing her gratitude later as the sound of thundering hooves coming her way startled her into reality. She took a few more precious seconds to look around, then she launched up to her feet, pulled her skirts up to her shins, and started running back toward the direction she thought would lead to the house.

She heard the horse getting closer and started dodging his swiping arms as he tried to catch her again. She bobbed away from the horse or stopped running until he was mid-adjustment in his direction before she started running again, but in another direction.

There wasn't anything to hide behind out here. The embankments on either side would be a good option, so she turned sharply to the right, determined to reach the steep embankment before the horse caught up to her.

Her skirts were heavy, and no matter how high she held them, they tangled in her legs. Her chest was heaving and starving for air, but Burns was still too close. She slid down the embankment, rocks, and dirt rolling under her boots. She nearly stumbled at the bottom but used the fall forward to jump into a run again. She took advantage of the darkness and the cover to weave her way into the brush.

And still, the horse came, its rider yelling, "Where are you going, woman? Do you think your God will save you? He's already forsaken you! You're being run down like a dog! Stop running, and we may not hurt you for this."

Her chest was burning, her lungs screaming in protest of the prolonged running after the wrestling she'd been doing on the horse. Her ribs were protesting, pushing on the boning in her corset as her lungs tried taking in more air. Tears of frustration leaked from the corners of her eyes, but she didn't slow down to wipe at them.

She ducked behind a row of thick bushes, taking her chances with the thorns. If she could stay hidden long enough, maybe Burns would give up looking for her and continue to protect himself.

She fought to keep her heaving breaths quiet and strained to listen over the sound of blood rushing in her ears. The sounds of the horse were distant and seemed to be going in the opposite direction from where she was.

She lost track of how long she stayed there, but after a little while, she didn't hear the horse any longer, and hope surged again. She counted in her head, passing two minutes before she crawled out from the brambles and rose gently to her feet.

Lydia's shoulders fell, and she rolled them, her steps taking her back toward the road, confident that Burns had decided she wasn't worth hunting in the dark. She caught a flash of movement to her left and gasped as he came toward her on foot. Lydia ran, the pain in her chest and legs making it more difficult. Her feet stumbled, too tired to lift high enough to fully clear the ground as she ran. Burns wasn't much better, and she kept ahead of him a few steps most of the way back to the road.

She saw the horse standing by the side of the road and felt a surge of... something... as she turned toward it. If she could get to the horse before him then she'd be off, and he couldn't catch up with the horse. She'd be truly free!

Before she could reach the clearing, she felt his full weight land on top of her as he toppled her to the ground. Her scream was a mix of shock, fear, and frustration but it was cut off as the breath was knocked out of her already starving lungs.

He had little trouble getting her back on the horse, this time using the reins to trap her wrists against the pommel. "That'll keep you from pulling that trick again. The next time you slide off, that horse will just drag you along." He climbed up behind her and leaned close to her ear. "And I will let him. It won't kill you, but I can guarantee you won't be using those arms to fight anyone off for a good while. Come to think of it, it might work better that way. Shall we try it?"

She shuddered, not giving him any other answer as she fought to get air into her lungs. Once she could breathe again, she returned to wiggling, rolling her head back violently, slamming her torso against him, trying to get free.

He tried everything to get her to stop, wrapping his arms around her tightly, hugging her to his chest so close she couldn't move her arms. Her upper body was pinned in and unable to get clearance enough to buck against him. Without her feet having anything to brace on, she had no way to rock into him. She shot her head back instead, hitting him square on the nose.

"Bugger it, woman!" he screamed, his hands leaving her sides and dropping the reins. This signaled the horse to stop. Burns slowed and halted in the middle of the road, his sides heaving. "I've had enough of you!"

She had no way to avoid the blow of the pistol grip to the side of her head, and she slid into unconsciousness without a sound.

***

Sometime later, Lydia winced and rolled onto her back, one hand moving her head and the other lying flat on the ground next to her, praying the world would stop rolling to one side. Her fingers came away from her temple sticky with blood, and she closed her eyes. She hung her head back, taking deep breaths. It slowly came back to her.

Burns had dropped her to the ground from the back of the horse. The fall made her ribs hurt even more than the pain slicing through her head like a knife. Was it possible she'd broken them? The corset would keep her body straight, but would it be enough to support her for more time on the horse?

The world spun a bit more when she turned her head to see where he'd gone, and she swallowed hard and tried to breathe to keep from emptying her stomach. Rolling to her side to avoid choking on it would only make her head spin more, which seemed to make the pain worse.

Her thoughts were slipping away, and she fought to remember what her father had said about head wounds when her brother had fallen from a tree behind the house. Her father's words had always brought her comfort before, and she needed all the calm she could get.

He'll be alright, mostly pain near the wound that may make him feel unsettled that might last for a while. He might need a few stitches on the cut, but head wounds always bleed more than anywhere else, so it looks worse than it is.

Lydia closed her eyes as the sharp pain stabbed through her head again. She wondered if this was what her brother had felt before the doctor arrived with the laudanum to help him sleep while he stitched up the wound. She had no idea whether she needed stitches, but the pain in her head was bad enough that even her vision was blurry for a few minutes after she opened them.

When her vision cleared, she focused on the brilliant array of stars overhead, then lowered her head to look around where he'd dropped her. She heard the sound of water moving from the general direction Burns had gone, so she could safely assume he was getting the horse watered and giving it a bit of a rest.

She raised her head a bit to see if she could find him, and there he was, about twenty feet away, on the side of the river next to the horse, whose head was bent to the water running a few inches from his feet.

She really should've made it a point to search the surroundings more in the time she'd been here, but as it was, she knew the water for the garden was channeled in from a river to the northwest of the house. If they'd ridden that direction, they were headed for the unsettled country, Native American territory. The idea froze the blood in her veins.

There hadn't been many attacks around Franklin, but she'd read harrowing stories about other towns that weren't so lucky. A pair of riders on a single horse riding through their land? Did they stand a chance of getting past them? Worse, not far from the bend in the river, the land was covered by dense forests.

The Natives in this area lived in those forests, she knew. Once or twice since she'd been there, a few of the men from the local tribe had come into town. She'd never met them but had seen them walking into the saloon. They were not small men, and the memory of the stories she'd heard, painting the Native people as merciless seemed to merge in her head. Now they were enough to make the blood rush in her ears again while another wave of nausea and pain threatened to empty her stomach.

Reining in her panic, she also had to note that Isaac wouldn't be able to find them if they got too far into the forests. She had to slow Burns down more. Her mind cleared, though her headache loomed. Burns seemed to notice since he dropped the reins for the horse to let him drink from the river and came to squat next to her. "There are towns in California and down past Silver City where a woman like you will draw a crowd. If you can sing, there'll be more money in it for you. Either way, I'm going to open a new saloon, and you'll be the star of the show. You owe me that much." His voice was oily, and he hissed a bit like a snake, which seemed only appropriate. She'd been comparing him to the devil while he spoke.

"I don't owe you a thing, and neither did Birdie," she cried out as his hand landed on her cheek and pain exploded under her eye. Lydia lifted her eyes and bared her teeth at him, hissing, "I'll die before I earn you a single cent."

"Possibly," he cackled, running his fingers down the side of her cheek, which she swatted away. "More talk like that, and I'll just put a bullet in that pretty skull and call it done. There are other women, other cities. You only make coin from mouthy women when the men who buy her services are given leave to discipline them. I'm not opposed to ensuring they're aware of how much I approve of it, either."

Lydia sneered at him but didn't answer, and after a minute, he turned back to the horse, leaving Lydia to survey the space they had stopped in. It was a lovely spot, especially as the night had fallen overhead. There was a mass of stars glittering overhead, cool grass under her hands, and crushed rocks along the riverbank where it met the small clearing. There were a few outcroppings of rocks behind them and a path between, which is probably why Burns had chosen it to water the horse. It would be a lovely secluded place for a picnic or a swim, and she made a note to bring it up to Isaac before she remembered who was standing a few feet away.

There is only one way into this little alcove and one way out, she thought, looking around the space for another route in. Anyone trying to get here would have to climb the boulders that flanked the small path, which would be a challenging climb.

They were either trapped in or well-protected from attackers. Lydia eyed the river running on her other side and shook her head. If Isaac caught them here, there would be a standoff, and there was no way out of this alcove alive. Did Burns know that?

She glanced at where he squatted next to the horse filling a canteen he'd gotten from the saddle and bit her lip. Did he think they were so far ahead of Isaac or that he wasn't coming after her? Is that why he seemed unhurried and not worried about their position? She knew the horse needed water and rest if he was planning on riding past Silver City, but did they have the time to sit here? He seemed unworried that she'd run, too.

She eased to sit up and took stock of herself. She could make a run for it, but she wouldn't get far before Burns shot her in the back. No, he'd be on her before she cleared the rocks, especially with this headache and the rolling it caused in her stomach. She eyed the horse, wondering if she had time to steal it and get out of here.

She shook her head again and laid her forehead on her crossed arms. She was in no fit state to even come close to disabling Burns enough to steal the horse. It would take time to get her bearings, get rid of this headache, and form a plan to get her out of this situation.

With her forehead laying on her forearms, she started praying for her safety. "Please keep them safe," she murmured, fear and disgust at Burns' intentions warring for dominance in her stomach. She began to think that if he killed her, he'd go back for Birdie and have to fight through Cora and Jack to get to her. She hoped Medina had recovered from his wound and would be able to protect them.

Then she heard it; the jingle of a horse's harness, the steady thunder of hoofbeats drawing closer. Her eyes flew to Burns, who stood and turned toward it, squinting as if he could see who approached through the dark. Hope surged in her chest, accompanied by fear. Burns looked apprehensive, so it wasn't anyone he'd been waiting for. He pulled a pistol free of the holster at his side and cocked it.

Could it be Isaac? Was it even possible he would have caught up with them that quickly? Had she delayed Burns enough to allow him to catch up? Questions chased each other in her head, and she rose to her feet unsteadily, her eyes fixed on the approaching horse. Then she raised her fingers to her lips with a gasp as the rider got close enough that she could see his shape more clearly. She'd know those shoulders anywhere. Even on a horse, leaning forward to urge the horse to move faster, she knew. As if an answer to the prayers, her husband had come to save her.

Love and hope surged like a wildflower in her chest, it was almost overwhelming and nearly made her forget the pain. The urge to run to him and be taken into those strong arms rose inside her, and she held back a sob of tears. He was the answer to so many of her prayers. It was ludicrous to be happy at a time like this, but as he drew closer, she drank up the sight of him like a man stranded in the desert guzzled water at an oasis.

Then, realization struck. If Isaac came between those rocks, Burns would shoot him. Her eyes wide, she opened her mother to yell and warn her husband as he raced toward them, to tell him he was riding right into a trap.

She did not doubt it was Isaac on that horse barreling toward them now. She could see his features, the squared jaw illustrating his determination, the hair flying loose around his head in a stream of cinnamon fire. In a few more feet, she'd be able to see those beautiful green eyes. But if he was close enough for that, he'd be dead.

She opened her mouth to shout at him, but Burn's hand clapped over her mouth as she started to scream, "Isa–"

She squirmed and bit his hand, fighting to get free again.

"I knew I should've killed you before I left the house," he cursed, placing his pistol on her still bleeding temple, waiting for her husband to enter their little hideaway.

Isaac slowed his horse and rode between the stones, sliding out of the saddle and raising his hands as he approached Fred. Lydia watched him walk closer, felt Fred's arm tighten around her neck, and made a strangling noise.

"You couldn't let her go, could you? You couldn't just leave me alone, leave Birdie and I alone, and now you've come to ruin my chances at starting new. I should just kill her, right here in front of you. You took my wife. It's time I returned the favor permanently."

She heard his finger squeezing on the trigger and pinned Isaac with her eyes, trying to tell him goodbye and that she loved him without saying anything. Her eyes moved over the lines of his face, memorizing each feature, committing them to her memory so they'd keep her warm in the cold nights that were sure to come.

The situation was grim, and Isaac's lovely eyes were hard, the green not sparkling with affection as he approached Lydia and Burns. Her avenging angel, her knight who didn't need shiny armor to stand in front of a man who wanted him dead and defend her, to rescue her.

The image of him covered in the protective light of God's power brought a smile to her lips, giving her the courage to consider they might make it out of there alive. Her gaze dropped to his hips as he walked toward her, and she narrowed her eyes. The guns on his hips were not any she'd seen him wear before, the gun belt was a deep black leather, and he wore it high on his hips where it stood out against the white linen of his shirt. Were they Jack's?

"Please, Fred," Isaac begged, stepping closer, his steps clear and deliberate. His voice was soothing like he was talking to a spooked horse. "I will give you anything you want. I will let you go. I will pay your creditors. I will wire the Marshal's office that you're dead, and you can start fresh. Just give me Lydia. Don't hurt her."

"It's too late," Fred hissed, spittle flying from his angry lips with every word and coating her cheek. Any other time, she'd have swiped it off in disgust, but she didn't dare move her hand. He'd hit her on the head, then slapped her, knowing her head was still in severe pain. He had no sense of humanity. He'd pull the trigger if he thought she was going to...

She froze, an idea blooming in her head. Bolstered by the need to protect Isaac, she slowly moved her left hand and dipped it into the pocket of her skirt, where she always kept a needle and thread. Glad for the habit she'd picked up at Mary's shop in Maysville, she retrieved that needle and, in a quick move, jabbed it into the arm around her neck.

Fred howled and released her in reflex, the pain in his arm distracting him for the split second Lydia needed to get free and fly to Isaac's side. Isaac's arms went around her immediately, and he turned, putting himself between her and Fred, his jaw clenched so hard she worried he'd break teeth.

"I knew you would come!" she exclaimed, tightening her hold on him.

"How could I not? If anything happened to you, I wouldn't be able to breathe," he murmured against her hair, where she was cradled against his chest.

She looked up at him with watery eyes and a smile on her lips. "I would fight every second to get back to you," she whispered. "I would not rest until I was back home."

Home. His smile was hesitant. "I wouldn't rest until I had you back at home."

She heard the click of a hammer and looked back at Burns, who had pulled the second pistol. Both were now pointed in their direction. Burns' slimy voice crossed the space to them. "You make me sick. I was just going to kill the Sheriff, but I think you'd be far too much of a nuisance to be of use to me, woman. I'll kill you both and dump your bodies in the river here. What's two more dead bodies on my record?"

Lydia closed her eyes tight and curled back into Isaac's warm body, drawing strength from his presence. If she was going to die, at least she'd die with him. The man she'd fallen in love with.

Chapter Thirty-Nine

Isaac stared at the guns pointed at them, holding Lydia against him tightly. The urge to charge the man and beat him until he lost consciousness had exploded in his head at the sight of his wife. He saw a gash at the side of her forehead, and the blood matting in her hair told him she'd been bleeding for a while.

Burns hadn't done anything to stop it but had callously laid her over his lap and let the blood run freely. That she seemed otherwise alright, just pale and worried, gave him the impression that it wasn't an emergency.

But with her now standing so close, the smell of blood stung his nostrils. Memories threatened, but his concern for Lydia overwhelmed them. He'd prayed the entire ride out here, with every ounce of faith he'd ever possessed, to allow him to catch them before anything terrible happened. Prayed that he wouldn't find her dead. Prayed that Burns hadn't gotten too far ahead of him to keep him from catching up.

He hadn't expected God to follow through with his prayers, not after He failed to act so many times. What was one more string of unanswered prayers? But now, having seen her and held her one more time before he left this earth, it was worth all of the prayers he'd sent to the heavens. He hadn't left this one, the most important prayer he'd ever uttered, unanswered.

He had a flash of connection to the words he had spoken in church after he'd skipped the part about love. 'Till death us do part,' took on a different meaning now – one he wished he didn't have to understand as he stood on the brink of death. He should've realized how he felt earlier. He should've protected her more. He should've... But he hadn't. And if this was what his unanswered prayers had brought them to, at least they'd die together.

Well, here was death, and he wasn't nearly as afraid of it as he had been on the battlefield. He'd danced with death so often that he'd grown accustomed to it. When those guns were leveled at him, he didn't fear them; he just raised his own and fired first. Now, though? He had so much more to lose than just his life as he had years ago. He would lose her. His salvation. His wife. She was curled in his arms, right where he needed her to be as he stared death down again.

"I'm sorry," he whispered to her, his eyes pinned on the barrel of the guns pointed at them and focused on the twitching of Burns' fingers on the trigger. "I had no right to put you in this position. I should've found another way to protect you from this."

"It's not your fault," she said, her voice soft as a breeze lifted her scent to his nose. Lilacs and lavender. He imagined it was what heaven smelled like, though he doubted he'd ever know. "I wouldn't change a thing, Isaac."

"Lydia, I–" He flinched and closed his eyes as the crack of gunfire split the air, cutting him off and echoing off the riverbanks and rocks lining the clearing. His ears started ringing, and his hold on Lydia tightened. His memories still didn't come for him, and he marveled at that as time slowed around him.

Gone was the nightmare of the day he'd been shot. He felt a calm peace move through him, and he silently thanked God that he had time to experience what it was to love someone as wonderful as the woman clinging to him in his arms. With a slow bloom of understanding, he realized God had answered his prayers.

He'd gone into battle asking God to protect his family. Before then, he'd prayed many times about returning home to apologize to his father. To find a good woman, settle down, and raise a family – to know what it felt like to love someone so much that you'd go to war to protect them.

This woman had stepped into his life, taken over caring for his house and his mother, and even loved him if he dared hope. God hadn't forsaken him. That war had nothing to do with Him. The battle that had seen his regiment destroyed had nothing to do with Him either. But this? This woman, this feeling, this understanding? This had everything to do with Him.

As quickly as that, the violent separation between him and God dissipated, and warmth filled his heart. He felt the acceptance of his fate and understood that if this was the end of his life, he'd die feeling the love of his wife and the love of God. Forgiveness flooded his soul, filling the space left by his sorrow for Lydia, who had never asked for this when she'd gotten on that train and was now dying after being married for only a few weeks.

Time lurched forward, but it took him a few seconds to realize that there was no pain. Had the Lord taken them before the pain to save them from feeling it? He opened his eyes to the sky and wrinkled his brow at the star-filled blanket overhead. His eyes fell on Fred lying on the ground a few feet away, the pistols still clutched in his hands. Neither pistol was smoking as if they'd been fired. There was a movement to the right, and Isaac's shocked gaze looked that way, his eyes wide as understanding dawned.

Jack walked down a side path from the right, pistols in both hands, one barrel smoking. Lydia raised her head and gasped, then fainted straight away, drawing Isaac's attention back to her. He scooped her up and settled her onto a patch of grass near the river. He set her head in his lap, and his fingers brushed the loose hair strands from her face. Jack walked the other way and checked on Burns, his eyes meeting Isaac's over Lydia's unconscious form. He didn't say anything, just nodded before looking back at the man in front of him.

Fred Burns was dead.

Chapter Forty

Isaac sighed heavily, and his shoulders dropped as if all of the weight was suddenly lifted free. The nightmare was over. His eyes fell to the woman's face in his lap, and he sighed, wishing he could tell her that she didn't have to worry anymore.

He heard the crunch of boots in the dirt as Jack crossed the space to them. Isaac lifted his eyes, feeling like he hadn't slept in a month. "I'll handle this. Take her home," he said, nodding at Lydia. His tone held none of his usual laughter, and his eyes were unexpectedly hard.

"Giving me orders, Deputy?" Isaac asked Jack, his nerves making the question shaky and high-pitched.

"I don't see a badge, Mister Branson. That puts me in charge here. And since I'm in charge, I want you to get your wife home, and I'll be around tomorrow for your statement. Take the day off," he grinned, flashing his white teeth.

Isaac pinned him with a look that said he wasn't buying the bravado and asked, "Are you alright? I know you've never..." He jerked his head toward the man lying dead on the ground a few feet away.

"I don't know," Jack said, his smile melting. "I don't know how I feel about it. It doesn't mean I wouldn't do it again if it was to save another person's life. That it was your life, one of the best men I've known, or Lydia's, one of the most amazing women I've ever met, means I would hesitate even less. I regret that it was necessary, and I know there will be prayers begging forgiveness for the string of events that led to it that I could've handled better. For now, I just..."

"I've been there," Isaac said, his voice low and soothing. "I'll be here whenever you need to talk about it. It's not an easy thing, taking a life. Even if it's for the right reason, the action goes against everything the Lord ever preached."

Isaac was shocked at how easily the words flowed from his lips, but even more so at how much he felt it. Jack nodded and looked up at Isaac questioningly. They'd worked together long enough that Jack was aware of his disdain for anything vaguely religious. The confusion on his face made Isaac's cheeks burn a bit in shame at having turned his back on God. "She's a miracle worker," Jack breathed, shaking his head.

Isaac let it be quiet for a minute before saying, "I will never be able to thank you enough for saving her, Jack. I owe you my life, as well. There are no words that can truly express that. But I will be here, ready to return the favor and more. Never forget that."

"Aww, shucks, Sheriff," Jack said. His face turned red, but his smile said he was glad for a topic he could smile about. "You'd do the same for me, for anyone in town. If doing it for you first finally gives me the upper hand, I will enjoy it as long as it lasts."

"I'm never going to hear the end of this, am I?" Isaac groaned, pulling his shirt out of his pants and ripping a long strip sideways. Jack laid his hand lightly on the makeshift bandage as Isaac tied it around the back of Lydia's head, trying to stop the wound that still seeped blood down the side of her face. From the look of her dress, even in the dark, he could see she'd lost a lot of blood. His worry must've shown because Jack piped up, adding a bit of humor to the situation.

"Name your first kid after me, and I'll consider dropping it," Jack negotiated.

"I'm not making any promises," Isaac laughed, scooping Lydia up and walking toward the horse standing outside the stone ridge. He handed her to Jack, who had followed him to the horse, then climbed onto his horse. Jack gently lifted Lydia to Isaac, and he tucked her into the protective curve of his arms. "But since taking her home is what I wanted to do most anyway, I will do as you say, Deputy." With a nod from Jack, he turned his horse back toward their home, his wife snuggled tightly against his chest.

He'd never been so annoyed at the gait of his horse as he was at that moment. He felt every breath catch in Lydia's chest as he clutched her tightly to his chest. The blood on Lydia's temple had soaked through the linen he'd used to bandage her. She stiffened and shifted as he held her close to keep her from falling off the horse. Was it pain or memory, he wondered, knowing Burns had likely held her similarly as they'd raced away from the safety of the house.

Time seemed to drag, and his horse's sides heaved. He apologized and whispered promises of apples and sugar cubes if they could just get Lydia home before it was too late. He didn't slow the horse as he traced his path backward. He'd been cursing under his breath about how far they'd gotten, so it shouldn't have surprised him that it took a while to get back to the house.

Finally, after what felt like hours, the peak of his roof came into view. He sighed in relief and barely restrained the urge to nudge the horse to run faster. He needed to tell Lydia about finding his faith, about Jack saving them, about how dangerously close to the border they'd been. But most of all, he needed to tell her he loved her. He needed to see in her eyes that she understood what a huge thing it was for him to have come so close to losing her.

He started praying, just as hard as he had when he'd been racing after them. "God, I know I've asked for a lot tonight, and I thank You for the prayers you've answered in getting me to this place. I will relish getting to hold her again for as long as I'm alive. But, please, don't take her yet. I have so much left to make up for, so many ways to show her how much I love her and treasure her. I will never forsake You again, but I beg You to help me keep her alive until we get home and the doctor can see her. Please, God," he breathed, tears pricking his eyes and streaming down his face. "I can't lose her. I couldn't earlier, and I can't now. You sent me an angel, and I fell in love with her. I can't be without her now. So please, just allow me to get her the help she needs so she can stay here and show me how to get closer to you again."

It was still dark when they arrived at the house, and Cora met them at the porch, her face pinched in worry. She reached for the reins as he halted at the porch, and he watched her eyes move to the woman in his lap as he eased out of the saddle holding her. It wasn't an easy feat, but his mother couldn't help him like Jack had. His mother simply stood silently, holding the reins as Isaac gained his feet and climbed the steps to the porch.

"Thank you," he murmured, and she kissed his cheek. Then he walked into the house and up the stairs, not stopping until he was in his room. Cora was there a few minutes later with a rag and bowl of water that she set on the table by his bed. She patted his back and gave Lydia a quick look before she left again. He sank onto the edge of the bed, using the rag to clean Lydia's face.

He cleaned the wound on her head the best he could, mildly annoyed that Jack had killed Fred Burns before he'd gotten the chance. After everything he'd put Birdie through, putting everyone in town at risk with his selfish ways. After everything he put Lydia through, it didn't seem fair that he'd died so quickly and not suffered as he'd caused others to suffer. The rage inside him had nowhere to go, and he restrained the urge to curse.

Lydia made a sound, and he looked down at her, brushing his fingers over her cheekbones and down to her jaw before moving back up to her hairline. The anger dissolved into concern so fast he was nearly lightheaded. "I'll have to get the doctor to look at your head and make sure you don't need stitches," Isaac said softly. She was still unconscious, but he had to talk to her.

He had so much he needed to say. He wrapped his arms under her shoulders and held her close to his chest, inhaling the coppery scent of blood mixing with the lilac and lavender of her skin. His eyes burned with tears he couldn't shed yet, but he had to tell her before something else took her away from him. "I was so scared when he pointed that gun at you, then dragged you out of the house. When I saw you next to that river, the blood running down your beautiful face, and that look in your eyes…"

"Lydia, I don't know how else to say this," he laid her back again and brushed his fingers down her cheek, his thumb stroking her bottom lip. The memory of the kiss they'd shared, the feel of her in his arms, and the ache in his chest at the thought of losing her filled his thoughts as he closed his eyes. "I love you, Lydia. I am so glad you came into my life. I promise I will do everything in my power to make you happy, even if you can't love me back."

"Isaac," she whispered, turning her head into his hand and opening her heavy eyelids. "I love you too."

He smiled down at her and gently touched his lips to hers, relishing the rush of happiness and fulfillment that filled his thoughts as she returned his kiss. When she moaned, he pulled out of the kiss and cursed himself for his selfishness as a fresh line of blood slid down her forehead. He cleaned it quickly and pressed a clean cloth to her forehead. "I'll send Ma in," he said, brushing her lips with a kiss again, not trusting himself to stay for longer. "I've got to get the doctor. When I get back, I will not leave your side until you're healed. I swear it."

He stopped at the door and looked back at her, lying pale in the moonlight coming through the window. He hadn't even lit the lamp. She reminded him of a fairy tale princess lying there, so still as she waited for her prince to rescue her. Not that this princess had waited for him to rescue her; the state of her clothes and the deep wound on her head were enough indication. No, this princess wouldn't have made it easy on anyone, least of all the villain taking her from her home. The thought made him smile, and he closed the door behind him and made his way down the stairs.

"I sent Birdie for the doctor," his mother said softly from her place by the door. She was looking through the window, and now he understood why. She was watching for the doctor. "For Mack," she added, not looking away from the window. They should be here any time now."

"Is Mack...?" Isaac couldn't bring himself to say anything more, and his mother shook her head before he had the chance.

"No, but I fear there may be more to his injuries than just the bullet wound. I didn't tell Birdie that, of course. He's bleeding too much. I've seen a bullet wound or two with your father's line of work. It's happened more than once. I've never seen one bleed like that, though."

Isaac looked up the stairs, but before he could say anything more, his mother the door open. "They're here."

In seconds, Birdie was hurrying the doctor into the house. His mother held the door open as they entered but didn't close it after them. "Is he...?" Birdie started to ask.

"No, child, but Doctor Jennings had best hurry," his mother led the way up the stairs, giving the doctor a heads up on what she'd observed about Mack, Birdie following closely.

They left Isaac standing by the open door by himself, and he took a deep breath. He should go back to Lydia, but he needed to talk to Birdie. She needed to know about her husband's fate. He wasn't sure she saw him as she'd come in the door. She hadn't made eye contact with him but kept staring up the stairs.

He climbed the stairs, moving slowly. He was exhausted and felt a deep ache forming in the muscles of his body. He needed to rest, but he knew there would be no true relaxing until he was sure Lydia would be alright.

As he reached the top step, his mother's bedroom door opened, and Birdie stepped out, one hand on her stomach. She saw him standing there and approached, her mind darting from one problem to another. "Did you find them? Is she alright?" The questions were rapid, not giving him a chance to answer before she threw out another. He couldn't help but notice that none of her questions were about her husband.

"She's laying down in my room. She has a head wound and looks like she put up a fight. She was unconscious and resting a few minutes ago." He smiled ruefully. "Which may be for the best. My Lydia would be harassing the doctor about what took him so long to get here for Mack if she could."

Birdie smiled for a second, relief filling her expression. It was a small smile, then it was gone, and he saw the weariness dragging on her posture. Her shoulders slumped, she had purple bags under her eyes, and her hands were clenched into fists, one hand covering the other at her belly.

"Birdie, I don't know how to tell you this, but..." Isaac closed his eyes and took a breath. When he opened them, he knew Birdie already knew. Maybe he'd given it away somehow. "Your husband is dead. He was killed by Deputy Sharpe when he tried to kill Lydia and me."

Birdie closed her eyes and lowered her head, breathing evenly. "He was a horrible man," she whispered. "But I never wished him dead."

"I'm very sorry, Birdie," Isaac said softly, his eyes dropping too. "I understand if you want a hearing on the matter. I'm sure Jack will be willing to–"

"No, it won't be necessary. Thank you, Isaac. If someone was going to die tonight, I'm glad it wasn't you or Lydia. Neither of you would be any good to anyone if the other were suddenly not there." Lydia shook her head, taking another deep breath and looking up at him. "No, it is as it was intended to be. I will bury him and mourn, but it won't be for the man I married. It will be for what could've been, for what I could've had if I'd gotten off the train earlier."

She paused, her head tilting slightly, then shook her head. "No, I won't mourn for that, either. If it had been different, I wouldn't have met a woman who looked out for me. I wouldn't change that." She smiled sadly. "I will pray that he finds what he needs, some peace, some humility, maybe some empathy?"

Isaac let her talk, not interrupting. She looked him square in the eye and asked, "What about you and Lydia?"

"I may not be prince charming," he said to her, who looked at him in confusion for a second before she understood. Then, he came up the last step and moved to his door, his hand curling around the knob. "But this tale will have a happy ending if I have anything to say about it."

Chapter Forty-One

The doctor took longer than expected to come to Lydia's room that night to check on her head. He gave her laudanum to help her sleep while he stitched her wound closed, and she drifted off to sleep. She woke once or twice during the night to find Isaac nearby, dozing in the chair next to the bed. He stirred when she did as if sensing that she was awake. After checking the time, he'd give her more laudanum to help her back to sleep, as the doctor had ordered.

Once, she'd been a bit slower to fall asleep and had time to ask after Mack. "Is he going to be alright?"

"Ma said Mack was bleeding too much, and she was right. When Doctor Jennings took the bullet out, he found an artery had been pierced, which explained the bleeding. He stitched it up the best he could, but I helped him put Mack in the wagon he'd brought, so he could take him to the clinic in town. He said he'd done field medicine and didn't want to rely on it.

So he was going to cut Mack's wound open in the morning and clean it out again, then check the work on the artery. He would have to take the sutures out of it and redo that part, but he'd have better equipment there." It was a lot of information, but Lydia nodded, biting her lip.

"I will pray for him," she said softly, closing her eyes.

"As will I," Isaac said softly. She fell asleep as his words became too fuzzy for her to understand. From the rhythm, he could only assume he was praying. She wished she could hear it and marveled at the transformation between him leaving for the Sheriff's office that morning and sitting next to her bed that night.

"The Lord works in mysterious ways," she murmured as she slipped into a dreamless sleep.

***

"Good morning, everyone! I trust you are all well. I bring great tidings! Mack is out of surgery," Jack said as he settled into a chair at the table in the kitchen the following morning. Lydia smiled and made to rise to get him breakfast, but Isaac sent her a glare that made her ease back into her chair, and Cora started fussing.

"And where are you going? The doctor said rest! Do you want your head to start spinning like it was this morning?" Cora asked, her mothering tone fully on. With a defeated sigh, she lifted her fingers to the bandage on her head. She was curious about the stitches in her skin, but she hadn't seen them yet.

Cora had laughed when she'd said she wanted to check his needlework, and Isaac asked, "Do you think you could identify which stitch he used if you saw it?" She'd wrinkled her brow, not having thought of that.

"What stitch did he use?" she'd asked, sitting up quickly in the bed, where she'd been, at the time, then slumping right back down to the pillow as the world began spinning again. "I don't know a thing about stitching skin. Which stitch would be able to hold the flesh together?" Her curiosity was truly peaked, not that either of them was taking her seriously!

But that could wait for later. Right now, Lydia was still worried. "How is Birdie? She didn't come back last night, so is she staying at the clinic?"

Jack wobbled his head from side to side. "During the day, yes. Doctor Jennings suggested she get a room at the hotel, so she'd be close enough that he could get her if he needed her assistance with anything. So, she went there for dinner, then returned for another hour or so before going back to it and going to sleep. At least, that's what the staff said."

Isaac poured Jack a cup of coffee and settled at the table with his own. Jack cast Lydia a bright smile that made her blush. "Your bandages make you look more like an avenging angel, Mrs. Branson. I wouldn't worry too much about the scar," he grinned.

Next to her, Isaac laughed and winked at Jack. "She's more concerned that the good doctor's needlework won't live up to her exacting standards, I think."

"Well, I read somewhere that if the stitches are too big, it'll leave a rather unappealing scar," Lydia complained.

"And you'll still look like an angel," Jack said, not putting off the idea no matter what she did.

Cora laughed and returned to the stove to take the steaming teapot from the fire. Lydia decided to change the subject. "Seeing you cook was very educational," she said with a wink.

"Educational?" he asked, raising an eyebrow. "What did you learn?"

"That you can't cook grits," Lydia responded, her free hand lifting a spoon full of the lumpy mixture from the bowl in front of her. "How have you existed so long without me?"

"I have no idea, but apparently, it wasn't with grits," Isaac laughed, shaking his head. "You think you can do it better?"

"How many lumpy and cold bowls of grits have you eaten since I arrived?" she asked pointedly, her eyebrows up.

"You're never going to win, Isaac. She's from Virginia. Those southern cooks know their way around grits, and I can only assume she's one of them." Cora laughed. "It's a point of pride, I believe."

"As are biscuits," Lydia confirmed, winking at Cora. "I have yet to meet someone who can make better biscuits than the ones my Pa taught me to make."

"Is that a challenge?" Jack asked, leaning across the table. "You know I can't leave a challenge on the table. I could use a distraction, and this sounds like the perfect way to spend some time over the next few days."

Lydia's grin faded in response, but Isaac cut in. "And you're not touching that stove until you've recovered, and the doctor says you're completely healed. It took months for me. That should give me plenty of time to perfect a biscuit."

They all dissolved into laughter at the look of horror on Lydia's face at the mention of how long she'd be required to stay immobile. She blinked.

Chapter Forty-Two

Isaac had refused to let her cook breakfast, saying she needed to rest. She'd argued that it was her place to cook him breakfast, and he'd simply stared at the bandage on her forehead. He'd won, and the plate of steaming grits and eggs on the table in front of her was his victory trophy. One he was very proud of until she'd poked holes in it by insulting his grits.

The conversation had turned to lighter things until everyone retreated to their thoughts and their meals.

"I'm glad to hear about Mack," Cora said softly from her chair, lifting her fork and taking a bite of eggs as she broke the silence. "His wound didn't look life-threatening, but anything can happen with a gunshot wound."

Birdie had ridden with the doctor who had taken Mack back to the clinic in town after he'd stitched up Lydia's forehead. She had refused to leave his side, saying she was protecting him as he'd protected her. She'd return by the end of the day unless the doctor let her stay with Mack overnight again.

The rest of them talked comfortably, if quietly, at the table over breakfast until Jack stood, slapping his thighs. "I'd best be heading into town," he said, nodding at the women and Isaac. "Someone has to work today."

Isaac laughed and shook his head. "The Deputy told me to stay home today, and I'm inclined to follow his sage advice."

"And well, you should!" Jack and Cora chorused, earning a round of laughter. Cora settled her dishes in the sink and made excuses about getting started on the laundry before Isaac released the animals to the yard. Isaac watched her go after she dropped a kiss on his forehead before doing the same to Lydia.

When they were alone, he allowed the mask he'd been wearing to fall off. He'd seen the crack in Jack's mask too. They were all pretending everything was alright, but it didn't change the fact that Fred Burns was dead and Mack had been in grave danger from the bullet wound. The sight of the bandage on Lydia's head reminded him that he'd come very close to losing her, too. He reached across the space between them, cupping his fingers under Lydia's and rubbing his thumb over her knuckles. "I am sorry you had to experience all of that," he said softly.

"I'm glad the situation is resolved," her smile melted away as she responded. "I'm sorry Fred Burns died, though. Life is precious, and death is never pleasant. No matter how terrible a man he was, I wish there had been a different way to reach him. I feel a bit guilty about my part in his death."

"No," he tightened his hold on her hand. "You were trying to help Birdie. I believe Mack when he said that Burns was beginning to cross lines and he feared for her life. I'm not sure what he was after, but I'm glad we saved Birdie from whatever it was. I just hope he finds what he was looking for now. Hope he finds peace."

Lydia nodded. "I'm not sure what demons were driving him, either, but I've forgiven him for his part in this. She lifted her hand to her head and then dropped it to her lap again. "I hope Birdie can do it, but it's for her to work through."

Isaac nodded and sighed, his eyes dropping to the table. The bandage angered him, and anger distracted him from what he was feeling in his heart. He took a deep breath, stilling the wild thumping of that heart, and asked without looking at her, "Will you pray with me? For forgiveness for him?"

Lydia's eyes watered, and she smiled, tightening her hold on his hand, then pulling on him until he was close enough for her to wrap her arms around him in a tight hug. "I would love to," she murmured, closing her eyes. "Why don't you lead the prayer?"

He nodded, and with a deep breath, he closed his eyes and started praying. "Lord, we thank you for bringing us all here together to share in your love and wisdom. We ask that you offer Fred Burns the peace he did not find while he was here and that you spread your healing warmth over Jack as he comes to terms with the burden he willingly carried to protect those he loves. We pray for the good health of our friends and our kin, for Mack to recover in such a way that he can serve You, and for Birdie to overcome the trials she's endured and find true happiness. I humbly ask forgiveness for not understanding your plan and not accepting my place in it, and for shutting you out of my heart while I grieved. I pray you protect this woman, who has brought us so much love and warmth that we found hope, not just to carry on but to thrive in Your name. And for bringing her to me, most of all. I don't know what I would do without her. We ask this in Jesus' name, Amen."

His eyes parted to see tears rolling down Lydia's cheeks. He lifted her hand to his lips and kissed her knuckles. "I will thank You every day for that one," he said solemnly.

"Amen," his mother said from the kitchen door, pulling their gaze to the door where she'd been standing the whole time. She lifted her hand to her lips, joy filling her eyes. Isaac smiled and turned his eyes to his wife again.

"Amen," Lydia breathed, her watery smile shining a light on his battered soul. Then she cried out as Isaac stood from his chair and pulled her into his arms with a lingering kiss on her laughing lips. She curled her arms around his shoulders and held him close. He'd never felt anything so amazing. They were alive. They were together, and nothing was going to stop him from proving to both Lydia and God that he would never abandon them again.

Epilogue

One Year Later

"Have you decided what you'll name the baby?" Essie asked Lydia. The room grew quiet as everyone waited for the answer. Lydia looked down at her rounded belly and ran her hand over it. The last year had been a whirlwind of happiness, and now, a few weeks from bringing her child into the world, she couldn't remember ever being happier.

"We haven't decided yet. We're considering a few names." She smiled up at everyone. "David William, or maybe William Abraham if it's a boy." She'd been worried that Isaac would balk at the Biblical names she'd suggested, but he'd smiled when she brought them up one morning.

"David standing up to Goliath is a good description of you, I think," he'd said softly, laying his hand on her swollen belly. "I think it's a good name for any son of the brave woman I love." He'd kissed her forehead at that.

Essie had gathered a few women to host a tea in honor of the impending birth, and they had gathered in the parlor. She'd even made the cucumber sandwiches piled on a tray nearby. She was now perched on Lydia's left side, making notes about presents and who they were from so Lydia could write letters of thanks later.

"Jack!" came a cheerful voice from the door, Jack Sharpe's wide grin appeared in the doorway. "They're going to name it Jack, of course!"

"What if it's a girl?" Birdie asked in the ensuing laughter from everyone in the room.

"Jaqueline!" He supplied without missing a beat, holding out a large box with a big blue bow on top to Lydia. "Ma apologizes for not being able to make it to the party today, but she wanted me to drop this off on my way to the Sheriff's Office."

"Oh, Jack, that's so sweet of her!" Lydia tried to take the box, but Jack held it firm, so she settled for pulling the bow off. Once the box lid had been removed, the room gasped in surprise as a box full of carved wooden toys and trinkets met their gaze. Lydia removed each item, breathing about how lovely they were.

"I carved them myself," Jack said proudly. "Ma painted them, of course. My hand isn't quite that steady."

"They're plenty steady when it matters," Lydia smiled and turned her attention to what remained in the box. She pulled the quilt from it, tears springing to her eyes at the attention to detail evident all over it. The quilt was a lovely six-pane farmhouse pattern done in an array of different colors. "This is gorgeous..." she breathed, her fingers stroking the pattern pieces of the house that looked like their home.

Tears pooled in her eyes at the care and detail stitched into the quilt, and Birdie handed her a handkerchief. She smiled gratefully, dabbing at her eyes and nose, then curling the fingers of one hand around it while she reached to touch the stitching on the quilt. She admired the neat stitches Jack's mother had used, not only to stitch the pieces together and apply the quilt pattern but also to add little embellishments to the houses like flower boxes and animals.

"She wanted you to remember where your home is, in case you ever got the idea to go back East," Jack said sheepishly. Lydia lifted it for everyone to see, and a collection of gasps and appreciative sounds erupted. "Please, pass along my thanks. I will be sure to visit as soon as I can," she said softly, holding the quilt against her chest as her tears ran freely down her cheeks.

"Oh, this baby is going to be so spoiled!" Cora cooed, pulling attention away from Lydia so she could get control over herself. Tears were ever-present lately, so they were used to their sudden appearance at the strangest times. Luckily, the queasy stomach had stopped, but now the swelling in her legs kept her from leaving the house most days.

When the doctor told her to get plenty of rest and not overdo it, Cora and Isaac decided she shouldn't do anything. They reprimanded her often if her feet weren't up while she was sewing. She was so tired most days that she didn't argue. Isaac had been busy converting the guest room Lydia had slept in when she'd arrived into a nursery.

He would often move a chair into the room with a footstool so she could give him her advice about the placement of decorations. Lydia felt loved and cared for and often sent a prayer of thanks to God for bringing her to this small town and helping her find the perfect husband for her. She finally felt as at home as she had in the house she'd grown up in. It was a wonderful feeling.

Lydia stared at her a second and then laughed, "You're planning your spoiling already?"

"It's my first grandchild! I have been making plans for years!" she said to another round of laughter. "You'll see! That's what you do once your children grow up."

Lydia looked around the room at the family she'd built here in Franklin, a smile blooming brightly on her lips as they dissolved into conversations. This town had accepted her for herself and did not pity her for the loss of her family. She had friends, family, and a community here that she adored.

Of course, she missed her father and brother and wished Nettie could see Franklin. She'd love it here, and Lydia knew they'd appreciate her cooking more than the people in Maysville did. She thought about that for a moment, a plan forming in her head.

Maybe she'd extend an invitation to visit once the baby was here. She imagined how Nettie would get along with the others around the room and smiled wider, knowing she'd fit in as if she'd been raised here. Much like Lydia had. Her eyes fell on each member of her new family, and she let the joy she felt for each of them fill her.

Birdie looked healthier than ever, with brightness in her eyes and more color in her cheeks that reminded Lydia of their time on the train on the way to Franklin. She had inherited the saloon after Fred's death, though she refused to step foot inside. Knowing she could use the money more than wanting any association with that horrid place, she'd sold it. She had used the money to buy a small lot and build a farmhouse on the other side of Isaac and Lydia.

With the house completed, she'd invited Mack to live there, getting him out of the saloon. She'd said she needed a man's help around the place since she'd never kept a house in her life, and there were a million things she'd need to do. Since he was one of the few men she trusted, she asked if she could offer him room and board if he'd help around the farm. He had agreed to move reluctantly, but insisted on building a small cabin about a quarter of a mile away from Birdie's house.

He paid rent on the land it sat on, saying it was highly inappropriate for him to share a roof with her, even if she was widowed. He'd taken on most of the hard labor involved in a farm and seemed to enjoy it. She saw how Mack and Birdie looked at each other, though, and knew there was more going on than just him fixing the barn and her cooking dinner. While she was scandalized that they were living together unwed, it was tempered by those looks they shared when they thought no one was looking.

Cora hadn't had an episode in almost nine months, and the doctor said she appeared to be in better health than she had been in years. He credited her excitement about the baby, and Lydia agreed with him. The love in Cora's eyes when she dropped her gaze to Lydia's belly was a thing of beauty, and she'd stepped up to do tasks that Lydia couldn't as her pregnancy advanced with no fuss. She'd even been seen in town more, using trips to the mercantile as her excuse to visit, though she'd come home more than once with seeds from Bishop Day's garden.

Lydia suspected they were developing a friendship, and she couldn't help but be happy for them both. He was far too nice a man to spend his days alone, even if he kept himself busy with his faith.

Essie was so shocked when she heard how things happened that she apologized to Birdie and Lydia every day when she came over. She'd learned to cook and had even given birth to a beautiful baby boy just before Christmas. Her husband had turned his catalog-buying habit toward buying things for the baby, and there was no end to the laughter that ensued the day following one of the deliveries.

As his experience with babies was sorely lacking, he bought the strangest things from the catalog that promised to help their baby stay healthy and happy. Her son, Jacob, who was a few months old, was just beginning to roll around on the floor at their feet. Essie had glowed during the long months she carried Jacob, and she was absolutely in love with him.

"You'll all have to wait behind me for any spoiling of my child. After all, I will live with him," Isaac said as he strolled through the door. His smile widened as his gaze found her settled into a wing-backed chair supporting her back and the growing bundle that swelled her middle. The love in his eyes made her shiver and wish there weren't so many people around.

If it was possible, she felt her eyes twinkling back at him, no longer hiding the love she felt for the Sheriff of Franklin one bit. Their relationship had grown significantly since their brush with death. Lately, Isaac had started to lead a few bible nights that he insisted be held at their home so his mother could be included. His nightmares were gone, and she'd blushed when he said it was all because of her.

As her belly grew, his swagger became more pronounced, and Lydia had heard more than one person liken him to a peacock. In truth, she knew he'd finally allowed his true nature to rise to the surface again, and she loved him more every day.

Friendly bantering rose between the others as they argued about who was planning to do the most spoiling. Lydia stayed quiet. She didn't want to put in that since she would be spending the most time with her baby, she'd be doing the spoiling long before any of them had a chance. Her eyes landed on Jack, who came around the farmhouse when he wasn't working.

He'd had a rough time accepting that he'd taken a life, but he'd reached out to Isaac, and they'd worked through most of it. Isaac said a man never really got over that feeling, so the best he could do was help Jack find ways to accept it so he could move on. These days, he was almost himself again. Only those closest to him caught the slight dimness of his smile, and they loved him through it, praying with him for forgiveness.

"It looks like you've got your fairy tale," Birdie said softly from her side, and Lydia turned her smile to her. Birdie continued, reaching a hand to curl around Lydia's where it laid on the soft swell of her belly. "I didn't think it was possible, but you sure look happier than Cinderella ever did in the books."

"I found my happily ever after. But I think it's more possible than you think," Lydia acknowledged. She raised her eyebrow at Mack Medina, who'd taken up a chair on the porch outside the windows.

He hadn't let Birdie out of his sight for a second since the incident with her husband, except when the doctor had asked Birdie to wait outside while he did the indelicate business of removing the bullet and stitching the big man up. Oh, the gossip in town had a lot to talk about with those two.

"Smiley?" Birdie laughed, shaking her head. "He's a good friend."

"I bet he can be even more than that." Lydia grinned, but Birdie waved her off.

"I'm not ready for anything like that," she said, her eyes going vacant for a moment. "I'm not sure if I ever will be."

"I know you will, someday. I understand, though. I can't imagine what you've been through," she said softly, patting Birdie's hands. "I am glad you have him around to help you, though. I don't think I'd sleep a wink if you were out there on your own all the time."

Birdie laughed and shook her head. "Didn't I tell you? I got a job!"

Lydia's eyebrows shot up, and she leaned closer. "No! What are you going to be doing?"

"I'm in charge of ordering for the Mercantile. I start Monday." She grinned. "I was laughing with George about Mister Gray's catalog habit, and I said there were more things he should stock so people didn't have to wait so long to get things. So, he gave me the job of ordering them!"

"Oh, Birdie, that's fantastic!" Lydia exclaimed, curling her fingers over Birdie's, clasped together in her lap. "I'm so glad you're not roaming around being bored all day!"

"As if you'd let me!" Birdie scoffed. "Do I really need to learn embroidery stitches? I haven't needed them in my entire life! Can't I just beg you to do it? I've got plenty of money to pay other people now, you know? I'll pay you to handle the needlework!"

Lydia put in. "How else are you going to occupy your free time and protect your reputation, what with the job and all the work you need done around the farm? All proper wealthy women sit around and work on their needlepoint all day." Lydia said the last with a haughty air. "I've helped dress them, so I should know!"

"You think I have a reputation left? That's funny," she grinned. "Wouldn't it be better if I shared that wealth with others? Doing all the work myself sounds rather miserly." She shook her head. "No, I believe I will pay someone else and save my fingers from the bloodletting of being too close to needles." She shook her head. "Though the men Mack suggested I hire refuse to let me help them with anything. They have done a wonderful job building the house. They even built a barn, and they're coming out next week to build a chicken coop and a sheep barn!"

"What a regular farmer you're turning into," Lydia laughed. They were laughing so loud that they drew the attention away from the argument.

"Oh, give it up! Do you think any child of mine will be that spoiled!" Isaac was asking incredulously. The answer was drowned in shouts and laughter, and Lydia felt warm all the way to her toes. Her family was here; her life was here. And she was so glad the sign at the depot in Maysville had caught her attention. She didn't know what her life would've become back east. But here? She couldn't imagine ever being happier.

Isaac brought a chair over and settled into it, reaching for her hand and kissing her knuckles. "It's me who is spoiled. God saw to that."

Lydia's smile broadened. "Unhappy Sheriffs make townsfolk unhappy. As long as I spoil you, everyone in town keeps smiling at me."

Isaac shook his head. "They smile at you because you are an angel, a miracle worker, right here in our little town. You saved me, Lydia. You saved my mother. You saved Birdie."

"I didn't save her, Isaac," she shook her head. "We all saved each other."

"And it's worth the time spent on my knees thanking God for knowing what I needed more than I did." He looked around the room and smiled. "Who am I, and who are my people, that we should be able to give as generously as this?"

Lydia's smile grew, and a sparkle lit her eye. "Everything comes from you, and we have given you only what comes from your hand," she finished. "First Chronicles," she nodded approvingly and looked at the gifts around them. "Perfect."

Isaac nodded. He'd thought for so long that he didn't need God in his life. He'd thought he could walk through this life without needing the comfort of knowing God was protecting him, loving him. He'd thought the war was a test he'd failed when his regiment died. But Lydia and all the things they'd been through, knowing she loved him through it all, had opened his eyes and heart.

And he knew that there was no love without God's love, and that his life was so much richer for having both. "But now faith, hope, and love abide these three," he smiled, then turned back toward her, lifting her hand to his and brushing a kiss over her knuckles. "But the greatest of these is love."

"Those Corinthians knew what they were talking about," Lydia laughed softly.

"As do I," he murmured, leaning forward to brush a kiss over her lips. "As do I."

THE END

Also, by Olivia Haywood

Thank you for reading **"A Blessed Love Arrives with the Bride Train"**!

I hope you enjoyed it! If you did, here you can also check out **my full Amazon Book Catalogue** at: https://go.oliviahaywood.com/bc-authorpage

Thank you for allowing me to keep doing what I love! ❤

Made in United States
Troutdale, OR
04/10/2025

30497709R00176